William Michael Davidson

TO: ED

DANCING LEMUR PRESS, L.L.C.
Pikeville, North Carolina
www.dancinglemurpress.com

For my parents

Part
I

1.1.1

Colton Pierce watched the interrogation from behind the window. Josh Mosley was about to confess, and if this didn't take long, Colton would be able to make it to the department's annual fundraising event that evening. He loved watching these confessions and wanted to hear Mosley say it. Something about confessions always made for a good night's sleep.

He watched Tracy Grover, interrogation specialist and long-time colleague, do what she did best: drill the subject relentlessly and from every angle until there was a genuine, honest confession. From there, she could get what she really wanted: more information. Colton watched silently from behind the observation window, which looked like a mirror inside the interrogation room, and checked his phone: 4:23 p.m.

Still time, he thought.

"Now, Josh," Tracy Grover said, folding her hands together in her lap. She glared at him sternly, like a principal addressing a problem child who had been marched into her office. Her long blonde hair was pulled back in a tight pony tail, and her slender cheeks, which just a moment before looked flushed, now appeared suddenly pale. "We technically don't need your confession. You know that, right? A judge has already deemed you guilty. You're already in our custody. But by confessing, you'll be starting with the truth, and from there, we're hoping you can give us more information. Perhaps there are others you know who may have done what you did? Birds of a feather, right? This is all pretty standard questioning, and you understand the gravity of what you've been telling me, but we need to finish this conversation. You understand how serious this is, don't you?"

Josh nodded.

"And you understand why you've been brought here? We take these actions very seriously."

"I know," he said. The guy looked like a nervous wreck.

"We're going to have to walk through this step by step," Tracy said. She reached over to the table beside her chair, picked up her tablet, and began to tap away at the illuminated screen. "I need to know exactly what happened."

"Can't I have a lawyer?"

"A lawyer?" Tracy smirked. "What year do you think you live in? And you've already been found guilty, remember? A lawyer doesn't apply to situations like this anyway. That law changed decades ago. Now, let's get back to the matter at hand. I need to know exactly what happened."

"Are you sure we need to go there?" Josh asked. "I never meant to do anything wrong. I'm sorry I tried to run. I never meant to—"

"But you did try to run, Mr. Mosley, and you realize the neuro-chip in your skull makes it impossible to get away from us. The Neurological Registry of Neurological Transmissions monitors you night and day. You know this, don't you Mr. Mosley? You haven't been living under a rock."

"Yes, I do, but I never meant to—"

"Mr. Mosley," she said, interrupting him. "I've already explained to you that we need to finish this sooner rather than later. I'm afraid we can't stop now. You must finish. Take me through this step by step."

Josh looked like he was trying to gather his thoughts but obviously wasn't doing a very good job of it. He didn't say anything.

"You were alone with your ten-year-old niece," Tracy reminded him. "You were alone with her in her bedroom, putting her to bed, because you were babysitting for your sister. She and her husband went out to dinner. That's what you told me, correct?"

"Yes," he said, voice trembling. "That's true."

"And then what happened?"

Josh sighed. Clearly, he didn't want to relive what had happened and probably didn't want to have to explain it to someone in graphic detail.

Come on, Colton thought, *hurry it up*. Any longer standing here waiting and he'd miss out on most of the appetizers at the fundraiser.

"Mr. Mosley, can you please continue by explaining to me exactly what happened? As you were saying, you were alone with her in her bedroom. You were putting her to bed."

"Yes," Josh said. "I was tucking her into bed, and she was really upset because her mom and dad have been fighting so much lately. Part of the reason they went on the date that night was as a last-ditch effort to save their marriage, but it's been clear for a while that it's over. I just wanted to help her. I wanted her to feel better."

Tracy cleared her throat, and her fingers danced across the illuminated screen of her tablet. "So tell me what happened. Exactly."

"Exactly?" Josh asked. "Do I have to walk through every detail?"

"Yes."

Josh slumped forward in his seat, defeated. Colton expected the confession would come any second. They always looked this way before confessing.

"I sat next to her on the bed," he admitted. "She was upset about all the fighting, and I wanted her to feel safe. To feel loved. I wanted her to know she'd be okay. She's always looked up to me as an uncle."

"Go ahead," Tracy said. "Let's just focus on what happened. We'll talk about your motivations in a moment."

Josh sighed.

"I kissed her on the cheek like I always do. And then I…then I…" He leaned forward and clawed at his hair. "Why do I have to say it? You know what happened. Why do I have to say it?"

"Because you need to," Tracy said. "You need to for yourself and for your niece. Just say it. Acceptance is the first stage, Mr. Mosley. This is just the starting point. From here, we can move on and discuss other things."

"I know."

He continued to scrape his nails along his scalp and, grunting, looked at the mirror. Colton suspected Josh knew it was a one-sided mirror and someone was standing on the other side of it, observing him.

"All right, I'll say it."

Tracy looked up expectantly from her tablet. Her fingers froze above the screen.

"I prayed," he said, forcing the words out of his throat like razor blades. "I prayed, okay! I prayed! I prayed for my niece! Now what? Does that mean I'm going to be taken to the Island?"

"Bingo," Colton said, and turned away from the observation window.

From here, the real questioning would begin, and Tracy would try to find out if Josh knew others who prayed. Such information could be handed off to the investigative branch of the agency, which would follow any leads for more possible extractions.

Colton checked his phone again as he made his way out of the building, pleased that he wouldn't be tardy for the fundraiser that evening.

1.1.2

The Center for Theological Control (CTC) held its fundraiser in the plush oceanfront Marriot in Long Beach, California. Last year's fundraiser had been held there as well, and Colton remembered it being just as grand. An enormous, sunlit ballroom teemed with endless tables of hors d'oeuvres; waiters and waitresses scrambling between everything while balancing trays of champagne flutes with impressive dexterity. A blues band had been hired for the occasion, filling the festive event with soulful tunes.

Colton arrived a little late. He adjusted his tie as he walked in, and he hardly had a chance to take in the enormous spectacle of a party before he was handed a glass of champagne by one of the waiters, who disappeared back into the crowd. He was greeted by several co-workers who all knew him to be the number one extractor the CTC had seen in recent years and, because of his impressive abilities on the field, also knew the rumors to be true: Colton Pierce was most likely be hired as the new Chief Officer of the CTC. Secretly, he liked the jokes that implied he was much too young and much too good-looking for such a serious role. Just over forty, he'd fought and clawed his way to where he was, and he hoped that soon—tonight perhaps—Brian Barclay would officially announce that he was stepping down from his post. Everyone knew the announcement was imminent; Brian had his sights set on sandy beaches and retirement these days.

Colton jested with colleagues and took several congratulatory slaps on the back for being the Extractor of the Month once again. Then he caught sight of Selma Grissom. She was at the hors d'oeuvres table, delicately picking sushi from the display and placing them on her plate. He completely lost awareness of his colleagues and what they were saying. Hoping not to be rude, he waved a friendly goodbye and drifted toward the hors d'oeuvres table, where he grabbed a plate and began to eye the sushi himself.

"My favorite," he said, and felt entirely fortunate that nobody else was near the spread. They were alone here, a little ways from the tables, the blues band, and the hordes of people.

"Sushi?" Selma asked.

"Yeah, that too."

Selma looked at him and grinned subtly. She was a new secretary for the CTC's Public Relations Office, and Colton had enjoyed the pleasure of a few brief conversations with her at meetings and in the lunch room. During those moments he'd thought the same thing he was thinking now: She was an amazingly beautiful woman. Her hair was long, not far above her belt-line, and black as the night itself. But her poise impressed Colton the most. She was confident in herself, or at least her posture seemed to broadcast that. She held herself in a way that conveyed she was valuable, rare, and confident, and Colton had been drawn to her from their first interaction. And there was something about her eyes—those green eyes of hers—that was almost mesmerizing.

"I hear you're the lead extractor again this month," she said.

"That's what they tell me," he said. He avoided the sushi altogether, and threw some delicious-looking sliders on his plate. He wasn't really a fan of sushi anyway. "It'll be my third month in a row as lead extractor, but who's counting?"

He grinned but couldn't read Selma's expression. Was she smiling back out of professional politeness?

"I've seen some pictures of you at old CTC functions," Selma said, and nibbled on a rainbow roll. "You were with a boy. Was that your son?"

"Yes, that's my son, Marty," Colton said, knowing that when it came to women, being a single dad and father to a pre-teen son was a deal-breaker for many of them. He watched her reaction very closely. "A good kid, actually. Twelve years old. Almost a teenager."

"Interesting," she said, and Colton, once again, felt frustrated that he couldn't get an exact read on her. Did this convey indifference? Rejection? What was she thinking? "Divorce, huh?"

"Kinda," he said. "She walked out almost seven years ago but died a few years after that."

"Oh, I'm terribly sorry to hear that."

"No need to be sorry," he said. "These things happen, and it's been a long time. So it's just the two of us in a bachelor pad of our own. It actually isn't all that bad."

"Well, it's good that you guys are happy," she said.

Colton was surprised to feel something that he hadn't felt in a long time: He was nervous. Something about this woman made him feel genuinely tongue-tied. It had been years since he'd felt this way, and part of him welcomed it. With his rising reputation at the CTC, many women—even the attractive ones—threw themselves at him. Sherry in the copy room, Barb in human resources, and Gina who worked in archives were only a few who'd made it abundantly clear they were available and willing. But something about Selma was more alluring. He'd been an extractor for so long that maybe it was his need for the hunt. The chase. Maybe it was in his DNA.

"Where did you work before the CTC?" he asked, and took a bite out of a slider.

"City of Long Beach, Gas and Water. Nothing special. I just needed a change."

"It's nice to work for a good cause, isn't it?" Colton wiped his lips with the back of his hand. "That's the thing you'll love about working here. You'll get up in the morning knowing you're doing something good for the sake of humanity, and you'll go to bed at night knowing you helped out in a meaningful way. Nothing more you can ask for."

"And that's how you feel?"

"Absolutely," he said. "I feel like this has become more than a job to me—it's become a passion. It's the reason I'm the lead extractor and why I might be running this whole division soon. I put everything I have into it. Nothing is more important than public safety."

She nodded, and he noted that she hadn't made any attempt to move away from the appetizer table. Maybe the mention of his son hadn't scared her away—yet.

A woman Colton had gone on a few dates with several months before, Amanda Morales, complained that Colton spent too much time talking about himself. The night she broke off the relationship, she said something that stuck with him: "If I could take every 'I' you say and turn them into pennies, I could fill up the Grand Canyon." It was a weird comment, spoken in anger, but Colton remembered it. The fact that his late wife had made the same observation on several occasions—without the imagery of pennies and Arizona geography—only made it that much more potent. So he questioned himself and his approach to Selma. *Am I talking too much about myself? Am I going to scare her off?*

"I'm afraid I'm not into causes," she said almost sheepishly, "but everyone here has been nice, and I'm having a wonderful time. Even right now, talking to you."

If that wasn't a direct invitation to take this to another level, he didn't know what was. He set down his plate of sliders and thought of how he could ask her out. There was a Lakers game next weekend, and he could easily get two tickets.

"I've enjoyed talking to you," he said. "Do you have any plans next—?"

"Colton, it's show time." Kramer, his personal aide, grabbed him by the shoulder. A short, stocky, curly-haired guy, Kramer was at least half the reason Colton made it to any CTC meetings on time. Already, Colton could hear Brian Barclay on stage, beginning his speech. He needed to get to his seat quickly. As lead extractor, it would be a political mishap to be out of his seat for the Chief Officer's presentation.

With Kramer pulling him away from the hors d'oeuvres table, Colton looked back and saw Selma, standing with her plate of sushi, watching him with her green, dreamy eyes.

"We'll talk soon," he said, and made a dash for his seat. "Very soon."

1.1.3

Colton listened to the opening of Brian Barclay's speech, but his mind wandered. He reflected on the organization he worked for and everything that had led to this point in history. The Super Flu of 2061 was infamous, and skeptics long debated the true source of the illness. Some said the Chinese government engineered the flu and released it intentionally, while others maintained that it was actually a product of the United States, and due to a security breach, accidentally spread amongst the public. Although some still debated its source, nobody debated what the Super Flu of 2061 really was: A genetically engineered virus with a 99.9% communicability rate that quickly and systematically destroyed a host's VMAT2 gene, the lone genetic reason humans had the ability to undergo spiritual experiences. After a couple days of coughing and a mild fever, a patient was rendered a guaranteed atheist.

Colton had always leaned toward the theory that the Super Flu of 2061 was the result of a United States attempt to infect the Middle East with a hacking cough that would rid the region of religious fundamentalism and, subsequently, acts of terrorism and violence. The United States had done all but admit responsibility for it, and while some conspiracy theorists still insisted it was the Chinese government or some other country, Colton had never given them much credence. But he was glad, like the rest of the population and the CTC, that the virus had been unleashed. Not only had religious fundamentalism and wars dissipated in the Middle East, but religious crime and intolerance had virtually evaporated from the globe.

"What we are doing here is one of the most important jobs we can offer society," Brian said. The audience was rapt. "Since the

14

VMAT2 gene was wiped off the face of the earth, all of you have benefitted from the results. Our great-grandparents could only imagine a world like the one we live in today—where terrorist attacks motivated by religious squabbles no longer dominate the news, and where wars are no longer ignited because of religious intolerance. This is a world they could only dream of, a world that is our reality.

"But we must not just remember the global benefits of the Super Flu of 2061; we must also remember the local ones. It may seem foreign to us today, living under the protection of the CTC in the aftermath of the destruction of the VMAT2 gene, but religious belief was one of the main links to violent criminal activity in the modern world. No more mass suicides or people drinking the Kool-Aid. Hey, speaking of Kool-Aid, can someone fetch me a bottle of water? I'm dying up here. Not Jim Jones Kool-Aid either, okay? Don't need any real life examples up here."

Brian wiped the sweat from his forehead, and some aide in the front row handed him a bottle of water. The crowd laughed while Brian took several gulps. The bottle of water looked unnaturally small in his big, beefy hands.

"Now that's better," he said, screwing the lid back on his water and placing it on his podium. Maybe it was due to the bright lights on him or the extra hundred pounds he was carrying, but he was dripping sweat. "Now, as I was saying, we live in a world that our great-grandparents simply couldn't imagine. Sure there's crime, and too much of it. We'll never be perfect. But could you imagine all of the out-of-their-wits extremists who would have gone into our schools, our hospitals, our parks, those now abandoned places of worship, and slaughtered us by the hundreds—by the thousands—if things were like they were? Some of you may not even be here. Some of your children may not be here. It's a sobering thought.

"But perhaps one of the most important benefits our society has felt since the advent of the CTC is simply the quality of life. It is difficult to quantify this, isn't it? But no longer do we have a society of people forgoing the advances and hopes of this world to store up treasures in the next! That kind of thinking undermines the very fabric of our society and deters every good possibility for justice. When that kind of thinking runs rampant, the poor starve, the needy go without, and the ill go unassisted. It is no wonder that since the destruction of the VMAT2 gene, medical science has taken massive leaps and bounds—not just because modern technology has advanced, but because the urgent need to deal with the here and the now has become that much more important.

"Crime has been taken more seriously. We no longer live in a day when we promise a grieving family the fictitious karma that will happen in some other life. For years and years our society functioned on this premise, and it became, over time, simply an excuse not to fix a terribly broken system. Justice has become swifter, more meaningful, and more precise in our modern society. All of us benefit from this. Every one of us does!

"When you walk down the beautiful streets of Long Beach, of local Los Angeles—of most cities in the United States—you notice the fruits of our labor in everything you see. In ancient societies, it was easy to endure broken and dilapidated streets when the masses foolishly clung to the false hopes of Streets of Gold in some mythological afterlife. Of course, there is still poverty, and there is still pollution. I saw some graffiti just yesterday while driving through Los Angeles to a meeting, but this is a just a shadow of what once was. We must not forget that our mission here at the CTC and the responsibility we have to our community is far and wide. We work hard, we work diligently, and…our extractors look pretty nice in those silver suits, don't they?"

Brian laughed, and the crowd went wild. He paced back and forth for a few moments, tossing the microphone back and forth between his hands. The guests clapped vigorously or held up glasses of champagne.

Colton scanned the crowd for Selma but didn't see her. Too difficult to find someone in the chaos. He would make sure to find her after, to finish his conversation with her.

When the applause faded, Brian raised the microphone to his lips and looked over the audience with a grim expression. It was clear that he was changing his tone. He took a deep, dramatic breath and waited until the silence became uncomfortable.

"This is an interesting time at the CTC," he said solemnly. "So much is happening, both here at CTC Headquarters and over in Washington. We all know there has been lots of debate recently about the quarantined and whether or not Congress will push through legislation to deem the quarantined non-human. When Washington makes the announcement, we must be ready for whatever the outcome is—and what such an outcome might entail for our jobs here at the CTC. I want to remind everyone to be patient, to be steadfast, as the CTC will continue to do our jobs while we wait for word on what laws—if any—may change."

"Kill 'em!" someone yelled from the back of the ballroom, and a few others joined in. There was some commotion and talking. Brian, holding up his pudgy hand to silence everyone, closed his eyes and waited it out like a patient school teacher standing in front of the class.

"I agree," Colton said in a low mumble. "Kill 'em all."

He looked out the windows and saw Catalina Island just twenty miles off the coast of Long Beach. On many days it was difficult to see, but on a day like today—crisp and clear—it was easily visible. At one time, long before Colton was born, it was a small community with schools, shopping, hospitals, golf courses, just a two-hour ride away on the Catalina Express. These days, it wasn't often referred to as Catalina Island; instead, it was referred to as the Quarantine Zone. Those who were apprehended by the CTC were sent there to live out their days where they would not be a danger to society nor spread such dangerous ideas. Many of the Aberrants were studied to answer the perplexing question of why such arcane beliefs had regenerated in them, though scientists had not yet publicized a concrete answer to that question. If the Aberrants were kept in society, they would begin to seek each other out, congregate, and the world would be thrown back to a far more dangerous time. It was better to keep them isolated or, even better, to have them killed; the deaths of a few now would save millions for future generations. And it made the public feel safe. So much of public safety, Colton had come to realize, was a matter of perception.

But Colton, like everyone else, knew the new legislation could change everything. Lobbyists had long been pleading with the politicians in Washington to enact a law deeming the Aberrants non-human; if this legislation passed, the ramifications would be significant. No longer beneficiaries of the Constitution, the Aberrants wouldn't be entitled to the same rights they were now. Many believed and rallied behind the idea of a mass extermination, and Colton found himself in this camp. Why waste billions of dollars shipping the Aberrants to the Island, guarding the Island, monitoring the Island, and supplying the inhabitants with basic needs such as food, water, and shelter? The country was broke as it was, and these superfluous costs only made matters worse.

Proponents of the new legislation rallied behind the idea that such a change in legislation would make a mass extermination imminent. Colton loved the idea and, even more, loved that the new possibility didn't threaten his job security. He would still be responsible for the seeking out and apprehension of those who were infected except, if the change in legislation went through, the theologically ill would be taken to a morgue rather than the Island. It just made sense from every possible angle, but Colton was well aware of the tensions it was creating. While most thought the new legislation was the right course of action, there were some—the humanists—who thought it crossed ethical lines. A very small minority believed the infected should at least have the right to live out the remainder of their lives on the Island.

He longed for the day when the Aberrants would be terminated. And since all the cells on the Island and the quarantine chambers at the CTC could be piped with cyanide gas, in what had always been a security measure to be used only in the event of a mass escape, it wouldn't take long for a change in the law to become a reality; every cell could easily be made into a tomb, and in record speed.

"As I was saying," Brian said, "this is a time of immense change for the CTC, and with Washington fighting it out over this new legislation, the future has a lot in store for us. It will take great leadership indeed for someone to guide us through this important time of change. I suppose, then, there is no better time to announce my retirement as Chief Officer of the CTC next month. I have enjoyed working for such a fine organization and think it's time for me to pass the torch to someone younger, someone with more vision, and someone who isn't as fat as I've gotten!"

The crowd went wild with applause and cheers. Some even called for a standing ovation and saluted him with half-drunk glasses of champagne. This wasn't news to anyone. The word had already gone through the office. These were the genuine, celebratory cheers of colleagues and guests who wished Brian the best in his early retirement and were happy that he had served so faithfully and for so long at one of the most important posts regarding public safety. When the applause simmered down, and people got back into their seats, Brian resumed.

"The next month will be very important, sorting through some things, particularly who will serve as the next Chief Officer for the Center for Theological Control. As you know, we believe in transparency and accountability, and all can rest assured that we will soon begin the process of selecting and appointing a new leader who has proven himself or herself in the field."

Colton smiled and looked over his shoulder to see if anyone was looking at him. While the news of Brian's retirement had circulated the offices, the rumors of who would replace him had circulated even more. Nine times out of ten that rumor was followed with speculation that he was the most likely and the best fit to replace Brian.

He nudged his assistant. "I think they're starting to chant my name."

Several in the crowd had begun to chant, and Colton wondered whether it would be appropriate to stand up and wave to his supporters. It couldn't hurt, and maybe it would help make it clear that he was, in fact, interested in stepping into that role.

He had barely gotten to his feet when Kramer reached up, grabbed him by his shirt, and pulled him back down into his seat.

"What'd you do that for?" He was about to stand back up when he noticed Kramer pointing across the room.

It was Ashton Lampson. All six feet three inches of him was standing and waving to the crowd. Colton realized they weren't chanting "Colton"; they were chanting "Ashton." He narrowed his eyes and looked hard at his fellow colleague—second in extractions over the last year—and realized then how much he had always disliked him. Ashton was tall and handsome in an overly manicured, feminine way with shiny wide teeth, a big horse-like smile, and hair that was always perfectly parted. Colton wondered what Ashton used to keep his hair in place, because every follicle was in order at all times—even after an extraction.

Colton cracked his knuckles and watched with distain while Ashton soaked up the crowd's admiration. Some were chanting *Colton*, and that took some of the edge off, but many people—possibly most of them—were chanting Ashton's name.

But that wasn't what made Colton the most upset.

When the applause faded away and the chanting stopped, Ashton sat down. Selma Grissom was sitting next to him.

1.1.4

Colton got home around ten o'clock. He'd stayed at the fundraiser for a few hours after the speech, had a couple more drinks, two plates for dinner, and did his best to socialize and rub elbows with his colleagues despite his misgivings over what had occurred. After a couple more glasses of champagne and a few conversations that encouraged him to apply for the soon-to-be-vacant position of Chief Officer, he'd convinced himself that he must have witnessed some kind of anomaly. Ashton Lampson couldn't be the favorite to replace Brian Barclay. It just wasn't humanly possible, and Ashton must have rounded up some of his inner-circle to get the crowd chanting. Once one person starts chanting, others tend to follow. It was almost a law of science. People would have chanted "Toilet Bowl Cleaner!" if the right number of people started and they were deep enough into their champagne.

He poured himself a brandy, kicked off his shoes, and walked onto his balcony, which overlooked the beach. He took a seat on one of his deck chairs. This was where Colton found himself most evenings. He often strolled onto the small balcony to reflect on his day and, when he could see the Quarantine Zone on a clear night, he would pride himself on how many Aberrants he'd personally been responsible for transporting there. It often eased his mind. It was too dark to see the Island now, but such a crisp breeze after a hot day felt refreshing.

Before long, Colton finished his glass of brandy and became restless. Marty was seeing a movie with a friend and his family and wouldn't be back till nearly midnight. The silence that filled the condominium—the silence that first began when Mona walked out—had never been easy to adjust to. Maybe he shouldn't have agreed for him to stay out so late. It was much later than his normal bedtime.

Unable to stand the silence any longer, Colton went back inside, poured himself another glass of brandy, and turned on the television to CNN. Drew Harrell was doing a story about the new legislation and various guests—scientists, teachers, politicians— were touting their opinions. A schoolteacher in Arkansas was discussing the safety of her classes and how, without fully exterminating the Aberrants, she feared a possible theological outbreak one day. It wasn't fair to the children and the country's future, she protested. The mayor of Chicago discussed how the city's unofficial polling had proven beyond a shadow of doubt that the people of his city—of the country, for that matter—were behind the new legislation and thought it a necessary step to ensure the public health and safety.

Wandering toward his bedroom, Colton looked at the long corridor covered with plaques, awards, and honorary certificates over the last sixteen years of working at the CTC. He referred to this as his Hall of Fame. He stopped, sipped his brandy, and absorbed the sight. At least twenty were certificates for EXTRACTOR OF THE MONTH, lining both sides of the hallway in mahogany frames. Eight trophies were for EXTRACTOR OF THE YEAR, four on each side of the hallway, sitting like golden artifacts on shelves. There were also five plaques for EMPLOYEE OF THE YEAR. It had occurred to Colton that soon he would have to find another hallway because there was barely any space left on the walls.

His late wife had hated the Hall of Fame. He could still hear her voice: *I don't want to see every award you've won, every honor you've gotten, every time I walk down the hall to go to our bedroom, okay? Do you realize, Colton, that every single thing you've put up on that wall is about you and you only? Does that mean anything to you? Anything at all? If your head gets any bigger, you won't even fit through this corridor.*

Colton grunted, because Mona had never been able to understand. Her parents were rich, and she had never really worked hard for anything she'd achieved. Colton, on the other hand, had come from virtual poverty. After his dad died in a factory accident, his mom supported him on a secretary's salary. And when she passed away from breast cancer when he was a senior in high school, he supported himself by working nights as a custodian for a local mall. Mona had no idea what it was to pull herself up by the bootstraps and fight for what she had in the world. He was convinced that if she had been through some of the things that he had, she would have seen the Hall of Fame in a different light.

He walked through the corridor and into his gym room. A couple years ago, this had been a second home office that became cluttered in too short a time. Now free weights lined one of the walls, a bench-press was in one corner, and Colton had one of the walls converted to a giant mirror; this way, he could see his progress. His head was swimming because of the brandy and champagne, but still he thought it might help him unwind to get a quick workout in. That always seemed to help when something was bothering him.

Standing in the center of the room, he looked at himself in the mirror. Just over six feet, he was considered tall—but not really as tall as he wanted to be. But he assumed he made up for his height with his muscle mass. Years of militant dieting and lean eating coupled with nightly visits to his workout room had resulted in a body that was strong and chiseled. He was as proud of it as the awards that lined the hall. He was fortunate enough to have avoided balding and had a thick crop of black hair that he liked to keep short enough to appear spiky and a bit messy with "artistic purpose." Kramer often joked that Colton had a "superhero chin," usually covered in five o'clock shadow, which was the way Colton liked it. All of the great superheroes had strong chins, so he'd always considered it a compliment.

But as he inspected himself in the mirror, he couldn't get his mind off Ashton Lampson.

"The popular consensus just couldn't be for him," he said to himself, while admiring his arms. He knew himself to be the very best extractor at the CTC, and he knew that everyone else at the agency knew that, too. It just had to be an anomaly. No way could some twiggy, overly-manicured, feminine extractor like Ashton get that many people on his side. Sure, he was good at what he did, but certainly not the best.

Admiring his side profile in the mirror, extending his right arm and flexing his bicep, Colton knew exactly what he had to do. On Monday, he would go into the office and throw his weight around. Maybe he'd been soft recently. Maybe a little too quiet. Next week he would make people more aware of his presence, his leadership, and his strength. He'd walk through the office like he was already the newly elected Chief Officer, and maybe that would put people in their place—especially people who actually believed that Ashton Lampson was cut out for such a job.

"I'll make sure everyone knows who's going to be the next Chief Officer," he said. He switched his brandy to the other hand and was admiring his left arm and bicep when the doorbell chimed.

Marty, he thought. *Back from the movies.*

He went to the front door and let in his son, who still had a giant cup of soda in his hand and a big box of Milk Duds wedged into his front pocket. Marty walked in along with his friend, eleven-year-old Kenny Payne, and Kenny's dad.

"So the movie was good?" Colton asked.

Kenny's dad was an auto mechanic, and every time Colton had met him, he looked like he had driven straight over from the shop. Even now, Michael looked like he'd just gotten out from under a vehicle. He wore blue jeans, a white T-shirt speckled with grease stains, and dirty sneakers. Colton couldn't remember a time when he didn't look this way.

"The boys had a good time tonight," Michael said with a crooked smile. His smile always looked asymmetrical beneath his bristly, unkempt mustache. "Took 'em to see *Deadly Force, Part Two*. Good one. Better than the first one."

"Yeah, Dad, it was really cool!" Marty said.

Kenny, a freckle-faced kid with an obnoxious bowl cut, nodded in agreement.

"Really? Good. Glad to hear it," Colton said, though he felt a little out of the loop. His son had talked on and on about how much he loved the first movie, but thinking back on it, Colton didn't have the vaguest clue what it was about. His son had also talked up the second one just a couple weeks ago and how excited he was to see it, but Colton couldn't remember the movie's premise. Something about astronauts going to a planet inhabited by humanoid-like aliens wearing sparkly silver suits. Something like that. It was impossible to keep all of his son's interests clear in his head.

"Yeah, we enjoyed it," Michael said. "Went through enough tubs of popcorn and soda to fill us up for the next year. Probably gained twenty pounds tonight."

"It was great!" Marty said, and sipped his soda. Colton wondered how many refills his son had gotten during the course of the movie. Two or three wouldn't surprise him at all.

"Wait, you had popcorn?" Colton asked.

"Yeah, why?" Marty frowned. He jiggled his straw up and down with adolescent hyperactivity, making an obnoxious squeaky noise. "Is that bad?"

"Just the butter. What about your allergies? You know that makes you stuffy."

Marty stopped moving his straw up and down and looked at him peculiarly. Kenny tilted his head sideways and looked confused as his fiery red hair listed to the left.

"Oh dear, I'm really sorry," Michael said, stroking his moustache nervously. "I had no idea—really—no idea. I should have asked first. Didn't even think about it."

"Dad, what are you talking about?" Marty asked. "Are you talking about the allergy I outgrew? Really, Dad? I'm not a kid anymore. Remember the last allergy test?"

"Yeah, of course I do."

But he didn't.

He remembered taking Marty to the doctor's office a couple years ago for a routine checkup—vaccinations, height and weight index, all of the basics—but couldn't pull up a memory of an allergy test.

"Then you should remember it's fine now. I can have dairy. It doesn't mess me up."

"Okay, okay, just playing it safe," Colton said, and tried not to be obvious in his ignorance. He hadn't eaten dairy himself for years and kept it out of the house entirely; this was mainly for his own dieting regime, but still, he should have known. Hadn't Marty just ordered pizza last week at dinner? Feeling pathetic and wanting to get out of this conversation as quickly as possible, he tried to change the subject.

"Well, I'm glad to hear you guys had a good time." Colton patted his son on the shoulder. He turned his attention to Kenny and his dad. "Thanks for taking my boy to the movies."

"Anytime," Michael said. He scratched his crooked moustache, and his forehead wrinkled in thought. "Listen, we're having a little barbecue in a couple weeks—you know, a way to kick off the summer—and we wanted to invite Marty. You, too. We'd love to have you over. Throw a few burgers on the grill. Lots of food and drinks."

"In a couple Fridays, huh?" Colton said, and maybe it was from watching Michael, but he felt himself scratching his own hairless upper lip. With the position of Chief Officer up for grabs and his newfound commitment to prove himself, he didn't want to commit to something that might pull him away from work. If he was leading a team that day, he could be tied up for hours. All night, possibly.

"Well, I thank you so much for the invite, but I'm afraid I won't really be able to commit that night. Work beckons."

"Oh, I understand completely," Michael said, and Marty pulled at Colton's shirt pleadingly.

"But listen, that doesn't mean Marty can't go. Consider it a done deal. I can have his babysitter drop him off, and if I can get out of the office on time, I'd love to join you."

Marty rolled his eyes at the word *babysitter*. He was twelve now, and he hated the use of that word. Once they were alone, Colton was pretty sure his son was going to harass him about using that vulgar expression in the presence of company.

"Well, that sounds great," Michael said.

Kenny and Marty gave each other a high five and, with the ice sloshing around in their sodas, they began to dance and clumsily gyrate their bodies in what could only be described as the Adolescent Happy Dance.

"If you don't mind me asking," Michael said, "what exactly do you do for a living?"

"What do I do?" Colton repeated. Given the great political unrest waging in the country over what to do with the Aberrants in quarantine, and in hope of sidestepping even a lukewarm debate, he dodged the question entirely. "Just government work. Nothing exciting. I wouldn't want to put you to sleep by explaining."

Slowly, a crooked smile grew on Michael's face. "Very well." He leaned close to Colton, whispering into his ear. "There's going to be several single ladies there, if you catch my drift. Pretty ones. Just think about it."

He winked, and Colton found it strange—almost perverse— to see a grown man wink at him, but he understood. Ever since Colton became a single dad, many of his friends and colleagues made it their personal mission in life to set him up with that special someone. It usually unnerved him, but this time he found himself thinking: *Is it Selma? If it's Selma, I might go.*

"Well, thank you so much for the offer," Colton said as politely as possible.

Michael wrote the date and address on the back of a business card and handed it to Colton. Kenny and Marty gave each other another high five. When the guests left, Colton told Marty to get ready for bed. It was late, and he wanted to get up early and get some work done around the condo.

"All right," Marty sighed and headed off to his bedroom.

Colton stood by the sliding glass door that led to the patio while he waited for Marty to finish getting ready for bed. He looked in the direction of the Quarantine Zone and thought again of the action he would take when he reported for duty on Monday. He would prove himself. Assert himself. Make his presence absolutely known.

"They'll never chant Ashton Lampson's name again," he said. His breath fogged the glass door he was leaning towards. "Never."

Taking his final sip of brandy, he carried the empty glass with him into his son's room. Marty was already in bed, his hands crossed behind his head, looking up in thought. Colton sat on the edge of his bed and wondered if Marty was getting too old to be tucked in every night. Colton wasn't sure. He was in that strange parental purgatory between things that are too "childish" and things that are too "grown up." He'd never thought himself very good at the whole nighttime routine anyway; these days he just tried to get Marty in bed with his teeth brushed and then ask him a couple questions about how his day went.

"So you liked the movie?" Colton asked. He was feeling the brandy now. The room was pleasantly spinning. "Lots of good action, huh?"

"Yeah, but I liked the costumes. Really cool. The soldier had these silver suits with cool triangle patterns on them. And the main girl—a good queen from another planet—had this amazing dress that changed colors constantly."

"You liked her dress?"

"Yeah."

"Well, weren't there explosions, guns, fights? Wasn't that cool?"

"Well, yeah, but I thought the costumes were really neat. And there was a love story, too."

"A love story?"

"Yeah. The lead solider, Markel, falls in love with Esmeralda. But the thing is, they actually knew each other from when they were children because Markel is really an alien from her planet, but his memory was erased when he was abducted and taken to planet Earth. But when they were kids and knew each other, they made a promise that they would always love each other. It was very sweet."

"Sweet, huh?

"Yes, I thought it was touching."

"Touching?"

Colton felt his shirt collar tighten around his neck, and he loosened it with his fingers. He never understood these conversations with his son. Why was a twelve-year-old boy coming back from a movie and making observations about things that were "sweet" and "touching?" What was wrong with him?

This just wasn't normal.

Colton hated that he had a difficult time relating to Marty. It was always this way. The first time he'd taken Marty to the shooting range to watch, the poor boy plugged his ears before they even entered the facility to get his ear protection, cried the whole time, and wouldn't stop until he was back in the car. All the gunfire scared him. He had no interest in any of it. Last summer, when he took Marty four-wheeling in the desert with a group of guys from work, Marty went on one ride for about five minutes and called it quits. He complained that it was too dusty, too loud, and sitting on top of that much power made him nervous. Sitting by a campfire with a group of dads and their sons during that trip, Colton wondered, *What's wrong with this kid? Did they switch babies on us at the hospital?*

But the worst of it happened just three months ago when Colton, desperate to instill some form of confidence and manliness in his son, enrolled him in karate. At the time, Marty had even showed some lukewarm interest. It was a martial art, and there was some kind of artistry to it, wasn't there? It actually went well for a couple months until it was time for Marty to test for his yellow belt. He was sparring with another kid, a twiggy little boy named Ambrose. Ambrose, who looked more like a kid in a karate outfit having an epileptic seizure than someone actually trying to spar, made accidental contact with Marty's face. It was minor—a powder-puff of a hit—but it was enough to cause Marty to run out of the facility and break down crying. Despite his best efforts, Colton couldn't convince him to go back inside. Not then and not later.

He even tried to cheer him up by taking him out for ice-cream. After a double scoop of Cookies & Cream, Marty pointed to the art store next door. Colton, desperate to rectify the situation, took him immediately. Colton watched as his son walked through the displays, marveling at the different paintings, and Colton felt the same thing he was feeling now: *Who is this kid? What's wrong with him?*

"Well, I'm glad you liked the movie," Colton said.

He looked at the walls of his son's room. They were covered

with paintings that Marty had done over the last few years: watercolors, pastels, chalks. All depicted exotic scenes: cascading waterfalls, unicorns, brightly colored parrots. They were good— at least, Colton assumed they were good. He never really had a taste for the visual arts. Marty had even asked recently if he could put one of his paintings in the Hall of Fame, but Colton wasn't about to go there quite yet. They were good, yes, but they weren't *that* good. Maybe after a few more years and some training, they could discuss it, but secretly Colton hoped his son's interests would change. He'd rather put up his son's own plaques and awards rather than some meaningless drawings.

"Dad," Marty said just as Colton was standing up to leave.

Colton felt suddenly tired and wanted to get to bed. "Yeah, Son, what is it?"

"The movie. There was a part in it that reminded me of Mom."

"Was there?"

Now Colton really wanted to go to bed. He hated these situations and loathed these discussions. He thought of something to say, something comforting, but when he opened his mouth to talk, he found no words—just empty breath. He wanted to comfort his son and thought for a moment that perhaps the right thing to do would be to kneel beside his bed, kiss him, and tell him that he missed her, too. But he couldn't bring himself to do it. Marty needed a strong example. He needed to see strength, not weakness.

"Go to bed, Son," he said, turning out the light.

"All right," Marty said.

Colton left the room but stopped just a few paces outside the door to listen. Sure enough, Marty was crying. It was just a soft whimper, a faint and sorrowful breeze rustling through a quiet home. Colton put his hands against the wall and leaned his forehead against it. As he listened to his son cry for his mom, the familiar feeling resurfaced. He recognized his complete lack of competency in this area and inability to deal with it.

Oh, what do I do?

He went to the wet bar and poured another glass of brandy. Downed it. Poured another one. Downed it, too.

Then, he walked back toward the patio and looked out toward the Island he couldn't see in the darkness.

"Good thing your God isn't real," he whispered, "because if He was, I'd hate Him."

1.1.5

When Colton pulled his Lexus into his parking space at the rear of CTC Headquarters, he reminded himself that today was all business. He had a point to prove. He would dispel any notion that Ashton Lampson was a reasonable candidate for Chief Officer, and he would do it with unflinching authority.

"Very big day today," Colton mumbled to himself as he stepped through the screening corridor.

A fatigued security officer sat behind a desk illuminated by several screens. He nodded approvingly when the first chime indicated that the NRNT chip in Colton's skull identified him positively as Colton Pierce; a second chime indicated that he was unarmed. As a green light above the security monitor flashed on, the officer waved him through.

The door behind the security monitors unlocked, slowly hissed open, and Colton walked into the large lobby with marble floors, spiraling staircases, windows pouring in sunlight, and the general commotion of CTC workers running around like ants. Typical for a Monday morning.

Colton stepped over to one of the coffee machines to replenish his portable mug, and Kramer, half-looking down at his tablet and half-looking up at Colton, waddled up to him.

"Good morning, Kramer," Colton said as he finished pouring himself a fresh cup. "Beautiful day out today, don't you think?"

"Um, yes, if you say so."

As usual, Kramer looked disheveled, slovenly dressed, with half of his white shirt tucked in and the other half hanging out. It seemed that Kramer employed all of his organizational talent on others but little, if any, on himself. In this way, Colton always found Kramer to be a contradiction. An interesting one. Kramer could probably tell Colton every appointment he had from now until his retirement, but at the same time, Kramer probably couldn't tell anyone what he himself was doing day-to-day.

"Listen, we have some important business to get to today. We have that new hire in Extraction Team Seven. You need to do a personal interview. PR stuff. Doug wants a copy of your opinion by the end of the day. At least three Senior Extractors are needed before a final decision is made, and you're the last one left."

"Okay, let's do that just before lunch. I'd like to walk around the offices for a little while. It's been too long. I'd like to see what's going on."

Kramer looked down at his tablet, back to Colton, back to his tablet. Colton thought, by the look on Kramer's face, that he had said something horribly offensive.

"Um, I'm afraid you don't have time," Kramer said. Now he was sweating, and he adjusted the tie that was already crooked to an even more crooked position. "They're filming a public service announcement today—you know, typical PR stuff. We need you to say something. There's some follow-up paperwork for your extraction last week regarding Josh Mosley. We need that before he can be sent off to the Quarantine Zone. And, of course, there's been such a surge in calls these last several months, you could get a call any minute. You might need to suit up and leave."

"Mondays are normally slow," Colton said assuredly. He sipped his new batch of coffee. It was black, the way he liked it, but not nearly as good as the stuff he brewed at home. "You mustn't forget, I have a little of my own PR work to do around here, Kramer. You don't want that scrawny Ashton character running this place, do you? You think this office is dysfunctional now? You let that guy get his hands on the wheel, and it'll only be a matter of time until this place falls apart completely."

Kramer was at a loss for what to say. The fingers holding his tablet turned white as he gripped it tighter.

"Come, follow me. Let's make a stop at the Command Center."

"The Command Center? Why the Command Center?"

"Why not?" Colton asked. "In addition to everything else, I need some cheering up. Listening to the news this morning, about how some of these humanists are protesting the new legislation and our right to terminate the Aberrants, put me on edge. Can you believe those people? Can you believe people actually are opposed to just eliminating them outright?"

"Uh…well…"

Kramer looked away and adjusted his glasses.

Oh no, Colton thought. *Not Kramer. No way could Kramer be sympathetic to the Aberrants.*

Colton shook his head and said, "Just follow me."

1.1.6

The Command Center looked like something out of the NASA space program. The room, or what seemed more like an aircraft hanger, was lined with desks, computers, screens, phones, and CTC workers clicking away at their keyboards and squawking away into their headpieces. A movie-theater-sized screen on the north wall displayed a digitalized map of the United States of America. There were always at least a few targets—little red dots on the screen—being monitored by the small paramilitary force in the southeast corner of the room.

Looking at the screen, Colton noticed there were only two current active targets—one in Charlotte, North Carolina and the other (this one flashing red, which indicated the target was armed and dangerous) appeared to be in the upstate New York area. The CTC would have referred such extractions to the local offices in that district but, once extracted, the Aberrants would be sent here in transport vehicles to be registered and delivered to their ultimate destination: the Quarantine Zone.

This was where it all began. As Colton looked over the rows of agents, he reminded himself that every call about every possible threat of theological outbreak began in this room. But few such calls resulted in a possible target and the need for an extraction team. This was the twenty-first century, not the Salem witch hunts of 1692. Every call was surgically monitored for the slightest possibility of fraud, and nobody became an extraction target without clear and compelling evidence: approval of local law enforcement and mandatory reporters, witness testimony, and a very careful examination of the suspect's activity by a close reading of the individual's NRNT chip as to his or her whereabouts and what could be considered anomalous behavior.

Colton had long prided himself on the extensive safety measures the agency had employed to ensure the public that anyone on the Island deserved to be there and, assuming the new legislation passed, anyone six feet under would deserve to be there as well.

He found Oswald Bane, director of the Command Center, near the front of the room. He stood at his podium directly before the gigantic map of the United States, where he was busy reading reports on his tablet and taking questions from agents who occasionally ran up to him from their stations. He was a short, plump, bald man with white wisps of hair. He wore giant, silver spectacles and pulled them down to the end of his nose to look over the rims when Colton and Kramer approached.

"Oh, hello, Colton," he said, sounding uncertain. He handed an agent some piece of paper that they had been discussing and turned his full attention to Colton. "What brings you to these parts?"

The Command Center and the extraction teams were two completely different entities and only mixed for special occasions: the staff winter party, Staff Appreciation Week, and community service projects. By and large, most workplace gossip suggested that the agents here thought the extraction teams didn't really respect the hard, mundane work of the Command Center—the first line of defense. Similarly, the extraction teams thought the Command Center agents were boring pencil-pushers who didn't really know what it was to get their hands dirty. Still, there was enough mild respect and cordiality to ensure any overlapping of those departments—during those few occasions—went smoothly enough.

"Not much," Colton said. "Just thought I'd stop by and have a look at how things were running on this side of the fence."

"Oh," Oswald said, unsure of what else to say. Holding his tablet, he shifted back and forth.

"Yep," Colton said. "You know, with the Chief Officer stepping down, I thought it only wise to walk around and see how operations were running throughout all departments. Doesn't hurt to know the whole picture."

"Oh, you're going for that position?"

"I most certainly am."

"Really? I heard Ashton Lampson was, but I didn't know that you were. That's great. I wish you the best of luck, really, the best of luck."

Colton ground his teeth and fumed. *What? Oswald knew that Ashton was pulling to be the new Chief Officer but not me? Wow. I really have been keeping too low a profile. I've been so concerned with my extraction numbers, I haven't gotten out there and thrown my weight around. Good thing that's going to change.* He turned around to look over the sea of Command Center agents sitting at their desks while they yapped into their phones and pecked at their tablets. He noticed one guy—a little, scrawny guy with a crooked nose and Dumbo ears—leaning back in his seat and glaring into his cell phone. What was he doing? Texting a friend? Surfing the web?

Colton thought this the perfect opportunity, and he reached for the small handheld speaker at the side of Oswald's podium that he had seen used when he'd been by the Command Center in the past.

"What are you doing?" Oswald asked and almost dropped the tablet. His eyes were gargantuan.

"Just gonna make myself known," Colton said. Kramer tried to say something as well, but Colton held out his hand to silence both of them. Speaking into the handheld radio, he heard his voice emanate from the giant speakers lining both sides of the room. The room went suddenly silent and tablets turned off, phones were put on hold, and movement came to a complete standstill. Every set of eyes looked to the Extractor of the Month standing at the director's podium with a microphone in his hand.

"Good morning, fellow workers at the CTC," Colton said. His voice shook the room. There was feedback, and he moved the microphone away from his mouth. He saw the ocean of faces looking at him. Silent. Squinting. Perplexed.

"Colton," Kramer said in one last effort to deter him, but Colton brushed him away like a gnat.

"I'm sure all of you know who I am, and if you don't, I won't hold it against you," he said, laughing. When nobody laughed back, he took the microphone in his other hand and tried to attack it from another angle. "You know that Brian Barclay has announced his retirement, and the most important thing a Chief Officer can do is improve morale and work ethic. We all know the important reputation we have here at the CTC, and when a new director is assigned, the committee will most certainly weigh opinions from every department—from this department, Quarantine Management, every department. And I want all of you to know that I will personally go above and beyond to ensure that this department will function better and be more productive than it has ever been. You can quote me on that!"

He backed away and lowered the microphone in anticipation of some kind of reaction, but there wasn't even lukewarm applause. Figuring he'd most certainly caught them at a busy hour and not wanting to take too much more of their time, he pointed to the skinny guy on the cell phone and barked into his microphone.

"Like, look at this guy," Colton said. His voice seemed louder than before, even though nobody had turned up the volume. "All of you are working hard, and this lazy excuse for a worker is just sitting there on his phone, texting his girlfriend, maybe? Or maybe he's looking up inappropriate images in the workplace? Perhaps I should call HR to have that phone confiscated."

The skinny guy leaned back in his seat and looked genuinely terrified.

"Colton." Oswald clutched him by the shoulder and whispered into his ear. "That's Larry Herrick. He was on break. He was Agent of the Month last month and—"

"Break?" Colton said. "Break? We don't break here. Theological threats don't break for us, and we won't break for them—and I can assure you, when I am Chief Officer of the CTC, I won't break for you."

He put down his microphone, slapped Oswald on the back, and marched out of the room with Kramer at his side. He felt everyone's eyes on him and, once outside, took a deep breath.

"See how they couldn't even talk after?" he said. "I think I shock-and-awed them. That went great."

"Yes, great," Kramer said, rubbing his eyes. "Shock and awe."

"Come on, let's swing by Quarantine Management. I'd like to make my presence known there, too."

"Oh dear," Kramer said, following.

1.1.7

Terrel Tyler, Director of Quarantine Management, looked a bit befuddled when Colton Pierce asked to do a walk-through with his assistant. He scrolled through something on his company tablet.

"Well," Terrel said, "I've looked through the calendar and I just can't seem to locate any—"

"Calendar?"

"Well, yes, the calendar."

"Oh, calendar schmallender, this is informal. I'm just coming by to do a quick, informal check on things. Nothing more. Nothing less."

"Informal, huh?"

Terrel was clearly the kind of guy who dotted his I's and crossed his T's and was having a painstaking internal conflict over this surprise visit. He glared down at whatever schedule was on his tablet, but Colton thought he was really trying to figure out how this inherent conflict in his daily schedule fit into his paradigm.

"Well, I suppose it's okay," Terrell said. "I don't see anything that would prohibit you from doing a walk-through, and I—"

"Of course."

"Of course, what?"

"Of course there wouldn't be anything that would stop me or anyone else from doing a walk-through. I'd love to get a look at this division. I feel like I haven't laid eyes on this place in years."

"Well, be my guest," Terrel said, and with absolute finality, looked up from his tablet and let go of the tethers binding him to the daily calendar. He punched a button on his desk, and the solid steel doors clicked, clicked again, and slowly slid open with a fatigued hiss. The cold, white corridor lined with doors lured Colton forward.

Terrel stepped aside, and Colton strutted down the corridor that housed the theologically ill who had been recently extracted. Kramer followed him. The hallway was sheer white with steel doors on both sides, each with a circular porthole-like window. A small, blipping keypad was adjacent to each cell. Colton looked in at the recently quarantined as he passed; he hadn't followed up much on the inner workings of this division, but a recent memo he'd read seemed to indicate that most of these Aberrants would be shipped out on Friday. These were fresh captives who still had several days to go before they reached their final destination.

He looked in at the first few cells as he passed: An elderly lady who looked like a librarian sat on a bench in the corner of her cell and stared dismally at the wall; a morbidly obese man picked his nails and glared nervously at the floor; a finely manicured man, maybe in his late twenties, sat upright in the corner of his cell with overactive fingers that were probably used to clutching the handle of a briefcase. All were clad in yellow jumpsuits, quarantine garb, with a number written across the chests. When Colton passed Quarantine Prisoner 2122, Josh Mosley, the man he'd extracted Friday afternoon, he stopped. Josh stared stoically into the corner of his chamber, waiting for the inevitable: his one-way cruise to the Quarantine Zone. Unable to resist the opportunity, Colton stopped, pressed the communication button on the keypad, and talked to the man he'd personally extracted.

"How you doing in there, Mr. Mosley?"

Josh, sitting on the edge of his cot, looked toward the door with weary, sleep-deprived eyes. Colton wasn't sure, but he thought he saw a faint glimmer of hope in those eyes—perhaps Josh thought Colton had come down here to give him good news.

"Did you hear me, Mr. Mosley? I asked how you were doing on this beautiful morning."

"I've been better," he said flatly.

"Colton, we really should go," Kramer said, nudging him. "We have so much to get done today and the public service announcement really needs our—"

"This will just take a moment," Colton said. He leaned closer to the bullet-proof glass.

"I need to see my family," Josh said, nervously fidgeting with his fingers. Colton realized that the red, irritated eyes weren't just from lack of sleep—this man had been crying. Weeping extensively, from the looks of things. "Please. I'll do anything. My wife and children. I need to see them."

"Oh, so you have children?"

"Yes. Two sons. Both in college. One is engaged to be married next week. Please, I must."

"Now, Mr. Mosley, this isn't a place for begging. This is part of the natural consequence of what happens when you break the law. You know the full consequence of what happens when you ignore the law, don't you?"

"Yes, but I never meant to—"

"Well, that may be true," Colton said. "Whether some mutation has caused your delusions or whether your delusions came first isn't for me to decide. I just enforce the law and leave those other issues to the scientists. But you could have at least—if you really cared for the society in which you live—checked yourself into a clinic the moment you started to experience symptoms. You could have called our toll-free number to report your condition. That could have proven quite advantageous to you."

"You would have taken me to the Island anyway!"

"Perhaps," Colton said. "Public safety is always our number one priority, but I can assure you, not all lodgings on the Quarantine Zone are created equal. For those who come willingly, without resistance, we offer the very best in accommodations and see to it that all privileges are bestowed to you. It could have been a nice trip for you, Mr. Mosley—a vacation."

"I don't want a vacation," he said, and now that desperate look was back in his eyes. "I want my family! I want my wife! I want my sons! Please! Have mercy!"

"Mercy," Colton said, chewing on the word like piece of gristle.

He knew, like all extractors did, that he had a reputation to uphold. Once word leaked that he'd gone soft, it would be almost impossible to earn back that reputation. Word spread quickly on the Island—both among the guards and the captives—and the last thing Colton needed was a bad mark on his record that would hurt his chances of becoming Chief Officer. He recalled what had happened to a now-retired extractor, Peter Huntley, who was a bit too kind to some of the captives' families when they visited their loved ones. As the humanist movement picked up steam, poor Peter became a target for them; he was bombarded by emails, letters, and calls in the political war to ensure humane treatment for the Aberrants. By the time he retired, Peter was known to have regretted every kind gesture he'd made toward the Aberrants. The last thing Peter wanted was to be a pawn in some political activist campaign, and Colton wasn't about to make that mistake.

"Please, sir," Josh Mosley implored. This time, Colton thought he might actually fall down on his knees and grovel. Wouldn't that be amusing? "Why? Why do I have to be taken to the Island? Why do any of us have to be taken? How will I hurt you? How will any of us hurt you?"

"Well, that's a complicated question, Mr. Mosley. Have you read your history books? Do you know what the world was like before the VMAT2 Gene was destroyed? The wars and the number of deaths that were a direct result from people like you and your foolish beliefs? I don't know why a minor percentage of the population believes these things again. That's a question the scientists are working on, and yes, Mr. Mosley, you will certainly be studied to determine why these arcane beliefs have regenerated in you. You can at least rest assured that you are giving your life to the advancement of modern science."

"But I'm not going to hurt anyone!"

"That's what you say now. I've heard it a thousand times. But if you were left in society, you would find others like you. You would seek each other out, wouldn't you? And over time you would become a threat to the peace our society enjoys. That is why, Mr. Mosley."

"But I won't—"

"I am a generous man," Colton said, and he thought, for just a brief moment, he saw hope flash across the captive's face again.

"In my great generosity, I will see to it that you leave as soon as possible on the next transport to the Island. I will make a personal call to make sure the process is expedited."

"But sir, I didn't—"

"No need to thank me." Colton tapped his assistant on the shoulder to indicate it was time to leave. "Have a good day, Mr. Mosley. Pleasant sailing."

As he walked down the corridor, the communication speaker was still activated, and he could hear Josh Mosley weeping.

Unlike listening to his son, however, the sounds of Josh whimpering filled him with a strange sense of pride.

1.1.8

Colton changed into one of the CTC's original extraction outfits for the public service announcement. Although he wished to spend more time making his rounds through headquarters, Kramer insisted that it was more important to film the announcement; the crew was on a tight schedule and it simply had to be done. He put on the silver, full-bodied, armored outfit with the coiled snake—the symbol of the CTC—across the breast, but opted not to wear the helmet. No need. When the CTC was first implemented, helmets had been used to protect the extractors from potential gangs of Aberrants who might fight back. The helmets were long and terrifying, with a breathing vent and two glowing eye filters that allowed extractors night vision when necessary. But the Aberrants rarely fought back and because it was just as easy for extractors to carry night vision goggles with their equipment, the helmets were deemed useless. Still, the public liked the old outfits. They had become a symbol of hope and security.

He checked his hair in the restroom, splashed some water on to tame it, and walked out to the south end of the CTC's cafeteria where filming was underway.

A film crew congregated by the large windows. Cords snaked across the floor and around tripods, cameras, and lighting equipment. Kramer ushered Colton to the set. A short, pudgy man wearing flannel pulled him in front of the camera and handed him a script. Colton realized that the short guy was the director and he was highly impatient to get this over with. Apparently it had been a long morning, he hadn't had his coffee yet (at least, Colton heard someone say that), and he had several other workers to film as part of this public service announcement. Colton wasn't sure who all these other people were, swarming around like gnats, but he assumed they had some purpose in the filming.

"You've looked at your lines, right?" the director barked.

"Of course."

"Usually, we bring in actors for these parts, so we're hoping you get this right."

"Not a problem. I can—"

Colton was interrupted when a lady with long blonde hair ran up to him and began to powder his face. He recoiled and began to cough, but the makeup woman hardly slowed down.

"So you have them memorized? Right?" the director barked for a second time.

"Yes, yes I do."

At least, he *thought* he did. He'd been given the script a week ago in preparation for this day and had looked it over for ten or fifteen minutes. It was quite short, and even if he was off on a few sections, how could it hurt? The whole point of the script was to remind the community to be vigilant in looking for Aberrants and to be aware of the symptoms. The best way to ensure public safety was simply to keep your eyes open and to be informed. Would it really hurt if he didn't do this word-for-word? It wasn't a big deal.

"Okay, okay," the director said. He paced back and forth for a few seconds and then took a seat in a folding chair. He looked over at the man operating the camera and gave him a quick thumbs up. "Just look at the camera, act confident, and say your lines. We have about twenty other people we need to film, so let's get this over with quickly, okay?"

"You got it," Colton said, and he turned just a bit sideways to make sure his good side was angled toward the camera.

"Okay, then," the director said. "On one, two, and…action!"

"Greetings out there," Colton said. "I'm Colton Pierce, Extractor of the Month and quite possibly the next Chief Officer of the CTC, and I want to—"

"Cut! Cut!" the director cried and violently began to wave a piece of paper around. He looked down at it to double-check something. "What is this about you being Extractor of the Month and the next Chief Officer? Where is that in the script?"

46

"Well, it doesn't hurt to give viewers some of my credentials, does it?"

The director stopped, thought about this, and waved his paper through the air with a sigh. "Fine, fine. Go ahead and put it in. Whatever. We can always edit out what we need to. Now let's try this again, okay? Stick to the lines, but add the credentials if you want. Ready?"

Colton nodded.

"And why are you turning a little? Face the camera directly."

"Okay." Colton turned to face the camera head-on, but once the director was assured, he turned just a little to give his good side a bit more prominence.

"Here we go," the director said. "On one, two, and…action!"

"Greetings out there," Colton said. "I'm Colton Pierce, Extractor of the Month and most likely the next Chief Officer of the CTC, and I want to remind you to look out for common theological threats that could be in your own neighborhood. Have you seen groups of people congregate secretly behind closed doors? Have you heard people utter strange, archaic beliefs concerning morality? Have you noticed seemingly sane, ordinary people mumbling softly to themselves or closing their eyes, particularly during meals or times of great distress? Don't hesitate to call our office. In fact, you can call me personally, because out of the all the extractors at the CTC, nobody has the track record that I do. Nobody can claim to—"

"Cut! Cut!" the director cried again and waved his paper through the air. For a moment, Colton thought he might tear it into pieces in rage. He got out of his chair, stomped toward Colton, and looked up at him. His face was beet red. "Why are you doing this? This is a public service announcement. This isn't a platform to promote what a great extractor you are, don't you realize that?"

"Well, yes."

"Then why are you making it all about yourself?"

"I'm not," Colton said, "but if I'm the best extractor at the CTC, I think the public has a right to know. In some cases, an individual might want to request a particular extractor, and if I'm the best at what I do, then I think—"

"Fine, whatever," the director said. He dropped the paper on the floor and walked back toward the cameraman. "We're gonna need a lot of edits on this one, I suppose. So we just need one more thing. I need you to look at the camera and say the motto of the CTC. We're going to overlay several clips of various workers saying the phrase at the end of the commercial. Can you do that for me, please?"

"Sure thing."

"Okay," the director said. "Now look toward the camera, smile handsomely, and say: *Protecting our new world.* On one, two, and...action!"

Colton looked at the camera, smiled, and said, "Protecting my new world."

"Cut!" the director said, and he rubbed his forehead with what could only have been the beginning of a pounding headache. "Did you hear what you just said?"

"I just said the motto, exactly what you wanted me to."

"No, no you didn't. You said, 'Protecting *my* new world.' Do you see a problem with that? It's not your world. I happen to live in it, too. And so do all of these people standing around here trying to film this. And so do the people who will see this. So let's try this again, okay? Just four words there, four words. Let's get it right. On one, two, and...action!"

Colton looked firmly at the camera and almost lost his concentration. He saw Selma, who had been eating on the other side of the cafeteria, walk to a trashcan and throw away her food. She looked toward him and smiled. She was wearing a black pencil skirt and a white blouse, and she looked—as usual—totally beautiful. Colton froze. The four words vanished from his mind. He had no idea what to say.

"Say your lines," the director said.

"Um, what were they again?" Colton asked.

The headache must have come back, because the director started rubbing his temples. "Protecting our new world."

"Ah, yes." Colton gathered himself, looked squarely at the camera, and said, with utter confidence, "Protecting our new world."

"Cut! Great." The director was going to say something more, but Colton didn't stick around to listen.

He walked past the crew and over the twisting cords to follow Selma.

1.1.9

Colton found Selma in the copy room. The coffee machine was there as well, so when he realized that he didn't have any actual purpose in being in the copy room and this might appear odd, he casually walked up to the complimentary coffee in the corner of the room, grabbed a cup, and filled it to the brim. As he stirred his coffee, he looked over at Selma, who had not yet—to his knowledge—looked up from the papers she was copying. She appeared entirely focused on the small stack of papers she had brought with her.

She does look quite amazing, Colton thought. He realized how dark and olive-toned her skin was, and he wondered again about her ethnicity. Some Asian? Some Hispanic? A blend of everything?

Selma looked up at him. He recognized the look to be more than just a casual glance upward—she saw him, looked back down, but then her eyes were back on him, and she perked up.

Every alarm in Colton's body sounded that this was a woman who was attracted to him. No questions there, and what better time to do something about it than right now—in the copy room—while they were alone?

"Hi there," she said, and her gaze lingered on him. The stack of papers she'd been so focused on just a moment before now seemed trivial. "Nice outfit. Playing the part of one of the old extractors, huh?"

"Yeah, I did my best. I think it went well."

"I hope so. I'm the one who scheduled all the filming now that I'm working for PR. I might try bringing in actors next time, but I thought, why not let the community see the faces of the real men and women at the CTC?"

"Good choice, of course. How are you doing?" Colton asked.

"I'm great."

"Got a big stack of copies there, huh?"

"Oh, these?" She looked down at the papers she was holding. The copy machine was spitting out fifteen copies of some kind of chart. "Yeah, just some PR calendars. Nothing that exciting. Planning more public service announcements."

"Any fun plans for this weekend?"

"This weekend," she said, puckering her lips in thought. "Well, I am going to an outdoor event down in Manhattan Beach. Very excited about it."

"Outdoor event?" This troubled Colton, because he'd seen the news and knew exactly what kinds of events were being planned around the city, and perhaps the whole country, for that matter. "You're not going to one of the humanist rallies, are you?"

"Humanist rallies?"

Her response eased his mind. "Yeah, there are some rallies going on this weekend, I think. You know, part of this whole social advocate movement to protest the possible new move in legislation to have the Aberrants killed rather than taken to quarantine. All that nonsense. Really ridiculous, if you ask me. We pay enough in taxes. Why pay more tax dollars keeping them alive? Burial prices are much less, and just on an inside level, I'd be willing to bet a passing of that legislation would mean a raise for everyone here at the CTC."

"A raise? Really? I haven't heard anything about that from HR."

"Well, it seems kind of logical, doesn't it?" he said. "If the CTC doesn't have to spend all that money to transport the Aberrants to the Island and keep them alive for years or even decades, that means more money for our salaries. Makes sense to me."

"Hmm," Selma said, puckering her lips again. "I never thought of that."

"You're not on the humanists' side, are you? I've heard there are some people at work that believe they should be quarantined for life rather than terminated."

"The humanists' side?" she asked, and seemed a little pinned down by the question. She clearly wasn't expecting it. Taking a deep breath, she readjusted her black-rimmed reading glasses, and her big green eyes blinked several times. "You know, I just like to stay out of all the politics in general. I try to just do my job and not get into all that."

"Oh, yeah, right, of course," Colton said, silently cursing himself for pushing this conversation into the realm of politics. That probably wasn't going to help him score a date with Selma. "Well, so, what event is it?"

"Oh, it's a Shakespeare play."

"Shakespeare?"

"Yeah, you've heard of him, right?"

"Of course I've heard of him. Didn't he write that play…um… what was it…I studied it in school."

Selma laughed. She folded her arms in front of her and looked Colton up and down with what seemed to be genuine amusement. "He wrote lots of plays."

"Yes, but there was this one we read in school. A son trying to get vengeance because someone killed his dad. Something like that. It was quite good, actually, once you got past the language and everything."

"*Hamlet*," she said.

"Yes! That was the one. It was good."

"Well, tomorrow night isn't *Hamlet,* but it's another good one. A comedy, actually. It's called *Much Ado About Nothing*, about people who fall in love. One of my favorites."

"So you've seen it before?"

"Of course. I've seen it several times. That's the great thing about theater…particularly Shakespeare. You can watch the same play a hundred times, and every time you see it, you see something different. It makes it almost magical, you know?"

"Wow," Colton said, "you sound like my son."

"Really? So he loves theater?"

"Oh yeah. Theater, music, art. Anything wei—" He caught himself before saying *weird*, and instead pumped out his chest with pride and said, "Wonderful. Anything *wonderful*."

"That's just great!"

It seemed much more natural for Selma to take a liking to such things. It made her more interesting, gave her more depth. There was a mystery to her, a mystery Colton longed to discover. He figured this was the time to strike and ask the question. Nobody had come into the copy room yet. They were connecting on some level, and he might not get another chance like this anytime soon.

Surprisingly, his hands were sweaty. He felt nervous, a new thing for him. *Why am I nervous? She's just a woman. Why?*

"Well, obviously you're booked for this weekend, but if you're not busy the following weekend, I can round up some Lakers tickets. It'd be fun to take you."

"Oh," she said, looking a little surprised. Colton tried to read the expression. Was she upset? Stunned? Excited? He genuinely couldn't tell. "Well, I think next weekend I would—"

The door to the copy room swung open, and Colton, cursing the ill timing of an interruption, looked over as Ashton Lampson walked into the room. Like usual, he was dressed in black slacks that looked a little too tight on him, a purple button-down shirt with a paisley pattern across the shoulders, and shiny black shoes that clicked-clacked on the floor when he walked. What were they, tap shoes? His hair, like always, was so perfectly combed and parted that it looked almost phony; if he were older, someone might accuse him of wearing a toupee, because his hair was always in the same condition and never seemed to change.

When he saw Colton, Ashton grinned widely, that obnoxious, false, plastic grin. His face was long and angular, clean-shaven, and his eyes—little brown beads on both sides of his sharp nose— always looked condescendingly on what they perused. At least, that was how Colton always saw them.

"Well, hello," Ashton said, and Colton wasn't sure who he was addressing—just Colton, Selma, or both of them. Ashton reached into the pocket of his slacks, took out a small can of mint breath spray, and shot himself twice in the mouth for good measure.

"Hello there, Ashton," Colton said.

Ashton, who held an empty mug, went to the coffee station and refilled it. He poured in a splash of cream and stirred it with one of the stirring sticks he plucked from a pile alongside the containers of cream. "I hear you've been making your rounds today, huh?" he asked.

"Making my rounds?"

"Yes, I just ran into Gregory Sullenger. Works in the Command Center. He said you put on quite a show there this morning."

"Did he?"

"Yes, he sure did," Ashton said. "Something about you putting everyone in their place, and how you're going to make the CTC function more efficiently, and how the whole organization will be better, run smoother, and be more accountable when you're at the helm."

It was difficult to be completely sure, but Colton sensed sarcasm in Ashton's tone.

"Yes, I suppose," Colton said. "I did say something to that effect."

"So you are planning on applying for the position?"

"Yes."

"Really," Ashton said, and he seemed to take a moment to absorb this. As he sipped his coffee, he squinted and peered through the tendrils of steam that rose from his mug. "Well, since we all know how nitpicky and backbiting this agency can be at times, perhaps we should make a gentleman's truce. Right here and right now."

"Right here and right now, huh?" Colton said, still wondering if he was correct in his detection of sarcasm. Was he imagining it? Perhaps Ashton was trying to wave an olive branch. He looked over and saw Selma, now done with her copies, watching both men with her stack of papers held against her chest.

"Yes, right here and right now," Ashton said, offering his hand. "Just because we're two extractors applying for the same position doesn't mean this needs to get personal. May the best man win. I think we can agree to that, don't you?"

Colton hesitated, but knowing it wouldn't do much good to deny this offer of goodwill—particularly in the presence of Selma—he shook Ashton's hand. Just as he suspected, it was cold and limp, certainly not a man's handshake; it was like clutching a dead fish.

Colton thought about saying something mildly conciliatory—perhaps a simple "good luck" or "I wish you the best" would be the right thing—but he just couldn't bring himself to do it. He didn't want to wish Ashton the best of anything. He would prove to the CTC, and to Ashton, exactly who the best man for the job was.

When they were done shaking hands, and Colton was fairly convinced that Ashton wasn't trying to be sarcastic, he decided to return to his conversation with Selma. Maybe she was busy this weekend, but there was always next weekend. He had barely turned his attention back to her, however, when Ashton stepped toward Selma and touched her delicately on the shoulder.

"Are we on for Saturday?" Ashton asked.

"Shakespeare?" she replied. "I believe so. Very much looking forward to it."

Colton froze. He felt something—his heart, his spleen, a host of internal organs—drop down to his toes. Was he hearing correctly? This just couldn't be. Ashton Lampson was taking Selma out on a date?

"Well, very good," Ashton said and, dipping his fingers back into his pocket, fished out his breath spray and shot two more quick puffs of peppermint in his mouth. "I'll pick you up at sixish? Does that work?

"Six is good."

"Wonderful. There's a lovely restaurant I'd like to take you to after, one I think you'd quite enjoy."

"Very nice," she said.

"Well, I wish both of you a good day," Ashton said. He opened the door to leave, but before he stepped out of the copy room, he looked back at Colton. This time, the sarcasm was obvious; all doubt was completely eliminated. "As I said before, let the best man win. The best man *always* wins."

He closed the door, and Colton felt completely stupefied. Although he hated entertaining the idea that his radar was off, maybe he'd been wrong about Selma's cues. He'd thought he'd sensed some kind of attraction.

"Colton, I'm sorry about that," Selma said.

"Sorry about what?"

"Well, it's just the way that Ashton—"

The wall speakers sounded: "Extraction Alert. Immediate presence needed on Extraction Deck Four. Repeat, Extraction Alert. Immediate presence needed on Extraction Deck Four."

Just as he'd been trained, Colton dropped everything he was doing, headed out of the copy room, and sprinted toward Deck Four.

As he stepped in the elevator, he promised himself that he'd hurt Ashton's chances at being elected as Chief Officer by making this extraction—and all the ones that followed—quicker and cleaner than he'd ever done before. He'd put up numbers that Ashton couldn't come close to competing with.

"The best man always wins," he whispered.

1.1.10

All extractions began the same, and this was no different. The acronym Colton had learned in training so many years before was APE: Access, Plan, and Execute. Before he even stepped off the elevator, Colton was already thinking of how he could make this extraction one of his quickest, most efficient yet.

The wall speakers sounded again: "Extraction Alert. Immediate presence needed on Extraction Deck Four. Repeat, Extraction Alert: Immediate presence needed on Extraction Deck Four."

He stepped into his private office and took a seat at his computer. As always, the extraction alert was already flashing on his monitor, and after a quick swipe of his finger across the security pad, the file opened completely, and he was able to access the current mission.

This one looked simple. A quick glance through the file indicated it was a 1TNT (One Team, No Threat), the simplest kind of job an extractor could hope for, though a part of Colton liked the more challenging ones. It meant that his team, and his team alone, would be the only ones assigned for this target and no special tactical team would be needed to assist with planning.

He rarely scanned the names of his targets—thinking it meaningless—and depended, instead, on his arm computer to take him straight to the source. He did, however, do a quick scan of the target's bio: a Mexican-American male, 5'8", medium build, who worked as a computer analyst for New Industries, a software company. As usual he had been monitored for weeks, and video evidence, phone warrants, and surveillance had accumulated since he was reported, leading to this final Extraction Order.

The CTC wasted no time; the moment an extraction was approved by a judge, the Aberrant was apprehended, whether at work, at home, or anywhere. Every minute in quarantine was a minute less for such dangerous ideas to proliferate in society, and the CTC prided itself on its efficiency. Years ago, Colton had entertained being part of the investigative branch of the CTC—a very quiet and elusive group of men and women in a separate facility, who gathered evidence and petitioned the courts to authorize extractions—but it did not seem nearly as exciting as being an extractor. Too much monotony and too many details, and Colton far preferred being out in the field as opposed to sitting behind a desk.

He scrolled through the pictures to get an image of the man and then, thinking the pictures too old to really be of any help, scrolled down to the formal accusation.

Target Accusation: Target formally accused of a theological threat as witnessed by target's brother, neighbor, and employer. Target seen harboring reckless hope, engaging in a form of prayer, and, in at least two documented instances, sharing such ideas with others. Target formally accused and sentenced to extraction per the Honorable Judge Whitefield.

Satisfied with what he'd read, Colton went into his wardrobe and changed out of the retro-extraction outfit and into his modern one. Like the older outfits, the new one was sleek and body armored but was also lighter and easier to move in. He attached his earpiece, which would keep him in real-time contact with the Command Center. They would closely monitor the hunt on a digital map, coordinate any assistance needed with local law enforcement, and follow Colton every step of the way.

He clipped his arm computer to his left forearm. This was, in many ways, the most important piece of equipment he took with him on any extraction. It fastened on at the wrist and the elbow. By simply glancing down at his arm, he could see the real-time tracking image of where the target was in relation to him. He referenced this constantly during extractions. A small secondary screen displayed maps and archives of information that he might need to assist him.

He placed his Shark 41-F tranquilizer gun into its holster. It could render any victim unconscious in a mere second. Although

Colton did place his Colt .45 in his other holster, the tranquilizer was always an extractor's first weapon of choice and the only weapon he could use legally unless he was in genuine fear for his life. Killing a target as opposed to extracting one equated to mountains of paperwork, a brief season of administrative leave, and endless media inquiry. So he only reached for his Colt in the most perilous of situations.

Making sure that his arm computer was fully attached and his guns in place, Colton left his office and walked into the central meeting room on Extraction Deck Four. This was a massive, dome-shaped room with yellow-and-white walls and large, oblong windows that looked out in all directions over Long Beach. There was no furniture except for a glass table that his team congregated around before any extraction. Both of his team members already stood beside the table, suited up in their extraction outfits, and ready to roll.

Marek was an extractor-in-training, and at only twenty-seven years old, the biggest brown-nose that Colton had ever worked with at CTC. Considering he was only a year or two from being a full extractor, Colton understood Marek's desire to not make any waves and secure his position.

If Colton could have had it his way, he would have worked alone. But that wasn't an option. Every extractor at the CTC was mandated to work with either a teammate or, at the least, a junior-level extractor. Preferring not to butt heads with someone else, Colton found the decision pretty easy. A junior extractor wouldn't question him. Someone like that was guaranteed to watch, follow, and take orders. Exactly what Colton wanted.

Petra, the team medic, stood beside Marek, scrolling through her cell phone. It was no big shock to Colton. For the last fourteen months that Petra had been assigned to his team, he rarely saw her go a full minute without glaring at her phone. It might have bothered him if Petra was an actual extractor, but being the medic and rarely needed, he didn't think much of it. The whole idea of having a medic assigned to him seemed asinine to begin with and was a ridiculous policy put into place nearly twenty years ago when a gun-toting target shot two extractors. One died and the other was badly injured. Ever since that unfortunate accident, it was department policy to have a medic assigned to any extraction team—both for the safety of the extractor and the general public.

"Well, it looks like the team is ready to go," Colton announced.

"Yes sir," Marek said. "Already read the target's profile. Marcos Quintero, computer analyst. No apparent threat."

Wow, Colton thought, *this guy really does play by the rulebook. He knows the name and everything. He'd probably wear pink panties under his extraction outfit if the policy said so.* "So you're ready. Guns loaded, computers on, everything?"

Petra, yawning, didn't look up from her phone.

"Oh yes," Marek said. He waved his arm in front of Colton's face to show that he was wearing his arm computer. As if Colton needed him to do that.

"And you went through your pre-extraction checklist of what to do before leaving, right? Can never be too sure."

"Um, yes." Marek went through several screens on his arm computer to bring up the checklist to look through it one more time. As he did so, Colton crossed his arms and looked at his trainee, amused. Oh yes, he was going to miss this. Marek was so determined to color between the lines that it was quite fun to put him off balance at times.

"Okay, so you're sure you're ready?"

"Yes, quite ready, sir."

"And you, Petra? Ready?"

Yawning again, she nodded, but still didn't look up from her phone. It was almost an impressive act of multitasking.

"Okay, well, then I think we're ready. One can never be too sure about following protocol. You must remember that when you're an extractor yourself, Marek."

"I will for sure," Marek said. His towheaded trainee looked younger than twenty-seven. Maybe it was his pale complexion and bowl-cut. Any grown man with a bowl cut was destined to look younger than his years. "Policy is the most important thing."

"It most certainly is," Colton said, trying to hold back laughter. He didn't know what was funnier, toying with his young pupil or the simple fact that Marek, in all of his ignorance and desire to be an extractor, had no idea that he was being toyed with. He seemed completely oblivious to Colton's sarcasm.

"All right, then let's go," Colton said. He walked to the wall, typed in his personal code on the small digital keypad, and the steel door slowly slid out of the way. Beyond it, a staircase illuminated in bright fluorescent lights descended toward the extraction vehicle lot. With Marek and Petra behind him, he walked down the stairs and confirmed communication with the Command Center. "This is Extraction Leader Four, checking in. Extraction Leader Four, checking in."

"Extraction Leader Four, we have you," a familiar woman's voice said. Colton had been told years ago that women were best suited to run the radio communication because their voices had a calming effect on the extractors.

"Request permission to leave premises to begin extraction."

"Permission granted."

At the bottom of the stairwell, Colton found himself in the parking lot for extraction team vehicles. His, as usual, was parked in the far northwest corner: a Ford Interceptor, all white, with a single black stripe running down the middle of it. The symbol of the CTC—a coiled snake—was emblazoned on the doors. This Interceptor was one of the newest models, faster than his last vehicle, and right now Colton felt that was exactly what he needed: speed. Still unable to accept the fact that Ashton Lampson was taking Selma out on a date, he figured that he simply must make this extraction his fastest yet. If he could make this one impressive, it would send a message.

He climbed into the driver's seat of his vehicle, and Marek took shotgun. Petra took her own vehicle, a slightly older model of the Interceptor, to follow behind. Her vehicle was yellow instead of black-and-white and loaded with medical supplies.

Colton started the engine, backed up, and pulled immediately down the exit ramp. He floored it and must have been going nearly fifty as he approached the exit gate—which was up since he'd called in permission to leave the premises.

Marek pressed a hand against the dashboard. It was a narrow exit out of the building, and pushing fifty miles an hour going through it clearly wasn't settling well with him. "Colton, too fast," he said.

"Too fast?"

"Yeah, policy. You're supposed to do twenty leaving the building!"

"Oh really," Colton said.

He was probably doing over sixty when he tore past the exit gate. The guard working in the booth looked about as terrified as Marek and recoiled as the vehicle sped past him like a missile.

Once out on the street, with sirens blazing and the open road ahead of them, Colton looked over at his young trainee. Marek was crouched down in his seat and gripping the handle of the side door with the determination of a drowning man clutching a life raft.

"You know what you were saying back there about that the policy of staying twenty or under leaving the building?"

Marek nodded. He didn't' say anything, and Colton wondered if he was too scared.

"Yeah, I've never been much of a reader. Must not have read that rule."

1.1.11

The target was somewhere on Pine Street, a popular and well-traveled road in Downtown Long Beach known mainly for its restaurants and nightlife. Right now, at a little after eleven, it would be less crowded than usual, but there would still be the early lunch crowd. His arm computer and communication with the Command Center confirmed that the target was hiding out in one of the buildings. Local law enforcement had already begun to evacuate the block and establish a perimeter.

As Colton pulled up to the crowd and brought his Interceptor to a stop, he looked down at his arm computer: 11:12. *Good*, he thought. Only four minutes since leaving headquarters. If he could get this extraction under fifteen minutes, or maybe ten minutes, that would be impressive; it would be something he could rub Ashton's nose in, and it certainly wouldn't hurt his campaign to become the new Chief Officer. He turned off the ignition and climbed out just as Petra pulled up behind him in her medical vehicle.

The crowd of bystanders stood behind the perimeter of yellow tape. Before Colton had time to get his bearings, he was approached by Officer Burrows, who pointed to one of the tall buildings about halfway down Pine Street.

"He's hiding out in that building," Burrows said. A police copter was circling it, and not far off, a couple media helicopters were hovering near the perimeter of the scene. "We have most of this block evacuated and have set up a perimeter. Let me know if there's anything else we can do."

"Sure thing," Colton said.

He walked toward the perimeter of yellow tape and the crowd parted as Colton, Marek, and Petra made their way through it. A few in the crowd began to clap, and when a few more began to cheer and whoop, it turned into an outright celebration. A young woman cried out, "I love you!" Two young brothers, one on dad's shoulder and one on mom's, pointed at them, and one—it was hard to tell which in all the commotion—cried out, "Look! Extractors! Better than firemen!" Colton felt so many people slap him on the back as he ducked beneath the yellow tape, he thought this was what a heavyweight boxer must feel like walking toward the ring before a title match. None of this was new to Colton, though. The presence of an extraction brought out the crowds, and because the CTC never wrote tickets or arrested the general public, the extractors had become an esteemed branch of public safety.

Once in the restricted area and away from the yellow tape, Colton withdrew his Shark 41-F tranquilizer. He heard Marek's tranquilizer gun slip out of its holster as well. Petra walked a fair distance behind. A few officers who were still in the restricted area ushered stragglers away from the Pine Center building. The police had done a good job evacuating the area, as was protocol; local law enforcement was prohibited from engaging a target except in extreme, violent cases in which public safety was in immediate danger. In most cases, such as this, local law enforcement played a secondary role only: evacuating an area, providing aerial surveillance, and assisting with the general public. Their job was to clear the path for the extractor, and Colton was thankful for that. With the people out of the way, this extraction—like all extractions—would go smoothly.

He stopped outside the front entrance to the Pine Center building. Burrows had told him the target was hiding out in this building, and Colton confirmed this by monitoring his arm computer. Sure enough, the red dot that indicated TARGET was a few feet in front of them. The question, of course, would be which floor. Tracking a target via NRNT chip was a sure bet, but it sometimes proved a little tricky when elevation was involved. Colton knew the target was only several feet ahead of him in the building, but on the first floor? The fifth? The eighth?

His own NRNT Chip activated, and a woman's voice said:

Please be advised, if you are on the block of Pine between First and Broadway, please evacuate immediately. An extraction is taking place by the Center for Theological Control. Please evacuate immediately.

Colton smirked. The National Registry for Neurological Tracking was sending a signal to warn people in the area. Warning signals like this had proved quite useful in past extractions, especially with sending such a message to a select group of people in a certain area. Law enforcement also used the same tactics. While some, from what Colton had read, thought such technology to be an intrusion on everyday life and invasion of privacy, it was clear that the benefits to public health and safety outweighed the arguments of the narrow-minded minority.

"So which floor?" Marek asked, looking at his arm computer as well.

"That's the question," Colton said as he opened the door to the gaudy lobby of the Pine Center building. The walls within were a shiny gold and lined with pictures of elderly men. Apart from a single plant sitting in the corner of the marble floor, there wasn't much within, but the oppressive gold made Colton feel like he was standing in some kind of mint; certainly, Pine Center hoped that was the impression the walls would have on clients walking through the front door. This was a place of money, and *lots* of it.

"Base to Extraction Team Four, do you have a read on target?" the dispatcher radioed in.

Colton didn't answer. He was scanning a list of names on the directory beside the two elevators.

"Base to Extraction Team Four, do you have a read on the target?"

"You gonna answer?" Marek asked.

Colton looked at his young trainee and could almost hear him say: *Don't forget, Colton, you need to respond back. This is policy. Don't forget to follow policy.*

"Yeah, I got it," Colton said, and then radioed in: "Extraction Team Four to base, we have a positive lock on target. But we need a little help with the signal. Elevation? Can you give us some help here?"

65

"Checking now," the woman said.

Colton continued to scan the list of names on the directory.

"The whole building's evacuated?" Marek asked.

"Most certainly," Colton said. "The moment the NRNT sends a signal, no one hesitates. Plus, you know the law—anyone ignoring an NRNT Warning and loitering in an area after an evacuation order serves jail time. My guess is everyone in this building ran out in one huge stampede. You can take my word on that. Where do *you* think he's hiding?" Colton was testing his trainee and genuinely interested in his response.

"My guess is his office. I read the profile. He works here. He didn't try to flee. My guess is he's hiding out in his office."

"Because targets often choose familiarity, right?"

"They sure do," Marek said proudly. "I paid attention to these things in training."

"Good," Colton said. He turned toward Petra, who was picking something out of her teeth, appearing totally disinterested in their conversation. "And you agree, Petra? That's been your experience, right? Targets always choose to go to someplace familiar?"

"Yep," she said, "that's about right."

"But what about cloaking?" Marek asked.

"Cloaking?" Colton repeated in genuine surprise.

"Yeah, you know, some speculate that if someone could hack into the NRNT or the neurological chip itself, then that person could throw their signal to appear to be somewhere else. Or they could displace it or maybe even eliminate the signal entirely."

Colton laughed. "And what are we going to talk about next? The Easter Bunny and the Tooth Fairy?"

Petra chuckled, and Colton thought, *Wow, maybe she is paying attention.*

"Well, I've just heard people speculate that someday, someone might attempt it. There's even been accounts of someone's signal—"

"Impossible," Colton said. "We can't remove the NRNT chip from our skulls without an instant lobotomy. There's never been a documented case of anyone successfully removing the chip or manipulating the chip without turning into a vegetable. Read your history books; after the procedure became law, a lot of whack-jobs tried it and ended up spending the rest of their days in padded cells. I'm sure people thought the same thing when the government issued Social Security numbers and freaked out because the government was going to keep tabs on them, but trust me, there's no way anyone could—"

"Base to Extraction Team Four, we have some info." It was the dispatcher at headquarters.

"Yes, I read," Colton said.

"Analysts looking at the signal believe you're ten, maybe twenty feet in elevation difference. Probably one flight of stairs, maybe two."

"Okay, I read you," Colton said.

"Where's his office?" Marek said, looking at the directory. He scrolled down the list of names with his finger until it fell upon Marcos Quintero. "Here it is. His office is on the second floor. That's where he should be."

Colton looked at his trainee with amusement. Marek, his finger pointing to their target's name, had a school-boy grin that suggested he wanted some kind of accolade and applause from his trainer. Colton didn't give it to him. He turned away from the directory and walked toward the door labeled STAIRS. Slowly, making as little noise as possible, Colton opened the door for his team.

Marek and Petra went through the doorway and walked halfway up the stairs to the second floor. Colton remained behind. "Why aren't you coming up?" Marek asked.

"So they taught you that a target always runs toward something familiar, hmm?" Colton asked.

"Absolutely."

"Really. And who did you do your policy and procedure training with before being assigned to me?"

"Um, with Ashton Lampson, of course."

"Really? Ashton Lampson? I should have known."

"Well, you just told me the same thing, didn't you? A target always runs toward something familiar. Isn't that true?"

"Yes, it's true, but it's not the whole truth," Colton said. He pointed toward the stairs that led down, to the word GARAGE written in large black letters on the wall alongside those stairs. "That's the problem with learning too many things from books. Yes, a target often wants to run toward something familiar, but a target always wants to get away. This target is a computer programmer, right? So I'm assuming he has a basic understanding of planning and strategy; if he locked himself in his office, he must know that it is only a matter of time and inevitability for him to be caught. Nobody can run from NRNT surveillance. Nobody. But his vehicle would be just as familiar to him as his office, right? Maybe even *more* familiar. And it would also give him the hope that he could use it to get away."

"Oh," Marek said, and Colton chucked because Marek really looked like that school kid again—a *dumb* school kid who'd made a complete imbecile of himself in front of his instructor. "So you're suggesting that he's…"

"Yes," Colton said, pointing down the stairwell. He radioed base: "Extraction Team Four, beginning extraction now. We have a lock. Radio silent until capture."

"Radio silent until capture," the woman responded.

Colton turned off his radio and began to slowly, quietly descend the stairs.

"Follow me and keep quiet," he said. "And remember, radio silent. That's policy."

1.1.12

The first thing Colton noticed when he stepped off the stairs and into the garage was an abandoned blue Mustang in the center. It was a vintage model. The driver's door was ajar, and the electric engine was on. This wasn't an entirely uncommon sight. When NRNT warnings sounded, people often wasted no time leaving the premises; the well-publicized threats of incarceration encouraged people to be swift in their exits. This warning, like many other such announcements, called for people to abandon their vehicles and walk to the outer perimeter of the capture zone if they were not already on the streets. Whoever owned the Mustang probably made a quick getaway.

One other vehicle—a white Mercedes—looked to be in similar condition. It was half-pulled out of one of the stalls, the door was ajar, lights on, engine running. No driver.

Colton walked deeper into the garage and stopped behind a black SUV. He looked down at his arm computer and scrolled through several screens.

"What are you doing?" Marek whispered.

"Finding out what kind of car our friend likes to drive," Colton said. Finally, after scanning through Marcos Quintero's profile, he found that a Toyota Star Runner was registered to him. He exited the background files and brought up the NRNT Map. According to the red dot on the far corner of the screen, the target was hiding out on the north side of the garage. Tracking via NRNT chip was a little tricky at close range, but Colton was willing to bet he'd find a Toyota Star Runner in the far corner of the garage, and he was more willing to bet he'd find his target hiding inside it.

Lifting his finger to indicate he was moving, he crept forward along the rows of cars. He passed a truck, a Volkswagen, and slew of other vehicles—all of these closed, locked, and engines off. As he neared the end of the row, he saw—just as he'd predicted—a Toyota Star Runner in the far corner.

Colton turned toward Marek. "Cover me," he mouthed.

Marek nodded, and Colton didn't like how nervous his trainee looked. It wasn't all that encouraging.

Colton inched toward the vehicle. The good thing—perhaps something those who served on the police force couldn't say—was that most targets were relatively harmless. By and large, they weren't murderers, rapists, or con-men, although there certainly had been some cases of that kind. Most of the targets were normal people—not criminals. A target was rarely armed, rarely dangerous, and often didn't fight back. That was encouraging, and Colton remembered this as he stepped toward the vehicle.

He needed one clean shot. Just one. The dart would penetrate the glass, no problem; Colton had done it on several occasions. As he stepped forward, he looked at his arm computer to verify his calculations had been correct. The blipping red dot confirmed what he already knew: Marcos Quintero hid in that vehicle, foolishly hoping he wouldn't be found.

Colton had turned to give the thumbs up—a clear confirmation that he was going in for a closer look—when the car engine started. Lights turned on. He saw a shadowy figure sit upright in the driver's seat, crank the car into drive, and all two tons of the Toyota Star Runner sped toward him.

Colton jumped out of the way, and the car blew past him. He watched Marek and Petra do the same. The Star Runner made a sharp left, its wheels screeching painfully in Colton's ears, and then it broke through the closed gate of the garage. There was a loud metallic cacophony as the gate burst open and clanged to the ground. The Star Runner sped up the ramp that read PARKING EXIT, and Colton heard the terrible screeching wheels on the garage floor as it made another turn. By the time he was on his feet and had gathered his wits, his target was out on the street.

"Follow him!" Colton yelled and began running toward the exit with his assistants.

It was Marek who brought up the obvious question. They had

only run a few feet when he stopped, waved his hands in the air, and asked how they were going to pursue the Star Runner on foot. He had barely finished his sentence before his question was answered; Colton jumped into the driver's seat of the blue Mustang and ordered the others to get in.

"Are you sure we can do this?" Marek asked. "We should call for back-up. We don't have to do this solo, you know. And don't we need to radio in to get approval for confiscating this vehicle? Isn't that—"

"Policy?" Colton said, finishing the sentence for him.

"Well, yes, isn't it—"

"Just shut up and buckle up, okay?" Colton said, and just as Marek started to say something else, Colton hit the pedal and peeled his way out of the parking lot onto Pine Street.

Once on the street, it was clear what had happened: The crowd of spectators had run from the street, and the Star Runner had torn through the yellow tape and now, from the looks of things, was making a turn onto Ocean Boulevard and heading west.

Colton floored it and wondered how fast he was traveling. Sixty? Maybe seventy? He saw Marek sink down in his seat. If he thought the fast exit out of the CTC's parking structure was a bit too much, then Colton couldn't imagine what Marek thought of this.

Colton slowed when he hit Ocean Boulevard, turned right, and accelerated again. Sure enough, he could see the black Star Runner ahead of them. Most of the vehicles on the street had pulled over to the side, and Colton knew why. Most certainly the Command Center back at CTC Headquarters was monitoring the pursuit and had sent out an advisory via the NRNT to warn drivers in the vicinity to pull over. This would make the roads ahead clear, and Colton was pretty sure he knew where the target was going. The 710 Freeway was ahead. Colton guessed that Quintero was heading straight to that onramp because, to Colton's continual disbelief, some people were still deluded into thinking that they could outrun an extractor.

Colton glanced down at his arm computer and read the time. 11:24. It was a much longer extraction than he had anticipated, but now it was a pursuit, and if he could at least get this down to under twenty minutes, that would be considered very good time for that kind of situation. He could live with that and wouldn't mind making Ashton Lampson aware of that fact.

He turned on his radio and made contact with the Command Center. "Extraction Team Four to Command Center. We are in pursuit. Believe suspect is heading to the 710 North."

"We read you, Team Four. Public advisory has gone out and streets should be clear."

The blue Mustang zoomed past a crowd of people along the row of houses on Ocean Boulevard who were pointing their fingers, raising their fists, and cursing. They were just a blur as the Mustang tore past, but Colton could make out a few of their cries. "Get ready for the Island!" a particularly large and voluminous lady yelled. Colton realized the crowd probably assumed that he—like the black Star Runner in front of him—was the target. If he'd been driving his Interceptor, the crowd most certainly would have been cheering him on. In some cases, during low-speed pursuits, when the public had time to prepare, it wasn't uncommon to see crowds of people with signs along the road, encouraging the extractors. He'd seen all kinds of signs over the years: WE LOVE OUR EXTRACTORS, GET THEM, and—his personal favorite—I'M STILL SINGLE!!! The public could be downright hilarious in their adoration of their theological protectors.

The road was clear ahead. Just as Colton had predicted, he followed the Star Runner through the heart of Downtown Long Beach. On the right, the tall buildings, offices, and restaurants blurred past him, and the beach was just to his left. He wasn't far from the harbor. Several cargo ships were slowly crawling across the blue waters. At this point, the Star Runner had one of two options: The target would either continue on Ocean Boulevard and go over the very large Vincent Thomas Bridge toward the same harbor the cargo ships were heading for, or—most likely—the target would cut off Ocean Boulevard and take the freeway. Colton was sure of it.

"Extraction Team Four to Command Center," Colton radioed

in. "Do you read?"

"Command Center here. I read you."

"Request spike strips set up on 710. A couple miles out. Near Artesia."

"Extraction Team Four, be advised target is not yet on freeway. CHP will not comply unless—"

"He's about to! Trust me!" Colton barked. "Get the strips set up. Set them up now!"

He looked down at his arm computer: *11:26*. Considering the nature of his circumstances, his time wasn't bad.

Just as he'd suspected, the Star Runner turned right and onto the 710 North. The target wasn't about to take the bridge, and Colton assumed that was because the target was no fool; it would be far, far too easy to trap him at the end of the bridge or near the harbor. This guy wanted open roads, and Colton couldn't blame him; if Colton ever found himself running from the authorities, that was what he would do.

Like Ocean Boulevard, the road was wide open. Several vehicles and even a couple big rigs had pulled to the shoulder. Colton was doing over eighty. He kept a distance behind the Star Runner and hoped that the CHP was quick to follow his lead.

His neuro-alert sounded again: *All drivers on the 710 North, please pull over to the side of the road. An extraction is in process. This is a public safety warning.*

"You think they'll get that strip down?" Marek asked.

"They better." For the first time since commandeering the vehicle, Colton checked the car's charge. It was almost out. Not good.

"The police are usually helpful," Petra said.

They were traveling so fast, it seemed like mere seconds before they reached the Artesia Boulevard exit. Colton backed off and let the Star Runner get some distance ahead of him. Just as he'd wanted, an officer on the side of the road had put down a long, collapsible strip of spikes across the center of the road. The Star Runner tore right through it, puncturing its tires. A moment after, the officer worked the contraption, and the long mechanical strip folded in and snapped back to the side of the road like a rubber band so that the Mustang could pass without shish-kabobbing its tires.

Pleased that it had worked, Colton narrowed the distance between himself and the Star Runner, which, now rolling on its rims and shredded tires, was quickly slumping to a dead stop in the middle of the freeway. When it was clear that the Star Runner wasn't going to move another inch, Colton leapt from his vehicle.

"Cover me," he told Marek who, getting out of the Mustang, took shelter behind the opened passenger door.

With his Shark 41-F drawn, Colton walked past the smell of burned rubber and through a minefield of tire chunks. The Star Runner's door suddenly opened, and a Hispanic man wearing black slacks and a white short-sleeve button-down shirt stepped out of the vehicle. He was crying uncontrollably. He held his hands up high in the air and began to plead for something, and Colton seized the opportunity for a clean shot.

He fired.

The target looked down at the small silver dart in his chest, as if contemplating it for a brief second, and then collapsed onto the asphalt.

"Extraction Complete," Colton said, radioing in. He looked at his arm computer: *11:29*. An impressive time for such a difficult extraction.

He looked back at Marek and gave him the thumbs up. Petra, as she had been trained to do, dashed toward the fallen target to make sure his vitals were stable and he wasn't having any adverse effect to the tranquilizer.

Then, as happened in many extractions, citizens who had been hiding out in their cars along the perimeter of the road climbed out of their vehicles and began to applaud. Pretty soon it was nothing but cheers, whoops, clapping, and verbal accolades running along the 710 North. One burly guy driving a big rig hung out of the driver's side of his vehicle and pulled down on the horn: a massive, celebratory blast.

Colton, out of duty and public service, smiled, waved hello, and bowed gracefully before the general public.

As he did so, he looked in the general direction of CTC

Headquarters and wondered what Ashton Lampson would think when he heard of Colton's extraction time.

"Not a bad time, is it, Ashton?" he said, bowing once again to the crowd of bystanders. "Not bad at all."

1.1.13

"Colton, glad you could make it," Brian Barclay said, opening the door to his office. It had been two weeks since the Marcos Quintero extraction.

Colton walked into the plush office of the Chief Officer—the office that he hoped would soon be his. It was situated on the top floor of CTC Headquarters, with a panoramic view of downtown Long Beach and the harbor. Brian put away the putter he'd held when he opened the door. A practice putting green lay in the center of the room, and a few golf balls sat to the side of it.

Brian welcomed Colton to take a seat on one of the large leather couches near the putting green and offered him a can of Diet Pepsi. Colton hadn't been to Brian's office that much over the years, but when he did, the large man always opened his little refrigerator in the corner of the room and offered him a can of Diet Pepsi. It was just the way he did business. Considering what a large man Brian was, Colton wondered if he should start stashing some other kind of refreshment in that refrigerator. Water, perhaps.

"Glad you could see me," Brian said, cracking open a can of soda and taking a seat on the other leather couch across from Colton. Brian seemed to enjoy meetings like this: away from the desk and in the central area of his mega-office where it felt more like sitting in a living room while catching up on old times rather than grinding through laborious work issues.

"Of course, not a problem. It's been a quiet morning."

In truth it was, but the last two weeks had been anything but quiet. Ever since the Marcos Quintero extraction, it seemed as if Colton had been swamped with extraction after extraction. From what he understood, the other extraction teams had been inundated with calls as well. Colton hadn't even gotten home until ten o'clock the night before due to a late extraction involving a young couple that tried to make a getaway on a small fishing boat. Fortunately, Colton had nabbed them, and based on all CTC data that he'd accessed, his times were still lower than Ashton Lampson. That thought alone made all of the recent overtime and effort well worth it.

"Well, I wanted to talk to you for a few minutes, Colton."

"Absolutely."

"It's about my imminent retirement, and all of the change that we're sure to see around here with the new administration and, of course, the recent change in the law."

"You mean the Extermination Act?"

"That would be the one."

"Good thing it's here, because it's been a long time coming."

Colton hadn't followed the news as much as he should, but the Extermination Act had passed through Congress. Starting in January, any Aberrants captured would not face a life sentence quarantined on the Island; instead, they would be taken to the Quarantine Zone to be terminated. Those already on the Island, of course, would be exterminated. At this time, those in the higher ranks were trying to figure out how to make the necessary transition. Colton knew that the new administration would certainly have some challenges, and implementing this new policy would be one of the primary issues.

"Yes, many such as yourself see the new law as a good thing, and that's fine, but I really wanted to call you here to ask you a simple question."

Colton shrugged and said, "Fire away."

"Do you still plan on running for my position? I've seen all of your paperwork is in, but I wanted to confirm one last time that you do, in fact, actually want the position."

"Well, of course I do. Why would I fill out all the paperwork if I wasn't serious about it?"

"That's true." Brian spun the can of soda in his hands, and Colton was pretty sure that he was looking for the right words; he had a serious look on his face, and Colton assumed that was because he was treading lightly. "How long have we been colleagues? And how long have we been friends, Colton?"

"How long?" Colton had to think about this. "A decade?"

"Yeah, that's about right. I've been Chief Officer for eleven years. Can you believe that? Oh, how the time flies."

"It does fly."

"And in that time, Colton, you have become probably one of the most dedicated extractors to ever work for the CTC. I really mean that. You'd be hard-pressed to find anyone who has won as many awards and gained as many accolades as you have, Colton. You are indeed a foot above the rest of 'em."

Colton nodded, accepting the compliment. He thought of his Hall of Fame, and yes, undoubtedly, he had won far more awards and put in far more time than any of the other extractors—and he was proud of it. At that moment, it occurred to him why Brian had called him into his office. Most certainly this was Brian's unofficial endorsement of his choosing to run. In a moment, Brian would toss the cans of soda and bring out the glasses of champagne, and they'd raise a toast to Colton and his new assignment. With Brian's full endorsement, his appointment was a sure thing.

"But there's one problem I've been seeing," Brian said, resituating himself on the couch. "It's the way you deal with people, Colton. It's not going to help you."

"The way I deal with people?"

"Yes, *people*," Brian said, grinning. "You know, those other individuals who work here with you? The other extractors and support staff."

"Well, what problem do I have with them?"

Brian set his soda on the small table beside the couch. He put his hands together, interlacing his chubby fingers, and looked sternly at Colton. He swallowed, and his white, blubbery double chin twitched. "I heard about the incident a couple weeks ago when you called out one of our workers in the Command Center."

"Oh, you mean the skinny guy who was on his phone when he should have been working?"

"Yes, him. And he was Employee of the Month as well. I also

heard you made a call to Art Murdock's home because he didn't show up to work for two days."

"Well, I signed up for that mentor program. He wants to be an extractor one day, and I just called him and told him that if he was really committed to our mission, then he would find a way to get to work."

Brian leaned forward and put his hands on his knees. He paused briefly for dramatic effect. "Colton, his mother had died."

"Yeah…and?"

Brian looked at him. His left eye twitched, a tic Colton had noticed when Brian was stressed.

"Colton, the fact that I have to explain this to you just proves my point. I want you to be the next Chief Officer…I really do. You are the extractor of extractors; nobody can hold a candle to you. But if you want to lead this place, then you need to learn to work with people better."

"So you're endorsing me?"

"In private, yes. But you know that I can't publicly endorse you—it's against policy."

"Policy, huh?" For a moment, Colton felt like he was having a conversation with Marek.

"Look," Brian said, folding his hands together again, "that's the only reason I've called you here. Just some friendly advice. As much as I want to see you as the next Chief Officer, you need to start working better with people. Tomorrow is Team Building Day. What better day to connect with people and show them you're a team player?"

Colton hated the annual Team Building Day and had been secretly dreading it. A day of playing games and completing tasks with fellow co-workers, all in the hope of building camaraderie and a sense of community in the workplace? No, thank you. Colton winced at the thought of it.

"Maybe you're right," he said, trying to be at least mildly diplomatic.

"I think you should seize the opportunity," Brian said. "Plus, as you well know, Ashton Lampson also wants the position, and he's more popular with some of the staff than you. And having a local senator as his father won't hurt his chances."

"You think that will make a difference?"

"Politics always makes a difference, Colton," Brian said. "His dad has been pleading for a long time to militarize the CTC more than it is now. He, like some others, thinks we're on the edge of real resistance. An organized uprising against us. I've never talked to Ashton personally about it, but I wouldn't be surprised to find out that he holds some of his father's same views. His father thinks that in the near future our facility will need to take a much more militarized approach to extractions because the numbers will increase to a point where we can't handle it anymore."

A frightening thought, to say the least. What made it most frightening to Colton was the simple truth that the number of extractions did seem to be steadily increasing. But an uprising? A more militarized CTC? That just seemed like fool's talk.

"And I suppose Ashton's father also believes that some of the infected have found ways to cloak their NRNT signals and stay off the grid?"

"Yes, you're quite right. He's expressed concern of that. How did you know?"

"Well, Marek hinted that he'd heard it, and Ashton was one of his trainers. The apple doesn't fall far from the tree."

"Yes, you're quite right." Brian reached for his soda and took a couple of long, greedy gulps. "There's going to be a few people buying into ridiculous ideas. You and I both know we don't want those rumors reaching the public. It could erode public confidence in us and generate paranoia, that kind of thing."

"Yes, I know," Colton said. But he wondered, *Why would such rumors start if it wasn't true? Why even make the statement? Is Brian keeping something from me? Is he keeping something from the public?*

"I fear that Ashton wants to militarize the CTC as much as his father. He very well may fan the flames of such gossip to procure more funding and more militarization. Like you, Colton, I have no desire to see Ashton elected as the new Chief Officer."

"Then I have no choice but to win."

"Yes," Brian said. "Just remember everything I told you about the people skills thing, okay? Really, I mean it for your own good. With the new law passed, the next Chief Officer is going to have a lot on his plate, and first and foremost, it is going to be making the transition of how to humanely exterminate the Aberrants on the Island. And you know there's going to be protesting. The vocal minority always protests things like this."

"Really? You think they'll cause a problem?"

"For a little while," Brian said. "It's human nature. People don't like change. It'll be like in the past when there were great changes—women being granted the right to vote, blacks being released from slavery—there'll be people up in arms, but surely, over time, they'll be seen as the eccentric whack-jobs who wanted to live in the past. Don't worry about that right now. Instead, focus on how you can build bridges with some of the staff tomorrow."

"Well, I thank you for the advice." Colton stood and made his way to the door. Brian followed him, shook his hand firmly, and Colton walked into the hall alone, contemplating the advice Brian had given him.

He hadn't gotten far when he noticed Selma, who had been walking down the hall with a stack of papers in her hands, stop and walk toward him.

1.1.14

"I've been trying to find you," Selma said.

Colton intentionally didn't stop to talk to her but allowed her to walk alongside him as he made his way back to his office on Extraction Deck Four. Ever since his meeting with her in the copy room, he'd made it a point to avoid her. The very idea that she was dating Ashton Lampson tarnished her in a way that Colton probably would have thought impossible a few weeks before; the fact that he'd misread her cues only made it that much worse. So he tried to act nonchalant, uninterested, and busy as he maintained a fairly rapid gait.

"You have, huh?"

"Yes, where have you been? I haven't seen you in the usual places."

"Oh, I've been busy."

In reality, Colton had avoided the "usual" places. Avoided them like the plague.

"Well, I was hoping we could finish our conversation," she said, and Colton, eyes straight ahead, didn't look over to acknowledge her. Not yet. When he reached the elevator, he pressed the down arrow and waited.

"And what conversation was that?" he asked. For the first time, he turned to look at her, and there she was, big green moons looking up at him. But there was something different about her, some sense of urgency.

"You know, the conversation we had. We were talking about Shakespeare and things."

"Oh yes," Colton said. The elevator hissed open and he stepped in along with Selma. He pushed DECK 4 and faced the stainless steel doors and they closed in front of him. "What exactly were we talking about that day? I can hardly remember. Forgive me; I've just been so overwhelmed lately. And weren't you wearing glasses the last time I saw you?"

"Oh," she said. "Those were my reading glasses. Just for reading. I was going through files."

"I see."

The doors hissed open and he walked out and toward his office door. For the first time, it occurred to him that Selma had followed him all the way here. Now that he was standing before his office door, he wasn't sure what to do.

"That day, you were asking me if I wanted to go out to dinner with you and I couldn't that weekend."

"Hmm, that kind of rings a bell. I think I do remember that."

"Yeah, well, I couldn't then. But I'm free tonight."

"You are?" Colton turned away from his office door and gave her his full attention. He looked her up and down—she wasn't joking. Had he misread her yet again? And yes, he couldn't help but think she was beautiful. Even the last time he saw her, wearing the big reading glasses, a spacey, artistic, book-nerdish kind of beautiful.

"Yes, I am!"

"But what about Ashton?"

"Ashton? What about him?"

"Well, aren't you two—"

"Me and Ashton?" Her nose wrinkled in disgust, and then, as she seemed to realize what Colton was implying, she had to hold back laughter. "Oh, that's silly. Absolutely not. We went on two dates, okay? Just two. And the second one was out of sheer pity. Trust me."

"Then you don't like him?"

"Like him?" she said matter-of-factly. "Um, no. Not at all—not like *that,* at least. Totally self-absorbed, egocentric, and hardly acknowledged me. And his breath is horrible. There's a reason he's always shooting himself with that breath stuff, and trust me, it's not enough."

Colton laughed and Selma, looking both ways down the hallway to make sure nobody had overheard her, joined him.

83

Wow, Colton thought. Her stock value had just gone up drastically in his mind. All her past offenses were exonerated.

"Um, well, yes, I'd love to go out with you," Colton said. "So you're asking me out, then?"

"I am," she said, and then stopped. Her forehead crinkled in thought. "No—wait—you asked me out. I'm responding to you asking me out. Remember?"

"Yes, I did ask you out, but you said no. So now you're asking me out."

"I am?" Her forehead crinkled again. She sighed but played into Colton's shenanigans. "Then so be it. Colton Pierce, would you like to go out on a date with me? I'm free tonight."

"Selma, I would love to go out on a date with you," he said teasingly. "Does this mean you pay for dinner as well?"

"Depends on what you order."

"Very witty," Colton said. "I like that. I'll swing by your office on the way out, okay? We can set up the time and place then."

"Very good." With one final flash of a smile, she walked back toward the elevator.

Colton went into his office and took a seat at his desk, but he couldn't focus at all. He was going on a date with Selma! All of a sudden the possibility of her became a reality to him, and he found himself for hours drifting in and out of imagining what it would be like to hold her hand, to sit and talk with her, to—once again—talk to someone about his day, the pain, the joy, and the frustrations.

It had been so long.

There was one thing he was convinced of. If Brian Barclay had seen how easily Colton was able to captivate Selma, he never would have thought Colton had any problem relating to people or dealing with people. He would surely have seen that Colton, like all great leaders, was completely astute in reading people, responding to people, and interacting with them accordingly.

"Yep, I must have the magic touch," Colton said, and leaned back in his leather desk chair. "If you got it, you got it."

1.1.15

"What do you mean you can't take me to the movies tonight?" Marty asked. It was half-question, half-whimper. Marty stood on the balcony with his easel and paints. Colton had already dressed and showered. He had chosen black slacks and a green button-down shirt and had decided on driving to Manhattan Beach to Mangiamo, a quaint Italian restaurant near the water with a menu to die for. The steak, particularly, was the best Colton had ever eaten.

"I'm taking out a friend from work tonight. Shelly's going to babysit. Remember her?"

"You mean the neighbor girl who spends the whole time on her phone talking to her boyfriend?"

"Yeah, that's the one."

"But what about you and me?" Marty said, pouting. Colton's son was exceptional at this, a true gifted thespian when it came to displaying his disappointment. He dabbed his brush into one of the colors on his palate, bright blue, and attended to whatever drawing he'd been working on. "I was excited to go see the movie. And I was going to give you my painting tonight. I'm almost done with it. It's called *My Hero*. It's taken me a whole two weeks."

"Yes, I understand," Colton said, vaguely glancing at the artwork. He was more concerned with how he could remedy the situation. "Listen, I'll tell you what, you know how I was going to take you to that rock-climbing place tomorrow after work?"

"Yeah," Marty said.

Colton knew Marty had never been very excited about going to begin with, but Colton thought it'd be good for him. It would teach him confidence. Plus, there were going to be lots of kids there. Maybe his son would make a friend or two.

"Well, I'll tell you what," Colton said, negotiating. "Since I'm not going to take you to the movies tonight, how about tomorrow night I cancel the whole rock-climbing deal and we'll do something tomorrow night? I promise. Is that a deal?"

"Tomorrow night is Kenny's barbecue. You know, the one we were invited to a couple weeks ago?"

"Okay, well great, let's do that." Colton took his wallet out of his pocket and looked at the card that Kenny's dad, Michael, had given him. "Looks like it starts early. I'll make sure that you're dropped off and I'll join you right when I get off work. It'll be fun. And if there's time, maybe we can still make a run to the movies afterward. Maybe we can do a midnight movie or something. Sound good?"

"Yeah," Marty said, but Colton was pretty sure he could still hear some amount of disappointment in his son's voice. "Do you like the drawing, Dad?"

"Yes, very good." But Colton didn't look. He was busy looking in the mirror, making sure his hair was in place. Selma was going to show up at any moment, and he wanted to be ready. She lived in Irvine, a thirty-minute drive on the 405 Sorth, and since Mangiamo was northbound, she decided to drive to Colton's; from there, Colton would drive to dinner.

Obviously upset, Marty threw down his palette, grabbed his canvas, and stormed down the Hall of Fame and into his bedroom. The door slammed closed behind him, and Colton found himself standing by the mirror, wondering what had happened. Without thinking, Colton went to his wet bar, poured himself half a shot of brandy, and downed it. He hated it when his son got like this; why did he have a son who was so emotional? Sometimes it felt like he was raising a daughter.

He looked at his watch and saw he had a few minutes. He didn't want to leave on such bad terms.

Slowly, Colton walked down the Hall of Fame and stopped just outside his son's door. He could hear Marty crying within and that made him even more uncomfortable.

Usually, Marty had these crying fits when he thought of

his mom, but this one was different. The kid had been overly emotional lately, and Colton chalked up this particular breakdown to his genuine disappointment at what had been a long-scheduled dad and son movie night. He knew he was going to have to make up for this, and in a serious way.

"Marty, can I come in?" Colton asked, knocking softly on his son's bedroom door.

Only sniffles within until finally, a whimpering childlike voice surfaced: "No, Dad…I wanna be alone."

"Marty," Colton said.

He hated moments like this. Loathed them. Every ounce of his own insecurity as a father surfaced in a great wave that slammed him mercilessly against the rocks; he was spun completely upside down. As he gazed despondently up and down his treasured Hall of Fame, he despised the fact that none of his accolades, plaques, and awards prepared him for fatherhood. How ill-equipped he was for this and how utterly without resource!

He leaned his head against his son's door and thought this through. "Marty," he said, trying to ignore the muffled whimpering within. "Look, Son, I know I'm not the best when it comes to… you know…talking about feelings and things. We really will go to the movies another time, and I really will make it up to you."

He paused, hesitated, and pressed his hands against the door.

"I know I don't tell you this all the time…" He sighed, remembering all the times he wished his own father, Victor Roland Pierce, had taken the time to acknowledge him, to at least spew out some semblance of affection. But it was never that way with Dad; Dad showed his violent approval through fist-bumps, grunts, and aggressive displays of domination. Perhaps his greatest moment of affection was the time when Dad tackled Colton during what was supposed to a family flag football game one Thanksgiving when Colton was only ten years old. That show of affection left Colton with bruises and, according to Dad, official "Pierce" approval. It was baptism by fire—or bruises and welts, in Colton's case.

"Again, Son, I know I'm not very good at this, but I really do…I really do…" He hesitated. His throat was dry. The words felt jagged, sharp against his throat. "I really do love you."

The doorbell rang.

Selma. He pulled up his sleeve and glanced at his watch. She was right on time, and that didn't surprise him at all. Those skills of organization and promptness were probably the very reasons she had been hired by the CTC.

Colton left the hallway and opened the front door. In the yellow luster of the hallway light, Selma stood outside the door in a black cocktail dress. Her green, starlit eyes blinked in excitement and anticipation, and Colton felt himself completely unable to speak. He could only gaze upon the dark-haired, green-eyed beauty.

"Well," Selma said after a rather long and uncomfortable silence. "Are you going to invite me in?"

He realized his mind had gone blank. Totally, completely blank. "Oh yes," he said, snapping out of it. "By all means, come on in."

Selma walked into the living room. She looked out at the ocean, the falling sun, and—in the distance—the faint rim of the Island about twenty miles deep in the Pacific. "Lovely view."

"Yes, very nice." Colton looked toward his son's room, where he could hear the faint sounds of whimpering; he was willing to bet that Selma could hear it, too.

"Something wrong?" she asked.

"Well, no," he explained. "And yes. You see, my son, Marty, can be really emotional. He thought we were going to a movie tonight, so I think he's upset. He's also really into his paintings, and I don't think I complimented him enough on this one or something. Who knows?"

"Oh, he's an artist?"

"Yeah, kind of."

"Wow," Selma said. "That's great. I love artwork. Anything of his out here? Even a sketch?" She looked around the room and her eyes lingered in the Hall of Fame, but seeing no artwork there, she lost interest and looked away.

"No, it's all in his room."

"Really? I'd love to see."

"Well, like I said, he's a bit upset right now. I try to talk to him, and maybe it's because his mom isn't around, but I just can't seem to connect with him."

"Why can't you connect with him?"

Colton didn't like this line of questioning. Somehow it just wasn't what he expected to be talking about on a first date.

"He's just into things I'm not. Things that are more…I don't know how to say it…feminine, perhaps."

"Feminine?"

"Yeah, feminine."

"So art is feminine?"

Colton nodded.

"So Van Gogh, Picasso, Shakespeare? All feminine, huh?"

"Who?" Colton asked. He wasn't dumb. He knew the Shakespeare reference and had heard of Picasso, but for some reason Van Gogh was eluding him.

Selma rolled her eyes. Colton thought he detected something playful in it; at least, he hoped she was being playful.

"I'll tell you what," she said, handing Colton her purse. He looked down at it, unsure what to do. "Give me a few minutes alone with him. Just to say hi. I was raised by a single dad myself, and I know how hard it can be when someone swoops in and takes your father away."

"Swooping me away? We're only going to dinner."

"Ah," Selma said, smirking, "you're seeing it through the eyes of a grown man. Just five minutes. I won't be long."

"Suit yourself." Colton pointed the way to his son's room.

Selma made her way there and Colton, standing with her purse cradled in his hands, walked over to his wet bar and poured himself another glass of brandy.

1.1.16

"So what exactly did you say to him?" Colton asked, leaning over his plate of steak. They were in Mangiamo, seated in the wine cellar; down here, surrounded by candlelight, the smells of steak and pasta rose in succulent aromas among the stony walls.

Selma was halfway through her French onion soup; it must have been good, because she'd been unusually quiet since the waitress—a blonde woman with a spray-on-tan—brought it to the table. "What do you mean, what did I say?"

"I mean, you must have said something to get through to him," Colton said.

The transformation had been nothing short of miraculous. Marty had come out of his bedroom ten minutes after Selma had gone in to meet him. He was wide-eyed, smiling, and after giving Colton a hug, he asked if Selma could come over again sometime soon. Colton, completely confused at his son's sudden change of demeanor, watched in awe as Marty gave Selma a hug goodbye and wished them a great night out on the town just as his babysitter, the sleepy-eyed teenager who lived a couple doors down, reported for duty.

Selma sipped her glass of champagne and grinned as only the bearer of such a secret could. It was playful, a bit sassy, and Colton loved it. This wasn't just a woman of beauty; she was a creature of substance.

"There's something you have to understand about kids." She held up her glass of champagne. Streams of carbonated bubbles raced to the surface. "They're a lot like women."

"Really?"

"Yes."

"Well, as strange as that sounds, it might actually be a little true in regards to my son."

"As I was saying," Selma said, gently veering the conversation back on course. She was only halfway through her glass, but Colton thought he saw the first stages of tipsiness. Or maybe this was just Selma: creative, fantastical, ethereal. He liked it. He liked it very much. "Little kids are like women. If you can understand one, you can understand the other, because they really desire the same thing."

"And what is that?"

She leaned forward and whispered: "Your undivided attention."

"My undivided attention?"

"Yes."

The waitress returned, topped off both their glasses of champagne, and was gone.

"That's all I did, really. Just ten minutes of giving him undivided attention. I looked at the painting he was working on and listened to him. Bright kid. For sure reminds me of myself when I was young. I wanted to be a writer more than a painter, but I understand the creative mind."

"So that's all you did?"

"Yes, that's all, because that's what we are: simple and complex at the same time."

"Simple, huh? I don't know about that. I would think a little more complex than simple."

"Such a contrarian. And has that been your experience? Was it that way with Marty's mom?"

Colton sighed and pushed away his plate; he was full, and considering the direction this conversation had veered, he might as well buy a whole new bottle of champagne. He spun his champagne flute in a circle on the table, wondering how to respond.

"My wife left because I was, according to her, a narcissistic, spoiled, self-centered, egotistical jerk who would turn our son into the same thing. She hated that, so she left."

"Wow, that's a lot of adjectives."

"Adjectives?"

"Nothing, go on."

"Well, that was pretty much her assessment of me. I hated it at first and got angry. But then, as time went on, I guess I got even angrier."

"Really? Why?"

Colton sighed. "Because I think she was right. She left, and then she died. Then it was just me and Marty, you know. I didn't know what I was doing. I've never felt so…so…"

"Incompetent?"

"Yeah." Colton couldn't even say the word. "Don't tell anyone, okay? This is top secret."

"You have my word," Selma said playfully. She held out her hand and they shook, but when done, neither let go. Colton couldn't figure out if *he* wasn't letting go of her hand or if *she* wasn't letting go of his. Maybe it was both. So they held hands on the table, and Colton felt something that could only be described as champagne bubbles tickling the tips of his fingers. How long had it been since he'd held a woman's hand?

"I didn't know what I was doing," he said. "My son would ask me questions about where his mom was and all of those kinds of things, and I had to be honest with him. False hope is a dangerous thing, and in today's world, very dangerous. Part of the reason I've tried to get him into karate, martial arts, or hunting is because this world is rough. It'll chew you up and spit you out, and there's nobody to look out for you but yourself."

Selma watched him with wide and damp eyes.

"Every time I catch one of those bastard Aberrants and send one to the Island, it's like payback for taking away my son's mom. For taking away my marriage. For leaving me with this kid who isn't interested in any of the things that I am."

"So it's personal?"

"Yeah, because I want him to see that if he's tough enough, if he fights enough, he can do anything he wants in this world. Anything! So every time I put away one of those Aberrants, it feels good. It feels like I'm doing my part. Anyone who believes in that nonsense is a threat to society anyway. A very grave threat."

Selma nodded.

"I mean, have you read some of the things they believe in?

What's that old story? You know, that one about the donkey? God talks through an ass? Really? I would hope to believe that if there really was some divine creator in all of this mess, he wouldn't talk through an ass! I mean, come on!"

"Well, I suppose, from their perspective, if there were such a thing, God could talk through just about anything."

Colton laughed. "I'll tell you what. If an ass walked into this room and started spouting out divine wisdom to me, I'd join all the others on the Island. But until then, I'm going to make sure my son has a safe world to grow up in. At least, the safest one I can give him. He deserves that much."

"Wow," Selma said. She looked Colton up and down as if she were seeing him for the first time. She leaned back in her chair, and Colton couldn't read her expression. Was she shocked? Confused? A little of both? Some battle played itself out on her face, a tug-of-war of conflicting expressions. He felt her hand still in his, soft and delicate fingers wrapped in his strong grip.

"What?" he asked. "What is it?"

She let go of his hand. "All of the talk about you in the office… the things your wife said about you…"

"Yeah," Colton said. "Pretty scary, huh? I know I'm not really running the best PR campaign for a guy going for Chief Officer."

"Maybe," she said. "But there's more to you. I was wrong. You're like a rocket."

"What? A rocket?"

"Yes. All this strength. All this passion. All this energy. If you could just be redirected, if you could just be—"

She stopped talking, and Colton saw her face flash with the fear. She pulled away her hand, wiped her mouth with her napkin, grabbed her purse, and hastily excused herself to use the restroom. Colton stood up as she left the table, wondering what had happened. What did he say? What went wrong?

As she slipped away, he thought he could hear her finish her sentence.

Only a slight whisper: "You'd be great."

1.1.17

Two hours later, Colton and Selma found themselves walking down the Manhattan Beach pier, each cradling a cup of coffee they'd picked up at Starbucks. Selma had returned from the restroom a bit more composed, a little less flirtatious, but the sense of mutual attraction was still almost palpable. Colton was surprised that everything had gone so well. Selma's momentary lapse and acknowledgement that she'd "said too much" must have been her wanting to pull back and proceed a little slower; typical of a woman.

Some kind of early summer fair was taking place. The sides of the pier were lined with booths selling various wares: jewelry, purses, pottery, rugs, mugs, bumper stickers, face paints, and so many other things Colton lost count. At one booth, they tried on hats. Colton found a traditional sombrero, and admiring himself in the mirror, was tempted to buy it out of sheer amusement when Selma said, "You look wonderful in it. Quite handsome." She tried on a little, pointed green elf hat, and unlike Selma's jest about the sombrero, he wasn't kidding when he said, "You really do look beautiful in it…really…beautiful."

So he bought it for her.

She agreed to wear it on their journey down the pier, and when they came to the game booths, Colton couldn't help but try his hand. He handed his coffee to Selma, rolled up his sleeves, and tried his luck at the penny toss; apparently, luck wasn't with him. As easy as it appeared to land a penny in one of the thirty or so milk jugs lined up on a folding table, it just didn't happen.

Next, he tried the ring toss at another booth. It didn't look that bad. Landing a rubber ring around an orange cone seemed easy enough, but after three tries and dropping six bucks for his efforts, he had to admit that he was starting to feel genuine frustration. Although he laughed it off to Selma, who was holding his arm and walking alongside him, he wanted to find something he could win. There had to be some game he'd be able to get a prize out of. It would make a perfect end to a truly exceptional evening.

At the very end of the pier he found what he was looking for: the Strong Man's Competition. The booth worker stood with a giant wooden mallet in his hands in front of a twenty-foot high board that lit up when the "strong man" pounded down on the target, indicating the contestant's strength: FEEBLE, WEAKLING, STRONG, MEGASTRONG, SUPERSTRENGTH, and, the crème de la crème, HERCULEAN.

"Now that's my kind of game," Colton said, pulling his wallet out of his pocket. The sign read: TWO DOLLARS PER ATTEMPT. He handed Selma his Starbucks cup again, paid the booth worker, got a good grip on the mallet, and took his position.

"What are you shooting for?" Selma asked. "Strong? Super strong?"

"All the way to the top," he said, pointing. "Going to see if I can surpass HERCULEAN."

"But it doesn't go any further than Herculean."

"That's because I've never used it." He looked down at the steel target, grimaced, raised his mallet high above his head, and then, crying out a battle cry, he drove the head of the mallet down onto the target with brute force. The mallet snapped, the handle broke off, and Colton lost his balance and fell to the ground. Humiliated, he got to his feet and saw the word WEAKLING illuminated in bright white lights and the booth worker with both pieces of the mallet in his hand, marveling over how he'd never seen a player break one of the mallets before.

"I'm sure if it didn't break, it would've hit Herculean," the worker said in an obvious attempt to console Colton. "When it broke, it probably threw off the detector."

Colton dusted himself off, and although he debated about giving it a second attempt, thought otherwise. Selma handed him his coffee.

"I wouldn't worry about it," she said. "I still think you're

Herculean."

"Well, you heard what he said. If it didn't break, it probably would have qualified."

"Yes, I'm sure it would have."

Feeling defeated and very un-Herculean, Colton walked past the remaining game booths to the end of the pier, where he stopped, rested both arms on the salt-weathered railing, and looked at the water. Selma, beside him, did the same thing. For the moment, all was quiet with the sounds of the games, the people, and the city all behind them. Ahead, the dark water lured their gaze, and the sounds of waves splashing into the pilings whispered below them.

Colton wondered what to say. The date, he thought, had gone well; the conversation had been most agreeable at dinner, the champagne had been wonderful, and so had the stroll down the pier, despite Colton's inability to prove his Herculean strength. He wondered if this would be a good time to ask for a second date. Or perhaps he should wait until the end of the night? What was the proper protocol? He had no idea.

But what he found himself contemplating most was Selma's quick exit at dinner, and her one mystic comment: "There's more to you. I was wrong."

What did that mean? What was she wrong about? Colton ached to know.

"Can I ask you a question?" he said.

"I think so." She adjusted the silly elf hat she was wearing and turned to look at him. He thought he saw flecks of starlight in her eyes, most certainly the reflection of the pier carnival lights.

"What did you mean when you said I wasn't what you thought?"

She grinned and looked back at the water, evading. But why? Why did she need to think through an answer?

"Well," she said slowly. With delicate fingers, she brushed strands of dark hair out of her face. A subtle, deft movement. "I guess you just weren't...just weren't what I expected."

"And what did you expect?"

"Honestly," she said, "I kinda expected a pompous ass tonight."

"Really?" Colton said, laughing. "Well, sorry to disappoint you."

"I didn't finish," she corrected him. "I'm not saying you aren't all of that…but you're something much more. Much, much more. It's there, just below the surface, but I think you have the potential to be…to be…"

"Herculean?"

"Yes, Herculean."

"Well, I think I proved just now that I don't exactly measure up to that."

She smiled, put her finger to her lips in thought, and then turned to get Colton's full attention. He looked down at her, wanting to kiss her, but he knew this wasn't the right moment. Her face, her olive complexion, defied definition. He wondered again: Did she have some Native American in her? Some Asian? Some Islander? Some African? She was all of them—and none of them—at the same time.

"I have one more piece of advice for you," she said, pointing at his chest. "Just one more lesson, and it might help with your son."

"Are you going to charge me?"

"Perhaps," she said, smiling. "All of this talk about strength? Marty even mentioned that you enrolled him in martial arts."

"Oh yeah, several times, but he wimps out. Can't take the hits."

"As I was saying," she said, "here's my last piece of advice. What makes a man—a father—strong isn't strength, but his ability to restrain his strength. The ability to stay his hand. If you can do that, you are truly Herculean…maybe even beyond that."

"Restrain my strength?"

"Yes."

"But why?

"When you figure that out," she said, "you will truly be strong."

"And where did you learn this?"

Her eyes darted to the ocean as she sought an answer. She returned his stare and said softly, "My father."

"Well, he must be a strong man."

"Yes."

"I'm not sure," Colton said. "I'm not sure I see the point in it. I don't know if I could do it."

"Exactly," she said. "Maybe you're not strong enough."

When she laughed, he found himself laughing with her. Maybe she had a point. He would think about and consider her words.

"And all of this talk about your son and you proving yourself to him," she said, turning away from the water. She began to walk back toward the start of the pier and Colton, mesmerized, shuffled alongside her. "I think you've already done that. One of the reasons he was so upset when I talked to him was because you didn't acknowledge the painting he was working on."

"Ah, yes," Colton said, sipping his coffee. "There's just so many of them. I can't keep them straight."

"Perhaps," she said. "This one was called MY HERO."

"Yeah, and what was it of? Shakespeare, or one of those artist guys you mentioned earlier?"

"Oh no," she said, stopping. She turned to him, and Colton almost ran into her. "The painting was quite good. It was of you."

1.1.18

The following day, Team Building Day, Colton found himself on the makeshift mound in the grassy knoll behind CTC Headquarters. He'd stepped in as pitcher during the bottom of the fifth and now, the bottom of the ninth, he'd thrown a no-hitter. His team, the Insurgents, a hodgepodge conglomerate of extractors and upper executives of the CTC, had a five-point advantage over the Rascals, an equally hodgepodge team consisting of Command Center agents, secretarial workers, and even some of the custodial staff. He pondered the score: 7-2. Two outs. Winning was an inevitability at this point; securing a no-hitter for the duration of his time on the plate would just be the cherry on top.

The last batter, Larry Herrick, the same man Colton had harassed weeks ago in the Command Center, stepped timidly to the plate. Out here, standing by home plate, he looked even punier dressed in baggy shorts and a white t-shirt. His arms looked like frail twigs, and the bat looked far too big for him.

Colton knew this would be easy. Larry had been to the plate three times already, striking out each time. Victory was sure. He looked to the side of the field and saw what looked to be hundreds of CTC workers sitting on picnic blankets, eating barbecued burgers and hot dogs, and downing sodas. Most took no interest in the game and were lost in their own conversations, but some, a small crowd composed mainly of the families of the players, stood along the first and third baselines cheering them on.

Colton thought he caught sight of Larry's family—a wife in a red dress with two equally skinny sons, each with a hot dog in his hand, jumping up and down and rooting for their dad. Colton couldn't help but laugh. Had they seen the score?

Colton threw a fastball. Poor Larry didn't even see it coming.

By the time he made a clumsy swing at the open air, the ball was already safe in Doug McCarty's glove. A few people along the baseline clapped, and Larry's sons, in between giant bites of hot dog, cried, "Get 'em, Dad! You can do it!"

Colton snickered again. How pathetic. He threw another fastball straight down the middle, and this time Larry didn't even swing at it. By the time he knew what had happened, the umpire, Clovis Beard, an extractor of ten years, was calling strike and McCarty had thrown the ball back.

"Come on, Dad!" one of Larry's sons screamed.

"Ease up there, Colton!" Someone—a faceless voice in the crowd—cried as well. "This is just a Team Building Day! No need to kill someone!"

Colton grinned. One more pitch and it'd be over. He'd spoken with Brian Barclay before the game. All of the applications had gone through—Colton's included—and the next Chief Officer would be announced any day now. Word was going around that the transition would be quick, considering all of the changes taking place in the organization. The new leader was going to have a lot on his plate, and the Powers that Be wanted to be sure that the transition was seamless and efficient. Brian himself seemed to like the idea. Wearing sunglasses and a Hawaiian shirt, he'd helped himself to two hotdogs and a can of Diet Pepsi.

"The sooner they replace me, the sooner I'll be sitting on a beach in Maui," he'd said cheerily, with bits of hot dog bun stuck to his lips. "I say the quicker the better."

What a way to celebrate. Winning the staff baseball game while being on the mound the same day—or a day or two before—being announced as the new Chief Officer would be exceptional. He contemplated this as he took his stance and held the baseball behind him. But then, as his eyes swept across the thin crowd of spectators, he saw Selma. She stood just beyond third base, arms folded in front of her, watching closely.

Her words came back to him: *What makes a man strong isn't his strength, but his ability to restrain his strength.*

Even though Selma didn't appear to be saying anything as she watched, Colton felt as if she were whispering those words in his ear. Somehow, he knew that was what she was thinking. She was watching him. Wondering.

He hesitated, thought about it, and decided he would give it a shot. Being the bottom of the ninth, two outs, two strikes, and no men on base, it wouldn't hurt to throw something "hittable." It might make Larry feel good, would certainly make his family feel good, and perhaps Larry, who was 0 for 3 at the moment, could walk off the field with some sort of dignity.

Colton took a deep breath and prepared to pitch.

"What makes a man strong isn't his strength," he whispered, still trying to make sense of the riddle, "but his ability to restrain his strength."

Not wholly convinced, Colton threw an easy ball right down the center. Larry saw it coming, swung, and made contact. It was a grounder right down the third baseline. Larry, semi-shocked that he'd actually made contact, stood in stupefied bewilderment before he took off running. He didn't stop until he reached second. He'd hit a double. His family jumped up and down in celebration and one of his sons became so excited that he dropped his hot dog on the grass.

The shortstop threw the ball back to Colton who, while waiting for the next batter to step up to the plate, looked over at Selma. She was clapping, but most importantly, she was looking at him and grinning ear to ear. She flexed her arm and pointed to her bicep, and then pointed back to him as if to say: *Well done there, Mr. Extractor. Now that took incredible strength. Herculean, maybe?*

He was thinking of what to pitch next when the facility alarms sounded.

Everyone froze.

Then a woman's voice broke through the loudspeakers: "Stage Three Alert. Stage Three Alert. All units to locations and extractors report to deck."

1.1.19

Colton raced back to the building. Everyone else did the same, and like a sea of ants, people poured back into the headquarters. As he entered, he glanced back to see that the grassy knoll behind the building was vacated and nothing remained but the barren makeshift baseball diamond, several barbecues, picnic blankets, and the families of CTC workers who barely comprehended what was taking place.

A Stage Three Alert? Even though Colton had been trained for such an event, he could hardly believe it was really happening. A Stage Three Alert meant one thing and one thing only: Every CTC extractor was needed on deck because a mass extraction was necessary. A group of theologically ill had been targeted, a very large group, and an extraction required the resources of several teams. To Colton's knowledge, this had never happened; in rare cases, a small group may require a team of two, perhaps three extractors to share the responsibilities, but all thirteen teams?

Colton avoided the elevators and raced up the stairs to Extraction Deck Four. Others did the same; all around him, workers moved to their stations. He suited up quickly, and then, in his office, he reviewed the extraction alert flashing on his monitor. This certainly wasn't a 1TNT; it was classified as ATMT—All Teams, Major Threat. He'd never seen that acronym flash on his monitor before.

Even though Colton had made it a habit to ignore the names of those he was apprehending, he couldn't help but notice the list. There were at least twenty. Maybe thirty. He simply couldn't believe it. That many targets in one place? He read the Target Accusation. Multiple targets had been monitored for weeks, and the mass extraction had been ordered due to cell phone records, witness testimony, and audio surveillance. This had, of course, happened with small groups before, but this was a very large number.

He clipped on his arm computer, placed his Shark 41-F tranquilizer gun in his holster, dropped his Colt 45 into his other holster, and walked out to the central meeting room of Extraction Deck Four, where Marek and Petra were waiting for him. Marek looked like he'd just seen a ghost, and his lack of experience clearly showed on his face. Surprisingly, Petra wasn't on her phone; maybe even she was aware of the significance of this kind of extraction.

"Well, ladies and gentleman," Colton said as he approached them. "Everyone ready? Big day, huh?"

"Yeah," Marek said. "Who's in charge? What is the policy when every team is involved?"

Colton grinned. There was that word again: *policy*. He wondered if Marek could go five minutes without saying it.

"Quite simple," Colton said. "We'll station ourselves outside of the gathering and formalize plans there, but unless notified otherwise, I'll be in charge. Only the senior extractor is in charge, and since that's me, I'll call the shots. That should be clear to all other teams involved, and if it isn't, I'll make it clear to them."

Petra nodded, satisfied, but Marek seemed to ponder this.

"Let's go, boys and girls." Colton led them down the stairs to the parking garage where the other teams, all twelve of them, rallied to their vehicles. As Colton headed through the parking garage toward his Interceptor, he radioed base.

"Extraction Team Four to base," he said. "This is Alpha Team. Preparing to depart. Do you read?"

"Yes, we read you, Alpha Team," a woman's voice said.

"Please fill me in as new information arrives," Colton said.

"Yes, Alpha Team. We will."

Colton, through his radio, addressed all the other teams: "All teams be advised we are Alpha Team. Please wait for my lead once we reach target destination."

A series of twelve squawky "yes sirs" and "roger thats" and "got its" followed as all other team leaders radioed in; one of them was Ashton, but Colton wasn't sure which one.

Colton and Marek climbed into their Interceptor, and as always, Petra took her own vehicle. Colton sped out of the parking lot with a fury. Even though Marek seemed to be white knuckling it, he didn't say anything about policy and remained silent. Glancing at his arm computer, Colton noted where this extraction was taking place: College Park Estates. A nice, affluent neighborhood not far from the university and hardly a ten-minute drive. He took note of the address: 5134 Atherton. Something about it seemed vaguely familiar, but Colton dismissed the thought entirely.

He looked out his rear mirror. He was in the lead, the other teams and their vehicles following. Along the road, pedestrians stopped, in awe at seeing so many CTC vehicles in one unified line with lights flashing, and some jumped up and down and cheered them as they passed. Colton, as he frequently did, waved, but most likely he was just a blur to them.

He arrived a block from the residence and brought his car to a stop. By then, he had killed the sirens. This was a silent extraction: They needed the element of the surprise to apprehend such a large group. Colton got out of his Interceptor just as an army of cars stopped behind him. A man who had been standing in front of his two-story home, gardening, noted the armada of CTC vehicles and quickly went inside.

All twelve extractors climbed out, along with all of the medics, and Colton, looking down at his arm computer, decided it would be best to set up a perimeter. The cluster of red dots on his screen indicated that all of the targets were together and unsuspecting.

"Team Four to base," Colton said.

"Team Four, we read you."

"We're going to set up a perimeter. Will be in contact once perimeter is established."

"Copy that, Team Four."

The twelve other Extractors, some with their own mentees—like Marek—circled around Colton in a great football-like huddle, waiting for their quarterback to call the play. Colton, referencing his arm computer, gave detailed instructions as to where each extractor should head. Four of them would establish a far outer perimeter, another four a middle perimeter, and the remaining five would be the inner perimeter that would advance upon the house. Colton, of course, chose to be part of this group, and he made sure that Ashton, who sneered at the directions, was one of the extractors working the far outer perimeter. Colton didn't want to share any of the glory with his competitor for Chief Officer.

When everyone understood their role, Colton and Marek headed toward their position as the rest dispersed and went to their designated places. Colton decided that he and Marek would approach the house from the south. Two other Extractors would approach from the north, one from the east, and one from the west.

Colton and Marek trotted down the sidewalk, Petra following, and they finally came to the house. It was a large Spanish-style home with a huge front lawn. Surprisingly, Colton thought he could hear laughter. Splashing. Lots of conversation. It sounded like a pool party was taking place in the backyard, and Colton caught the scent of grilled hamburgers.

He grinned. These people had no idea they were about to be extracted, and considering that it sounded like there were children here, the job would be even easier. Children rarely resisted.

Colton was about to radio the others to begin their advance toward the house when his eyes fell upon the address: 5134 Atherton. Something about that address was just so familiar. He was sure he'd seen it recently or heard it. Maybe it was—

His heart froze. His fingers went stiff.

He dug into the pocket of his uniform and pulled out his wallet. He flipped through it and took out the card that Michael, Kenny's dad, had given him a couple weeks ago—the one he'd written his address on. This was the barbecue he'd been invited to. The one that would supposedly be attended by some single women.

The one his son was at.

Colton was so shocked, he dropped the card. It fell to his feet.

Marek, standing beside him, tranquilizer gun drawn, nudged his mentor and asked, "Colton, what's wrong? What's going on?"

Colton couldn't answer. He looked at Marek blankly, back to the house, and then down to the crumpled paper at his feet.

"Oh no," he said in a faint whisper.

Part II

1.2.1

Colton had little time to make a decision. For the time being, he knew he had to go along with the normal procedure. If he said anything or did anything unusual, Marek would notice; so would the twelve other extractors taking their positions along the perimeter. So as his mind raced with all the possibilities, he decided, for now at least, to conduct business as usual.

"Team Four to inner perimeter," he radioed, "begin your advance. Please keep an eye-out."

All inner-perimeter extractors confirmed their advance via radio.

Colton crept toward the house with Marek by his side, tranquilizer guns drawn. The back yard could be accessed by a side gate in the fence and, behind it, he could still hear laughter, splashing, and what sounded like a typical summer barbecue. Under normal situations, he would sneak up to the fence, wait quietly, and when all extractors confirmed their position along the fence, they would advance all at once; but Colton couldn't let that happen. He had to look for himself to see what he was dealing with, and more importantly, to see if Marty was there—even though, in his heart of hearts, Colton knew his son was there.

He radioed again before he had advanced far: "Team Four to perimeter teams, halt your advance. I suspect some unusual behavior. I'm going to take a close look myself first. Stay back until advised."

All the other perimeter teams confirmed, and Marek, who had been trotting alongside Colton, looked at him in confusion.

"What unusual behavior?" Marek asked.

"I just need to check something out."

"Like what?"

"Wait here," Colton said. Marek shrugged and Petra, several feet behind him, nodded.

Colton inched toward the fence and, very slowly and very quietly, looked over the edge. As he suspected, this was the barbecue he'd been invited to. Several kids his son's age were splashing in the pool. Michael was manning the barbecue, and a group of parents stood around him, engaged in conversation. He scanned the large backyard and pool area, and while he saw several clusters of kids and parents, he didn't see his son anywhere. He could see people moving inside the house, and he was sure Marty was in there.

He backed away from the fence, looked back at Marek and Petra, and knew this was the moment of decision.

What am I going to do? His mind raced with the possibilities. His heart hammered in his chest, and he found himself shaking. It felt like someone had their hands around his neck, slowly throttling him, and he knew he couldn't take this much longer. He had to make a decision, and he had to do it quickly.

In a daze, he walked back and stood right in front of Marek.

"So what did you see?" Marek asked.

Colton couldn't talk; he knew what he had to do.

"What's wrong?" Marek asked. "What did you—"

Colton moved so quickly that Marek didn't have time to react. With his tranquilizer gun already drawn, he shot his colleague in the arm. By the time Marek realized what had just happened, he crumpled to the ground unconscious. Colton fired at Petra a moment after, and like his other colleague, she collapsed onto the grass. He stood there for a moment, looked at both of his team members on the grass, fully absorbed the visual symbol of his imminent demise, and knew there was no turning back. He was in neck-deep now.

He raced back to the fence, looked over, and knew he had to find his son. Where was Marty? Why wasn't he out in the pool like everyone else?

He looked at his arm computer, at the cluster of targets on his screen, and knew that his son was one of them. He was in the house somewhere. Colton had to warn him. But how? He had a minute tops before the other extractors would become suspicious and start to radio in. He thought of only one solution: He would have the targets scatter. It was the best way to escape. He would warn them, order them to flee in every direction, and he'd take Marty with him. He knew he'd most likely run into an extractor, maybe two, but he had a plan for that.

Holstering his tranquilizer gun, he knew he would use the handgun if necessary. Colton was aware that his life was over, and a stark reality nagged at him: *Even if you run, Colton, you can't run far. You'll be tracked. Your son will be tracked. You'll both be tracked, and the inevitable conclusion will reveal itself. Isn't that the same thing you've told all of the targets you've apprehended?*

Colton dismissed the thought. He had no choice. With no time to think, Colton grabbed the top of the fence, climbed over it, and jumped down on the other side. He landed in a planter. Most of the kids playing in the pool didn't notice him, but the adults did. Michael, who had taken a break from flipping burgers on the grill, turned ghostly white and stopped whatever conversation he'd been engaged in. All the adults went suddenly still; two dropped their plastic cups; one, an overweight lady biting into a hot dog, started to hyperventilate.

Knowing what was going on in their heads, Colton raised his hands. "I'm here to help," he pled. He hoped they wouldn't run yet. He wanted to explain to them.

Some of the kids in the pool finally saw him, clung onto the edge, and watched. The adults were silent, but a couple of them— the hyperventilating woman with the hot dog and her husband, a little tubby man wearing giant glasses—started to inch their way toward the sliding glass door that led into the house.

"Colton, what do you see? What's going on?" It was Ashton on the radio. Extractors were trained to extract and to extract quickly, like theological dentists pulling the rotted thinkers out of humanity; it shouldn't be taking this long to move in. Colton knew that and he knew that Ashton, and any extractor who'd been properly trained, would know that, too.

"Trying to get a…get a…get a read," Colton radioed back, knowing he sounded shaky.

"Read of what?" Ashton radioed back. "Is everything okay? Marek? Do you read?"

Nothing but silence, and now Colton knew he had seconds.

"You need to run," Colton said. Kids began climbing out of the pool, running toward their parents. The fuse was lit; an explosion was about to take place. In a moment, Colton would lose all control. "There are twelve other teams of extractors moving in from all directions. They *will* find you. Your best bet is to run away in all directions at once. Some of you may get free. But you have to run now in all directions, and I—"

Pandemonium ensued. Parents ran for their children, children clung and wept in their parents' arms, and Colton heard crying and screaming from inside the house. But in some ways, they took his advice. He could hear a stampede of bodies pouring out of the front door, several people ran out of the back door, and some even climbed over the fence.

In the turmoil, Colton was losing track of the one thing he wanted: his son. He ran into the house and nearly collided with a young blonde woman who screamed and fell backwards when she saw him. Another young woman, cradling a baby in her arms, put out a defensive hand and yelled, "Stay away from me!"

"Where's my son? Marty Pierce?" he asked her.

She didn't answer. She was scared of him. They were all scared of him.

He tried to ask a few others where his son was but nobody answered. They just ran past him. In a matter of seconds, the house was abandoned.

Colton cried out to the newly vacated house: "Marty, where are you? It's Dad! Marty!"

No answer. Nothing. What had happened to him? Most certainly, he ran away like everyone else. Another adult probably shepherded him away from the threat.

"Damn you!" Colton looked down at his arm computer and saw the red dots dispersing from the residence. Then he heard Ashton on the radio.

"Team Eight to base, we have a situation, Team Four unresponsive. Request lead."

111

"Request granted."

Ashton again: "All teams are advised, all targets fleeing. They may be armed and dangerous. Use lethal force if necessary."

"No!" Colton screamed. He radioed in: "This is Team Four. No lethal force! They are not armed!"

"Team Four, I am now Alpha," Ashton said. "Use force if necessary!"

Colton fell to his knees and slammed his fist on the ground. Why? Why hadn't he been able to find his son?

He had one last idea. He looked at his arm computer and modified his view to isolate his son's NRNT signal. Marty was one blip in a cluster of multiple targets, moving to the north. Colton would go after him. Even if his son was captured, he might be able to free him. Just maybe.

He got to his feet and was making his way toward the front door when, to his horror, he heard gunfire.

Fortunately, it was to the south, but it paralyzed him anyway. Most of the extractors would still use the tranquilizers, but some of them, loathing the Aberrants and relishing the opportunity to kill a few, might opt for gunfire. The imminent enactment of the new death law concerning Aberrants might come into play as well—why not just shoot them if they were destined to die soon anyway?

You would have done the same if your son wasn't involved, a voice nagged at him. *You know that, don't you?*

He looked down at his arm computer and saw several of the targets turning blue, and that meant apprehensions—or, in some cases, deaths. The escape wasn't working, and Colton, although he hated to admit it, knew that they'd had slim odds. It was hard to run from hunters when you had a GPS device in your skull. Still, maybe he'd be able to get to his son. He'd kill the extractor who had him. He didn't care who it was or how long he'd worked with him. Marty's GPS target was still red, and that meant there was still time.

As he was reaching for the doorknob, someone kicked it open from the outside. Colton jumped back. Ashton stood there with his tranquilizer gun drawn.

"Well, look what we have here," Ashton said. Colton knew he had no time to go for his weapon. Ashton was, as much as Colton hated to admit it, a great shooter, and at this close range, a miss would be impossible.

"What are you doing?" Colton didn't have any option other than to lie his way out of the situation. "Why aren't you out there extracting these Aberrants? What are you doing threatening me for?"

"I think you know exactly why," Ashton said.

Colton shook his head, feigning ignorance.

"You've made it too much of a habit not to check your target's names," Ashton said. "I'm not sure when you realized your son was one of the Aberrants this time, but I suspect it was when you radioed in your strange request to advance forward alone. At that point, I realized you'd figured it out. Why else would you give such a bizarre order? But *I* figured it out way back on my extraction deck, Colton, because I actually take the time to perform proper protocol. The last name Pierce isn't all that uncommon, but when I saw the first name Marty and his age, I was pretty sure this extraction was going to be an interesting one."

"What do you want from me?"

"What do I want from you?" Ashton said, laughing. He wiped his thin, angular nose and grinned in his perverse way. "You've already given me exactly what I want."

Colton glanced down at his arm computer as several red targets bleeped and turned blue. They'd been extracted. His son's target indicator was still red, but one by one, they were all converting to blue. It was only a matter of time.

"And what have I given you?

"Exactly the evidence that I need." Ashton pointed to a belt pouch that held his small, tubular video camera. "You didn't think I followed your orders about where to be stationed along the perimeter, did you? Oh, no. I assure you that when the CTC sees the video of you, Colton Pierce, lead extractor—and potential candidate for new Chief Officer—tranquilizing two other members of your team and assisting the Aberrants in escaping, they're gonna have a field day with it. Your face is going to be on every major newscast for weeks. The media's gonna have a blast with this one."

"No." Colton stepped forward. His hands in the air, Colton knew he didn't have time to reach for a weapon. At point-blank range, Ashton would tranquilize him easily.

"Don't bother to try to attack me," Ashton said. "You know as well as I do that everything I filmed is already backed up in the CTC's hard drive. You could kill me, take the camera, destroy it, but—at the end of the day—it'll be there for everyone to see."

Colton looked down and saw several other red dots convert to blue, but then, strangely, two red targets along the perimeter vanished. They didn't convert to blue; they were simply gone.

"I want my son," Colton found himself saying. At a complete loss, he had no idea what to do now but to plead with his captor. Maybe Ashton, despite his obtuse and annoying personality, would listen to the plea of a father. He had no other hope. "I don't care about being Chief Officer, okay? I don't care about the job. I just want my son. Please! Help me, Ashton! Help me!"

Ashton tilted his head to the side in amusement. He puckered his lips, contemplating this. "Am I hearing this correctly? Is Colton Pierce actually begging?"

"Yes," Colton said, looking again at his arm computer. Two more reds turned to blues, but his son was still out there. Running.

"Then if you're going to beg," Ashton said, "perhaps you should get down on your knees and beg properly."

What? Colton was disgusted. Ashton was relishing this. But hoping it might buy him time and that Ashton might listen to him, he collapsed to his knees. It was a horribly awkward position, and he felt overwhelmed by the shame of it. Considering the circumstances, Colton felt he had no choice.

"Ashton, I don't have time for this! Please! My son is out there!"

"Yes, he is," Ashton said, "but not for long. Soon, like the others, he'll be caught. And I'll be happy to take credit for it. I'll also be able to take credit for apprehending you as well. When I report to the CTC how you attacked me and I had no choice but to tranq you, I'll be more than happy to accept the accolades."

"What?"

"You heard me."

Colton knew it was over. He saw Ashton preparing to fire, and on his knees, Colton thought about lowering his head, closing his eyes, and quietly submitting to the inevitable. But he just couldn't go quietly. He lunged toward his opponent, hoping that perhaps in the frenzy Ashton would miss, but something else happened— something Colton never would have expected.

As he leapt like a lion toward Ashton, a man emerged through the front door. He shot Ashton with a tranquilizer gun. Ashton never saw it coming. The dart struck his back, and when Ashton swiveled around to see what had hit him, his own tranquilizer gun went off and struck the wall. His knees went out from under him, and he collapsed onto the floor, unconscious.

Colton looked at the stranger in the doorway. Who had saved him? And why?

He wasn't a member of the CTC but was dressed in camo gear and, like a CTC worker, wore a radio earpiece. He also appeared to be wielding a CTC department-issued Shark 41-F. With shoulder-length black hair and a salt-and-pepper goatee, he resembled a pirate.

Colton held his hands in the air when the stranger pointed his gun at him. *Maybe he isn't here to save me. Maybe he's here to save the Aberrants and take down anyone wearing a CTC uniform.*

1.2.2

"**I** have the target," the stranger said into his radio.

Colton, back on his knees with his hands in the air, hadn't the slightest clue who this man was or what he was doing. *And why is he calling me a target? What does he want from me?*

The stranger listened to whomever he was conversing with on the radio, nodded, and then drew his full attention back to Colton.

"Who are you?" Colton asked. The man had an intense stare with thick, angular eyebrows. Something about him looked vaguely familiar. Colton was sure he'd seen him before, somewhere, but couldn't place it.

"Bayard," he said flatly.

Bayard? A strange name.

"We need to get you out of here," Bayard said. He had a low, raspy voice. "We only have a few minutes, maybe less, before your team makes its way back here. If you want to live and have any hope of seeing your son alive, then you need to follow me. Understand?"

"My son? You know about him?"

"Yes." Bayard holstered his weapon and headed toward the vacated backyard of the home.

Colton got to his feet and followed. Whoever this stranger was, he wasn't interested in hurting Colton. Bayard had possessed an open shot, and if that was what he wanted, he surely would have taken it. For whatever reason, this man was helping Colton.

By the time Colton reached the backyard, Bayard had climbed over the back fence. Colton scrambled after him. He passed Marek and Petra, who were still out cold in the grass. He thought he could hear Marek snoring. Ahead of him, Bayard stopped at the curb where, at his arrival, a white van pulled to a stop. A faded advertisement—GINA'S MAID SERVICE—was on the side of the van with the image of a young, attractive blonde smiling while holding up a duster.

The back door of the van slid open, and Bayard climbed in.

Colton looked down at his arm computer. Most of the reds had turned to blue; there were only a few reds left, and one of them was his son. He had to admit he was impressed. The boy was running. Maybe he hadn't given Marty the credit he should have; most people didn't make it this far, especially with a whole team of extractors bearing down on them.

When Colton got to the van, he was a surprised to see what was inside. The driver was a large, muscular black man, smoking a cigar. He wore a black, sleeveless vest and had arms that looked like bronze tree trunks. He took the cigar out of his mouth when Colton approached and squinted in suspicion; it was evident he wasn't happy about Colton being there, and he offered the newcomer a cold stare as smoke escaped his large, flaring nostrils.

Suddenly, it became clear what was happening: Bayard and this other man were saving the Aberrants from the extractors. This was some kind of rogue operation, and although Colton had heard stories about these things, he'd never believed that they existed.

Colton stopped just outside of the van, wondering what to do. The back of the van was mostly gutted except for a few seats, some boxes, electronics, and weapons—what appeared to be more tranquilizer guns as well as some real artillery.

"Get in," Bayard said. He opened a laptop that had been sitting on a seat. "And close the door behind you."

Colton climbed in and slid the door closed. The black man looked at him, chewed on his cigar, and then pulled away from the curb and onto the street.

"What's going on?" Colton asked. "Where are you taking me? You said you'd help me get my son."

"We will," Bayard said, not looking up. "But right now we want to make sure that we're not being followed, okay? We're making sure no other extractors have identified our vehicle and are in pursuit."

"What?" Colton said. "How can you tell through the computer?"

Bayard, sighing, as if to ease Colton's mind, flipped the computer around for a moment. It was a digital map of the area, very similar to the one on his arm computer, only instead of red dots turning into blue dots, there were yellow dots. Thirteen of them.

"What are they?" Colton asked.

"They're extractors. You and your colleagues. We're monitoring their movements."

"What? How?"

"The same way your organization tracks us. Through their NRNT chips."

Colton couldn't believe it. No way could anyone hack into the NRNT computers; it had been tried and tested by the best hackers in the country, and the system was, for all practical purposes, bulletproof. No way could anyone—let alone these two guys— have the knowledge or the expertise to pull off something like that.

"Impossible." Colton looked at his arm computer and saw one of the red targets—Marty—suddenly turn blue.

He closed his eyes and, for the first time in years, began to weep. He didn't care that the other men in the van were listening to him, watching him. His life was over, and so was his son's. He wept unabashedly, and being out of shape at this kind of thing, didn't know how to stop.

Bayard set down his computer. "I think your definition of possible and impossible is about to change."

Then, before Colton had a moment to react, Bayard shot him with a taser. Colton wasn't even sure where it came from or how Bayard did it so fast. Colton convulsed and flopped around on the carpeted van floor as fifty-thousand volts shook his body. When it was over, he felt Bayard place some kind of metal clamp around his head; he was too weak to resist. He could feel the metal tighten, it beeped a couple times, and then a firecracker went off inside his skull.

It felt like a two-hour migraine hitting him all at once, a

purified cerebral stream of pain. He screamed, grabbed the steel collar around his head, and then his vision flickered out like a dying light bulb.

Colton was blind.

1.2.3

"Where am I?" Colton asked. He'd been unconscious and he wasn't sure how long.

"We're in a Motel 6 parking lot," Bayard said.

Colton's body had gone completely rigid during the tasing, and now he felt weak and limp. His head hurt more than anything else. He wasn't sure what Bayard had done to him or why, but the clamp over his head and the firecracker feeling in his brain had been worse than the taser. The clamp had been removed, but Colton still couldn't see. Everything was dark.

"Why? Who are you, and what did you do to me?"

"We took you off the grid," Bayard said. "Just like I'm off the grid, just like Big Al is off the grid. They won't be able to track you. Your NRNT Chip is dismantled, mostly. You'll still receive the emergency transmissions, but the tracking feature is completely destroyed. Your colleagues at the CTC have no idea where you are right now. No one does."

"I saw two targets go completely off the grid earlier today," Colton said, remembering the two dots he'd seen disappear on his arm computer.

"Oh yes, we were able to save two. Another team was able to get them. We wish we could have done more, but it wasn't possible. This was a unique circumstance. So many extractors in one place. Usually, when we take people off the grid, we don't like it to be so obvious; we try to do it quietly before the extraction begins. In those cases, the NRNT computers just chalk it up to a death. But we had no choice today. We did what we had to do."

"So there's more of you? Who are you?"

"We call ourselves the Remnant," Bayard said, and Colton heard him lean back in his seat. It indicated that this could become a lengthy discussion with lots of follow-up questions. "We are a group of people—men, women, and children—who have gone off the grid to avoid being taken by your agency. We are Aberrants, as you would call us, and we've dedicated ourselves to stopping your agency from apprehending others."

"Why can't I see? What did you do to me?"

"Like I said, I disrupted the tracking feature of your NRNT chip. It affects your optical nerve, unfortunately, so you won't be able to see for a couple days. But don't worry, your vision will come back. You're just going to have to grope around in the dark for a while."

"But why did you take me off the grid?"

There was a pause, and Colton suspected that Bayard was thinking carefully of how to answer.

"Well, you did help our cause today, didn't you? If it wasn't for you, we wouldn't have saved anyone. Our commander specifically ordered that you be taken off the grid, so you might think of this as a case of following orders. Plus, we've been watching you. There was reason to believe that, once your son was taken, you might be the exact thing we needed. So I'm just following orders here, bud. This is protocol."

Ordered? So they must have a Chief Officer, too. A thousand questions swirled through Colton's head. *How many are there? How many have they taken off the grid? How do they coordinate it all?*

"Like I said, today was pretty messy," Bayard said. "Most of the time, we work preemptively. We try to take people off the grid long before they're reported to your agency. A small percentage of what the government statistically thinks are suicides is, in fact, a result of what just happened to you—the dismantling of an NRNT chip. When someone in society disappears and their NRNT chip goes blank, the government has always chalked it up to one thing: someone went out and jumped off a bridge, shot themselves in the desert, or drowned in the ocean. We've also been able to create a ghost signal."

"A ghost signal?"

"Yeah. After we take a person off the grid, we can create a

substitution signal that seems normal in all ways. It doesn't create any glitches in the NRNT's system, and because that person is off the grid anyway, there's no chance they'll be reported and pursued. The false signal follows the GPS coordinates we give it, but if someone were to track it, they'd find nothing but air."

"But all of this is impossible," Colton said. "The NRNT system is unprecedented. Nobody can crack that code."

"As I said, you're going to have redefine your idea of possible and impossible."

"But the government would recognize these anomalies, wouldn't it? They'd be on to it."

"Well, some probably are...but they're not about to allow the public to think that, are they? Come on, this is the government we're talking about. We're pretty sure some of the higher-ups suspect we exist, but until they have to, they're not going to admit it."

"So what now? Why are we here?"

"Good question. Deactivating the tracking system on your NRNT chip works most of the time, but sometimes the deactivation doesn't work properly. It takes a day or two to know for sure. In the unlikely event that the deactivation didn't work, we are going to check you into this hotel for a few days. You can rest, recuperate, and wait for your vision to return while we monitor to make sure your signal doesn't begin transmitting again. But we will come back for you. You'll just have to be patient."

"What? You're going to leave me here? Where's my son? You told me that you would help me get my son."

"Yes," Bayard said, "but you must be patient. We can't take you with us. This is protocol, okay? We can't have you at our operations base if your signal starts to transmit. Everyone's going to be looking for you, and we can't risk the exposure of our whole operation."

"But you can't leave me here alone. I can't see."

"You won't be completely alone," Bayard said. The front door of the van opened, and Colton heard Big Al exit. The whole van listed to the side and then righted itself when he stepped out. Most likely he was going to the motel office to book a room. "You'll hear from someone soon, probably via your NRNT chip."

"What? How?"

"Direct two-way communication through your chip. Be patient and keep listening. You will probably hear from our leader. Be alert."

Colton hardly knew what to say. Only the Neurological Registry of Neurological Transmissions had the ability or the resources to transmit signals for neuro-alerts, and the idea that this band of pirates—this Remnant—was able to transmit their own signals certainly pushed all of this far into the realm of sheer impossibility. This was science fiction. At this point, Colton genuinely wondered if he was dreaming. Maybe he'd wake up soon and discover this was all part of a bad nightmare.

"Enough questions for now," Bayard said. A pair of pants and a T-shirt fell into Colton's lap. "Go ahead and change. We don't want anyone here to see an extractor walking around. I'm going to step outside for a moment. Leave your weapons and equipment in the van. When I return, we'll take you to your room."

The side door of the van slid open, and Colton felt warm sunlight pour into the vehicle. Bayard jumped out.

"One last thing," Colton said. "Why me? Why did your leader choose me?"

He thought he heard a bit of laughter. "Good question. Truth be told, not everyone in the Remnant is happy about you. It's not a usual day when we take one of our chief persecutors off the grid. But we have some inside sources, and what you did today changes things a bit, doesn't it? You might just prove to be one of the most valuable extractions we've ever performed."

Inside source? What inside source?

"Remember, I'm just following orders," Bayard said. "So don't take this personally. We were ordered to take you off the grid, and that's what we did."

"I see." Colton wondered where Marty was right now. But he didn't have to wonder much. Right now, Marty was in a semi-unconscious state in the back of some extractor's Interceptor, headed toward his quarantine cell. He'd awake in a bland, colorless room to lukewarm food and no human interaction, waiting to be shipped off to the Quarantine Zone. It would only be a matter of days before he'd be taken, and once there, due to the new law, it wouldn't be long before he would be killed in one "merciful act of extermination."

Blind and disorientated, Colton felt sick to his stomach.

"Wait here. I'll be back," Bayard said. "I'm going to see what room Big Al got for you. Change into the normal clothes."

"I want my son…please…I want my son…."

"I'll be back," Bayard said, and he closed the van door.

1.2.4

Colton spent two days in the hotel room; at least, he thought it was two days.

Bayard and his associate had taken him to a room on the second floor and given him a chance to get a "feel" for where everything was. He stumbled around the room in his blindness, and Bayard helped him comprehend where the bathroom was, where the front door was, where the television was, and ordered him to stay put until he was notified. The blindness would last at least two days—perhaps three—and once the Remnant was certain that his NRNT chip was completely off the grid for good, he could join them at their base. Until that time, Colton was to relax, listen to the television, and keep a low profile, which didn't seem like a hard thing to do considering that he couldn't see and didn't know where he was. Bayard and his friend had the courtesy to leave a small *hospitality pack* as they called it—a small cooler filled with sodas and sandwiches—and then they were gone.

At first, the silence of the small hotel room was terrible. Colton longed for his home, where he could at least sit outside on the balcony and listen to the ocean. But by now, Colton knew, the authorities had swarmed his house. The thought of other CTC workers sweeping through his home while touching things, moving things, rearranging things made him sick to his stomach. He was convinced that, by now, every police officer and extractor in the city was looking for him—or his body, at least. Since his neurological signal had disappeared, he wondered if they assumed that he had died in flight. Either that or this would create a whole firestorm of speculation as to whether or not the NRNT chips could be deactivated and their signals cloaked. The disappearance of Colton Pierce could be the spark that ignited a great fire.

For the first time that day, Colton thought about his son. He lay on the bed and fell in and out of sleep, though the little sleep he did find was filled with night terrors. Several times he awoke in a cold sweat with an image of Marty sitting in an isolated prison cell at CTC Headquarters. Blood rolled down his forehead, and he reached toward Colton, whimpering, "Why, Daddy? Why did you let them take me?" Colton sat up in bed, hyperventilating, half-crying, wishing he could have stopped it. Why couldn't he stop them from taking his son? Why wasn't he strong enough?

I've always been strong enough. Why not this time?

He knew Marty would have a terrible time as a prisoner. The boy cried at everything. Colton couldn't imagine what a mess he would be sitting in that prison cell, while waiting to be hauled off to the Island. If only he could be there to help comfort Marty, to talk to him, to get him out of there, because he knew they would treat little Marty just like they treated the adults—horribly.

For the first time, Colton began to put the pieces together as to how Marty came to be a target in the first place. What had they been doing at that summer barbecue? Was it some kind of religious meeting? Some kind of prayer group?

And then the ultimate question presented itself: *Is Marty, my son, really one of them? Is he one of those Aberrants? How did I not notice?*

Colton knew that his son had always been different and he had hated that fact, but he never would have guessed that Marty was actually one of them.

But now, the more he thought about it, he realized there was something different about Michael Payne, Kenny's dad. Maybe this was one of those underground cult operations designed to lure in followers; it had happened before. Last March, Colton had extracted five individuals meeting in a house in Downtown Long Beach. It had been a swift, clean operation, and all five were shipped immediately to the Island. That seemed quite small compared to this one, but maybe there was hope that his son wasn't actually one of them. Maybe he was just in the wrong place at the wrong time and had been listed as a target accidentally. If Colton could get out of this predicament, he could clear Marty's name, bring his case before the court, and plead that all of this was an unfortunate accident and his son was not a theological threat in the slightest.

But despite such dim hope, Colton recalled what he had told every target who had pled the same thing while in custody. "The system doesn't make mistakes." And he was right. To his knowledge, no person ever targeted as a theological threat was taken off the registry. All trips to the Quarantine Zone were one-way tickets.

Once ill, always ill.

By day two, Colton was getting antsy, and his vision didn't seem to be coming back in the slightest. He was still completely blind, and there was no indication that anything was going to change. He began to worry that, at any moment, a team of extractors led by Ashton Lampson would kick down the door, throw him in the back of an Interceptor, and put him into the same cell as his son. Bayard had never told him exactly when somebody would come for him or when he would be contacted. If his NRNT chip suddenly went back on the grid, he would have no way of knowing.

He flipped on the television and began to surf through stations, hoping to listen to the news and find out what the world was saying about the situation. Unsurprisingly, everyone seemed to be talking about him, the rogue extractor who had turned against the CTC and had suddenly disappeared off the registry.

He stopped to listen to a gravelly-voiced man who Colton thought was a reporter for CNN. "Nothing much has changed in the last twenty-four hours. Colton Pierce has been an extractor for the CTC for sixteen years and has been considered to be one of the best. Some speculated that he may have even been the next Chief Officer, with Brian Barclay stepping down. His whereabouts still remain unknown, but nobody has any doubt that his intent was to assist in the escape of this group of Aberrants and to turn on his fellow colleagues. In the next hour, we will play the full video of Mr. Pierce tranquilizing two of his colleagues just before his disappearance."

The video? Colton cringed. *It's gone public? Now I'm a traitor in the eyes of everyone. I won't make it a block without someone recognizing me.*

"All of this has certainly brought on speculation as to whether or not Mr. Pierce has died," a female reporter said. Colton imagined both reporters sitting behind a desk, shuffling papers, looking earnestly into the camera. "Ever since Mr. Pierce's attack upon his fellow colleagues, the NRNT has been unable to locate him. It's also been reported that two other Aberrants targeted for extraction have also disappeared, and the NRNT has been unable to locate them as well."

"Well, Shelly," the other reporter said, "this obviously has led many to ask the obvious question: Is it possible that Colton Pierce and these others somehow deactivated their neurological tracking chips, or did they somehow perish in the escape? Because of this, we are going to bring in two experts: Sean Cole, a former programmer with the NRNT, who insists there is absolutely no way a chip could be deactivated, and Laura Alshin, a lead programmer with Compucare, who believes Colton Pierce may have discovered a way to deactivate the NRNT Chip. We'll be hearing from both sides of the aisle in what we hope will be—"

Colton turned off the television.

He didn't want to hear more. The mere thought that the entire world was out looking for him made him feel sick. This was going to complicate matters. He began to curse Bayard and this group that called itself the Remnant. Why did they leave him here? What if they didn't come back? What if he sat in here for days and ran out of food? What if his vision didn't come back? After all, this was the second day of waiting, and his vision didn't show the slightest bit of improvement. He couldn't see his own hand in front of his face.

He fumbled his way into the bathroom to wash his face. Groping for the faucet, he eventually found it, adjusted the temperature to create a lukewarm stream, and splashed water across his face. Maybe there was just a bit of improvement; he could see little flashes of lights—white sparks in the darkness— and he wondered if this was the beginning of his vision returning.

But how long would it take? An hour? Ten hours? Was there any way to know?

"Colton," a man said.

Startled, Colton spun around. He hadn't heard anyone enter.

"Who is there? Identify yourself! Who are you?"

He held his hands out in front of him and swept them through the air, but nobody was there.

"Colton," the voice said again, but this time it didn't sound like it was coming from right next to him. Maybe it was coming from the living room. Maybe someone had cracked open the door and was calling to him.

Colton stumbled out of the bathroom and felt his way back toward the bed, where he took a seat. "Yes? Where are you?"

"Colton, I'm here to get you out of here."

"I don't understand," Colton said, realizing something about this voice was difficult to pin down. It was everywhere and nowhere at the same time, both in front and behind him. "Where are you? Who are you?"

"I'm the commander of the Remnant. Bayard told you I might contact you."

Now Colton remembered. Somehow, they not only had discovered how to deactivate the tracking feature of the NRNT chip, but they'd also learned how to communicate through it. Quite impressive. They had turned what was supposed to be the one-way message device for neuro-alerts into a two-way communication feature. If Colton wasn't actually experiencing it, he wouldn't have thought it possible.

"When are you going to get me out of here?" he asked.

"In a short time," the voice said. "It is going to be dark soon. You are going to leave in a couple hours and meet one of our members who will take you to the base. You have to walk up Bellflower Boulevard and turn off into a neighborhood. There's a small park there, and that's where you'll meet."

"Wait a minute," Colton said. "Wait a minute, do you remember? I'm blind."

"Yes. And?"

"And how am I supposed to get to this park when I can't see?"

"I'll guide you," the commander said. "I have the entire grid of Long Beach here at my disposal, and I can tell you exactly where to go. You don't need to worry about that."

"Well, why can't he just come get me? Wouldn't that be easier?"

"Consider it a precaution," the commander said. "Movement on your part—particularly a few miles of walking—will determine once and for all if the NRNT chip was successfully deactivated; it's what we call the litmus test. Right now everyone would like some assurances, and I'm going to give it to them. Most are busy making preparations anyway."

"Preparations? Preparations for—"

"If you make it there without the authorities apprehending you, everyone can be assured that all has been successful."

Colton didn't like the sound of this. The only way to determine if everything worked was to put himself in harm's way? There had to be another solution to this.

"Hold on," he said. "You want me—a blind man—to walk down the street a few miles in the hope that my NRNT chip is deactivated? You're telling me the only way to know if it worked is to have me do this?"

"Nobody said this was going to be easy, Colton."

"Easy? Who said easy? This sounds suicidal!"

"It's your only chance. If you want to get out of that hotel room and free your son, you're going to do it."

Colton felt his shoulders slump. If only he could see. If only he had some semblance of power in the situation. He'd never felt so helpless, so at the mercy of someone else.

"Okay, okay," he said after a long silence. He had no choice. He knew he had to comply. "So when do I leave? When do I go?"

"In a couple hours when it's dark. I'll tell you when."

Colton nodded. For the first time, he realized how alone he was. He thought of his son and wondered what was happening to him at that moment. He contemplated the dark trek he must make down the street without the ability to see. At least, if he was shipped off to the Island, he would be with his son. Maybe that was where he should be.

"I'm afraid," he whispered. He rubbed his inoperative eyes and dragged his fingers down his stubbly chin.

"I know," the commander said softly.

Colton had forgotten that he was listening.

1.2.5

"Continue forward for about a hundred yards," the commander said, and Colton, still blind, did just that. It had been this way for the last twenty minutes. He had left the hotel room, climbed down the stairs, walked around the parking lot, and was now—to his knowledge—walking north on Bellflower Boulevard. It was a busy street and occasional cars zoomed by, but by and large it wasn't frequented by pedestrians much, so his sightless stroll down the sidewalk was uneventful.

He was still blind, but the little white sparks had intensified, and he could feel his vision returning. Occasionally, after a white spark appeared in the darkness, he saw a brief muddled image of what lay ahead of him: a long sidewalk, concrete light poles hanging over the street, black asphalt, the red taillights of vehicles ahead. The images were few and scarce, but in a strange way, Colton could *feel* his vision returning like he could feel circulation returning to an arm that had fallen asleep. It was that same prickly-tingling sensation. It was emerging, slowly but surely.

"I think my vision might be coming back soon," he said.

"Of course it will. Like you were told, the loss of vision is temporary."

"Then isn't that proof that it worked? Can't you just have someone pick me up?"

"Not necessarily. There is always a chance that—move to the left a little, you're going to run into a pole—there's always a chance that the signal could come back within this window. And we'll know soon enough."

"Wait a minute. How are you doing this? You have street poles on your map? And how are you tracking me? I thought my tracker was disabled."

"I'm not tracking you through your chip."

"Then how?"

"You wouldn't understand. Not yet. I'll explain later."

Satellite? Colton wondered. Did these guys somehow tap into satellite monitoring or something like that? He hadn't the vaguest clue.

Colton put his hands out in front of him, moved to the left, and felt his way around the concrete pole. He continued down the road in the jeans and T-shirt Bayard had left him. Stumbling down the sidewalk on a main street wearing an extractor outfit wouldn't have been the greatest of ideas now that everyone was looking for him.

He walked another hundred yards or so and came to an intersection. The commander asked him to stop, and Colton, following directions and able to discern the distance to the curb through one momentary flash of sight, stopped at the corner and rested his hand on the light pole. Though he couldn't see, he could hear cars zooming by.

"All right, the light is green. You can walk forward."

Colton put the toe of his shoe down on the asphalt but hesitated. It didn't sound right. He could hear cars zooming by, could feel the vibration in his feet.

"Colton, listen to me. Walk forward. The coast is clear."

"It doesn't sound like it. I can hear the cars. This isn't right."

"Colton, you have to move forward now. I didn't want to tell you this, but there may be a problem. We've picked up the signal of three extractors moving in a couple miles behind you. They are moving up Bellflower, and they are moving fast. We don't have time for this."

"What are you talking about? Are you kidding me?"

"No, I'm afraid I'm not."

"What? What does this mean?"

One of the firecrackers exploded in his vision, and he caught a brief glimpse of someone passing by on the sidewalk. Colton realized he must look like a crazy person, leaning on a light pole and engaged in a heated debate with himself. But he didn't have time to be embarrassed.

"It means you need to cross the street right now. You don't have a second to lose, okay?"

Colton swallowed. His mouth was dry and coppery.

He put his foot down on the asphalt and stepped forward, wondering if this was the end of the road. Maybe the commander and his team had realized that his signal was transmitting, and he was being directed into oncoming traffic to put him out of his misery.

Colton walked forward, cradling himself like a man in the arctic, prepared to become road kill. But it never happened. He kept walking, and though he heard cars whisk past him, they were going the same direction he was. The commander was right. The light was green.

"Be careful," the commander said, and then directed him to step up onto the curb. Colton however, preoccupied by the news that there were extractors in pursuit, ran into the curb and fell flat on his face.

Now I really look like a crazy guy, he thought, getting to his feet.

"You have to run, Colton. Run straight, two blocks. Then make a left. I'll guide you. They are advancing."

"If they're tracking me, why run?"

"They're not tracking you via chip. You were reported. Probably a passerby called you in. They can only visually find you. If you can outrun them, if you can get to the park, we can get you out of there. You have time. Run!"

Colton didn't take the time to contemplate but ran at full speed. He had only gone a few feet when he realized how difficult it was to run without being able to see. Instinctively, he kept his hands in front of him and expected to run into a street pole or a person. The commander helped guide him to stay out of the street and directed him when the curbs were ahead. Though it felt like an eternity, Colton eventually made it the two blocks. The commander ordered him to run down the center of a small residential road. There were no vehicles, and it would be far less hazardous than an obstacle-ridden sidewalk.

Out of breath and panting, Colton asked, "Where are they? Are they behind me?"

"Yes, a couple of blocks."

A couple of blocks? Colton hated how nonchalantly the commander said those words. He might as well have said, *You're dead.*

"What do I do?"

"Keep running. The park is a block ahead and on your right. You're going to have to—"

Static. Suddenly, the commander's voice was diluted by the sounds of interference. The signal was fading. Maybe Colton had entered a dead zone for whatever frequency the Remnant was using. It didn't matter anyway, though. Colton had already decided that whoever he was speaking to wasn't thinking clearly. Running down the middle of the street with extractors on his tail wasn't a good idea. He'd be taken by the time he made it to the park.

Instead of going to the park, Colton decided to run to the side of the road and hide behind or under a car. The extractors would drive right past him.

He felt his way to the side of the road and found the hood of a car. Another flash of vision illuminated what he thought to be a Mercedes. Hurriedly, he felt his way around the car and collapsed onto the ground beside the curb. He lay there, inhaling the fragrance of cement and asphalt. Two vehicles drove past. His vision was dark again, but he would have sworn they were Interceptors. They sure *sounded* like Interceptors. He knew their sound well, and he wondered who was driving them. Ashton? Marek? One of the others? He didn't want to stay to find out.

Another burst of light brought his vision back, but this time it didn't leave completely. He could see the Mercedes he was hiding behind. And he could see, only ten feet away, an alleyway. That was where he'd go. It was no use going to the park now because the extractors were there and no way was he going to risk it.

Looking around and discerning what little he could, Colton stood up and dashed for the alley. He didn't hear any cars or see anyone moving. He jogged down the dark alley, blinking, regaining his vision, wondering where he was, and noticed he was running straight toward a wall. The alley came to a dead end, and the walls on both sides of him were high security fences for neighboring condominium units; there was no hope of scaling them. He would have to turn around and try again. As he made an about-face, he heard more static, and the commander's voice materialized out of nowhere and everywhere.

"What are you doing?" he demanded. "The park. Not an alley. The park."

"They would have gotten me. I wouldn't have made it on time."

"You just complicated matters," he said. "You're putting yourself in danger."

"Look," Colton said, exasperated. "I don't even know who you are, I don't know anything about your renegade team, but you just asked me to run miles through a city while blind and being hunted. You need to cut me some slack, okay? I'm doing my best."

"Don't do that again," the commander said, and for the first time Colton realized something about this man's voice reminded him of his dad. It made him a little uneasy.

"Okay, so what do you want me to do?"

No response.

"Well," Colton said, "tell me what to do. My vision's back. I can see. Everything is dim, but I can see—"

Colton stopped and fear gripped his heart when he saw two headlights turn into the alley. A vehicle—probably an Interceptor—drove toward him. Loose gravel crunched beneath the weight of the tires, and because of the darkness and his weakened vision, Colton could only see headlights. They advanced toward him like glowing Will-O-Wisps, and Colton was forced to cover his weakened eyes.

"Someone's here," he said. "What do I do?"

No answer. No static. Nothing.

"I said someone's here. What do I do?"

His heart thundered mercilessly in his chest. The vehicle came to a stop. The door opened. He heard two feet hit the ground and

136

walk toward him, but he couldn't look. The light hurt his eyes too much.

Helplessly, he raised his hands above his head. He knew resistance was futile.

"Don't be afraid," the commander said. "This is one of us. The one you were supposed to meet."

"One of us," Colton whispered. Holding his fingers in front of his eyes and blocking as much of the headlights as he could, he saw the dark silhouette of a figure moving toward him. It was a woman. He saw the dark outline of feminine legs, a narrow waist, and long hair.

Then the light was behind her, and he could see she wasn't just any woman. Clad in black pants and a sleeveless leather top, with guns, ammo, radio, and rope holstered to her belt, he recognized her immediately.

"Selma?"

She grinned and said, "Hi there. I hear you need a ride."

1.2.6

Colton climbed inside a black Corvette, buckled up, and tried to make sense of what was happening. Selma pulled back onto the street, took a few side streets, and finally found the onramp to the 405. By the time they were nearing North Long Beach, most of Colton's vision had returned, and so had his questions. He leaned back in the black leather seat, looked out the window toward the waning moon, and wondered how he'd gotten into this predicament.

He looked at Selma's profile as she drove—still beautiful, but now she appeared more stoic, more poised. With both hands on the wheel and looking straight ahead, she looked like a woman on a mission. The reality, of course, was clear—she had never been interested in Colton. It had all been a ruse to infiltrate the CTC. That, most likely, had been the reason for the date, the reason for the flirting, and the reason for everything. No wonder she also went out with Ashton Lampson. She wasn't looking for a man. She was looking for information.

"So," Colton said, breaking an icy silence, "you drive a Corvette, huh? How much are they paying you at the CTC?"

"I saved for a long time. My dad drove one, so it has sentimental value."

"How long have you been working for this…this Remnant?"

She looked at him and grinned; that same playful expression was there, but now Colton doubted the motive for it. "I was taken off the grid five years ago."

"Five years ago, huh?" Colton said. For some reason it struck him that his ex-wife, Mona, had died five years ago. Those were long, miserable days of trying to console Marty. Nothing he said ever helped. And anything he tried seemed to make it worse.

138

"Yes," she said. "I was taken completely off the grid and given a new identity. I was Tina before. The old me was about to be apprehended by your lovely organization, but according to the government, I was abducted and killed. My new chip identifies me as Selma—like when I walk through the security entrance of the CTC—but they can't track me with it. From the government's perspective, I just follow the same physical route every day of the week."

"A ghost signal?"

Selma looked at him, surprised. "Yeah. How'd you know?"

"I paid attention. So this is what you guys do, huh? Switch identities and start a new life?"

"No. Most of us are completely in hiding. In the shadows. Delivering others. Only a few, like me, have their NRNT chips reprogrammed to reenter society. And there's a good reason for it. I've been trying for years to get that job at the CTC. Years!"

"Wow, you're telling me some pretty top secret information right now. You sure you should do that?"

Selma laughed.

Colton looked at her strangely. *Did I say something funny?*

"I think the CTC is much more interested in you than me at the moment," she said. "I'm just a secretarial worker. You, on the other hand, are public enemy number one. I don't think you're going to take this information and run to the authorities now, are you?"

"Good point," Colton said.

They made brief eye contact, and Selma, grinning again, rolled her head back and laughed. That was the Selma he knew— at least, the one he was starting to know. The one he liked. The one he would give himself to, if the opportunity afforded itself. Her lightheartedness brought with it a reassuring thought: If what he knew of Selma had been the real Selma, then maybe it wasn't all just a sham. Maybe she hadn't been acting the *whole* time.

"So where exactly are you taking me?"

"Good question," she said. "I'm taking you to our chief operations base. Next time you get orders, you should follow them. Honestly, that was a close one. Two Interceptors almost apprehended you. If you had just listened, it wouldn't have been so risky."

"Are you kidding me?" Colton asked. "Your commander had me run miles through the city when I could hardly see."

"Would you prefer to be back in your hotel room?"

"Well, no, but there's got to be a better way to do this. If I had listened to him, those Interceptors would have been on me for sure. No way could I have made it to the park on time. It would have been impossible."

"I wouldn't be so sure about that," Selma said. "He has the entire city grid at his disposal, the NRNT tracking data, you name it. If you don't listen next time, you just might get yourself killed."

"Really?" Colton said. Then reality struck him.

Selma was one of the Aberrants.

She must be one if she had been on the CTC's watch list, and had been near apprehension. Her conversations with him had led him to believe that she was highly creative, and now that made more sense. She carried the archaic belief that some divine power was holding the world together.

A more frightening thought struck him: *She is taking me into the den of those who share that belief.* Colton, the chief persecutor of these people who had found a means to live in the shadows, was walking right into their lair. Undoubtedly, he may have been the one to put some of their own brothers, sisters, mothers, and fathers on the Island.

"Oh no," he whispered. They would hate him. And how could he blame them?

He couldn't go there. Under no circumstances could he go there.

"What's wrong?" Selma asked.

"You can't take me to your base. I can't go there."

"But why?"

"Because these are the same people I've been sending to the Island my whole career. They'll hate me. Are you kidding me? I just can't walk in there."

"You needn't worry about that," Selma said in what was supposed to be a reassuring voice. "They've been prepared.

140

We've all been prepared. Don't forget, I'm one of those people, and I'm helping you."

"Yes, but I doubt they're all like you."

"True," she said. "There may be some…um…adjustment. I'll give you that. But by and large, we've known you've been coming for a long time. We've known that someone from the inside was going to help us and lead the captives off the Island. That's part of why I was working at the CTC, because we knew it was just a matter of time before someone stepped over to our side. We just never imagined it would happen like this."

"Oh, I see, so you were there looking for *someone*."

"Yes," she said flatly.

Colton didn't mean anything by it, but he realized, after the words escaped his mouth, that it sounded like a loaded comment. *Just someone, huh, some guy to take the bait of your green eyes, your dark hair, and your olive skin? So the whole date was just a sham, huh? The little elf hat I bought you, the giggles over champagne, the walk down the boardwalk—all part of the plan, huh? So I'm just the sucker.*

"Time is short," Selma said again.

She pulled the Corvette off the freeway and into a neighborhood somewhere in North Long Beach. It wasn't a nice area. This was the kind of neighborhood you drove through with your doors locked, and as Selma sped down the graffiti-covered, crumbling outer-rim of Long Beach, Colton couldn't help but wonder where exactly this base of operations was.

"You didn't listen to much of the news during your stay in the hotel, did you?" she said.

"A little. Why?"

"Then you know Ashton has been officially appointed the new Chief Officer?"

"Ashton?" Even though he had more than obliterated any opportunity of working for the CTC ever again, the thought of Ashton winning the battle for Chief Officer made him nauseous. "Really? Already?"

"Yes. Your betrayal of the CTC, coupled with what has already been a huge influx of reports, expedited the whole process of putting a new Chief Officer at the helm. They didn't waste any time. He was sworn in yesterday evening, and you know how all that goes. He promised to be the best Chief Officer yet, and his number one priority is to bring you into custody. According to him, he's got every man, woman, and child looking for you."

"So Ashton Lampson is the new Chief Officer of the CTC?" Colton was really having a hard time getting over that fact.

"Unfortunately."

She turned the Corvette down a narrow street where half of the buildings appeared to be abandoned and the other half were crumbling. This was some kind of dilapidated commercial zone on the outer fringe of the city. Slowly, Selma pulled the Corvette behind a dumpster, killed the ignition, and clicked off the headlights.

All was dark.

"Wait here for a moment. They'll find us."

"Wait here?" Colton asked, looking up and down the alley. "Why?"

"They'll take us below to base," Selma said, "and they'll hurry. Everyone's hurrying now. We have until tomorrow at midnight."

"Tomorrow at midnight for what?"

"You didn't hear that either, I take it? I should have known. You would be much more upset if you had." Selma turned toward him, looking worried. "Well, there's no easy way to say this—there's been a change in termination plans."

Colton was now paying close attention to her. Selma bore a look of worry, fear, and incredible sadness all rolled into one. She didn't want to tell him—he immediately recognized the trepidation in her voice—and Colton recognized this look as the same one the doctor had worn during one of the last visits to Marty's mom in the hospital. This was a look of death, or *near* death.

"What is it?" he asked again. "What's wrong?"

"The Island," she said softly. "With you being AWOL, and the sudden media coverage of the possibility of an underground organization, Ashton has been given everything he needs to expedite the Termination Order. Congress met into the wee hours of the morning to approve the emergency order. This was exactly what the CTC needed to take things to the next step."

"Termination?" Colton gasped. He pictured Marty sitting in his cell, frightened, clinging onto his own scrawny arms in fear.

"Yes. All the Aberrants on the Island will be exterminated, and those who haven't already been transported will be terminated at CTC Headquarters. Gas."

The words sounded far off, surreal. *This can't be happening,* he thought. *It just can't.*

"When?" he asked. "That law wasn't supposed to take effect until next year."

Selma squeezed his hand. She closed her eyes.

"Tomorrow night. Midnight."

1.2.7

"Who are they?" Colton asked, as two shadowy figures approached them from the alley.

The men emerged from the back door of one of the dilapidated buildings, and Colton had a difficult time discerning them in the darkness. One was slim, angular, and appeared to be toting a rifle. The other, a massive beast of a man, lumbered beside the shorter one.

Colton looked to Selma in hopes she would start the ignition and leave, but she just smiled and opened her door.

"This is them," she said, and climbed out of the vehicle.

Colton got out of the passenger side and realized, as the men drew nearer, that he knew them. This was Bayard, still clad in camo and looking like he hadn't shaven in days. Big Al stood beside Bayard and appeared just as disgruntled and angry as he had the last time Colton saw him. If this was what he looked like normally, Colton couldn't imagine what he looked like when he was upset.

"Glad you made it in one piece," Bayard said.

"Barely," Colton responded.

Selma walked past Colton, threw her arms around Bayard, and hugged him. It wasn't a long, sensual hug, but it lasted long enough to make Colton feel uncomfortable, and when Selma let go of Bayard, he heard Bayard whisper, "I love you" in her ear. Despite the circumstances—his son having barely twenty-four hours to live—watching Selma hug her boyfriend or husband in front of him felt like a slap in the face. Salt on the wound. He was completely at these people's mercy, and that was the one thing he had never shown the Aberrants in his years working at the CTC.

"Well, I guess introductions aren't necessary," Bayard said.

"You know Selma, obviously."

"Yeah," Colton said dryly. "We've met."

"Good," Bayard said. "Now we're about to have you meet some people you normally wouldn't have the chance to meet. We're going to take you down to our base, the hive of our operation. I really do apologize for the inconvenience of that hotel stay, but we can't be sloppy. Too much is riding on this."

"I just want my son back."

"We want him back, too. We want them all back."

"Then why are you taking me down into your base?" Colton asked. For the first time, anger boiled inside. Maybe it was because his confusion had worn off and now, standing in the back alley of a washed up part of North Long Beach, he failed to understand exactly how going to this base would take him one step further in getting his son. "What am I going to do here? How is this going to help? They're gonna hate me here. I've been hunting these people for half my life."

"You have a point," Bayard said, and Big Al, smoking a cigar, grunted in what seemed to be agreement. "But we've warned them you're coming, okay? Some might have a hard time with it—and you have to see where they're coming from—but you're just going to have to make do. You have a bounty on your head, Mr. Pierce. Our station is probably the safest place around for you."

"I want to talk to your leader. What is his name?"

"We call him Gus."

"I want to talk to him about what's being done to get my son out of the CTC. And if he has more plans for me running down the street blind and making a fool of myself and nearly getting killed in the process, then maybe I'd be better off on my own."

"Oh, I'm sure Gus has more interesting plans than that," Bayard said, laughing. Selma joined him, and Colton couldn't figure out if they were being sarcastic or serious. "Listen, you got this far, didn't you? You're alive and in one piece. Your son is alive and in one piece. And you have a chance to save him. That's more than a lot of people."

"Shouldn't there be more of a sense of urgency?" Colton

asked. "My son is going to die tomorrow night, and so are all of the people on the Island—the same people you claim that you want to protect. Shouldn't we be doing something? If all those people on the Island are going to be killed tomorrow night, then shouldn't we—"

"Ah, so you call them people now and not Aberrants. Things change when your own blood is in the mix, huh?"

"Yeah, people, Aberrants, whatever you want to call them. What are we going to do?"

"Do you have any suggestions, my friend?" Bayard asked.

"Me? No, I don't, but haven't you guys been planning for this? It's been all over the news for months, this idea that the Aberrants are all going to be killed. Didn't you put some thought into this?"

"Glad you asked, actually," Bayard said. "We do have a plan for this, and if you're patient enough, you'll get a chance to hear it. You see, this has been orchestrated for months. Selma finally infiltrating the CTC was one step. Our commander has it all planned, and we've been working out the mechanics."

"Then I want to meet him. I want to hear it."

"Well, you can't meet him yet. He's at Station One."

"Station One?"

"Think of it as the Intelligence Base."

"Then I want to talk to whoever's in charge at *this* base."

"You are." Bayard winked. "Listen, we have a plan, and all will be explained. The fact of the matter is that we have a candidate to infiltrate the offices of the CTC and put our plan in action."

Colton half-laughed. "What loon did you free from the insane asylum to agree to that? It's impossible to infiltrate the CTC. The White House itself doesn't have that good of security! Look, I know you guys believe in miracles and those kinds of things, but that's just nonsense."

"We shall see," Bayard said. "Follow me." Bayard and Big Al turned and walked toward the shadowy building they had emerged from.

Selma put her arm around Colton and reminded him that everyone in the base was happy he was coming, but some of them might have a hard time trusting him. Colton listened but didn't like the sensation of her arm around him. Had she forgotten the other night? At dinner? On the pier?

They walked a short ways down the alley, past graffiti-covered dumpsters, boarded windows and doors, and a family of cats scurrying along the walls. At last they found themselves behind an abandoned shop with a faded sign that read: MARLEY'S AUTOMOTIVE. Bayard looked several times down the alley, though it was apparent nobody was in the vicinity, and then knocked in a strange cadence on the back door.

A moment later, the door opened, revealing three men brandishing weapons. They were dressed in black body armor, but the weapons made the greatest impression on Colton. They were military-issued automatic weapons. Somehow, it wasn't what he was expecting from an underground remnant of people being hunted down for their theistic beliefs.

One of the men had a black patch covering his left eye, and he introduced himself as Sadie. The two quieter men at Sadie's side looked Colton up and down with awe and a palpable sense of repugnancy. It was clear they weren't altogether thrilled at his arrival. Sadie led them into the crumbling remains of the building, through a massive sliding steel door that took several of the men's strength to roll away, and into a dark stairwell that descended into the bowels of the earth.

The walls of the underground passage oozed with moisture and after several minutes of descending, they found themselves walking along a very narrow and seemingly unending passage to nowhere. The cavern ceiling was low, and all of them had to duck to make clearance. Big Al almost had to walk on all fours.

"What do you do down here?" Colton asked Selma.

"We plan extractions, coordinate, and keep a close eye on the city above. Our base is below Fire Station 41. We've tapped into their computer, and it's proved useful in learning the comings and goings of law enforcement and extraction units." Their voices echoed off the damp walls.

"Wow," Colton said. "You guys have been hiding here all this time?"

"Yep. But remember, we can't be tracked, so we're up above in the city all the time as well. We meet here for planning purposes and to coordinate, but we do get out. We dedicate ourselves to prayer down here so we won't be reported. Once you're taken off the grid, you have to be really careful not to be reported, because if the government realizes you have no signal, everything could collapse like a house of cards. Fortunately, it's never happened. Not yet. We've gone to great lengths, trust me."

The downgrade of the corridor increased, and Colton had to hold onto the sides of the rocky walls to keep from falling forward. But far ahead, in front of the black-clad soldiers walking in front of him, he thought he could see light. Soon they found themselves in a large chamber that looked like a tactical command room. A row of computers were lined against one of the rocky walls, and several men sat in front of them in black chairs, making calculations and charting coordinates. Pairs of other men and women—all carrying firearms and wearing body armor—talked quietly. In the middle of the chamber, a holographic map depicted the entire city, and several men and women stood around it, mumbling to each other, discussing seemingly important matters. The three-dimensional map rotated, turned, zoomed in and out, and manipulated in every way possible at their verbal commands.

The room grew quiet as the men and women stopped what they were doing and turned their attention to the men entering the chamber. It was more than clear that everyone was most interested in Colton. He wasn't entirely sure how to read their expressions. Were they happy? Surprised? Upset?

"Everyone's looking at me," Colton whispered to Selma.

"Of course," she said. "They've been expecting you for a while now, and you've made quite a name for yourself. I think they're surprised to actually see you here."

"Some of them look a little pissed off," he mumbled.

"Give it time."

"Well, I can tell by the looks on all of your faces that you've been waiting for us," Bayard said to everyone in the underground war room. "The mission was a success. We've extracted Colton Pierce, who—just a few days ago—was the most determined of our hunters. But he's here now with us and ready for the second part of our plan."

The men and women offered a lukewarm applause, and Colton chalked it up to the fact that some of them seemed genuinely in awe. Unsure of what to do or say, Colton simply offered everyone a friendly wave and smile and hoped that would convey that he was happy and thankful that they'd taken him off the grid.

"And now that he's here, we're ready to initiate part two of the plan. The next step will be to infiltrate the CTC tomorrow evening. We have little time. We'll spend tonight and tomorrow coordinating all the details."

The proposition sounded even more ridiculous upon hearing it the second time, but this time Colton noticed Bayard look at him as he mentioned those words: *Infiltrate the CTC.* A terrible thought struck him. *He* was the one they were going to send into the CTC on some fool's quest to save all of the Aberrants. It was a terrible thought. They had brought him here only to send him back into the dragon's lair, where any chance of saving his son and the other Aberrants was only a sliver of a possibility.

"Who are you sending to infiltrate the CTC?" Colton asked, already aware of the answer.

Bayard smiled and slapped him on the shoulder. "You're the loon we're going to send in."

1.2.8

"**I** want to remind every United States citizen that we will stop at nothing until Colton Pierce is in our custody," Ashton Lampson pronounced boldly from behind a podium. A gaggle of news reporters filled the chairs, took pictures, and waited not-so-patiently for Ashton to finish his speech so they could ask questions.

Colton watched all of this on a large projection screen in an underground conference room. He sat next to Selma, Bayard, and Big Al. Aaron, an older man with salt and pepper hair pulled into a ponytail, had brought them to the room and then taken a seat at the head of the old oak table.

"And I would like to remind every United States citizen that all of the Aberrants will be eliminated tomorrow at midnight," Ashton said. He looked down at some papers on the podium. "If there is any good fortune that has come of this incident, it has been the acceleration we have needed to move this bill through Congress. Now that we have received the green light, we will not tarry in our responsibilities. Tomorrow evening, the prisoners of the Quarantine Zone will be exterminated in the most humane way we know how. Their cells will be gassed, and they will die a more peaceful death than most of us will ever have the opportunity to experience. Those Aberrants who still remain in holding tanks in our Long Beach facility—or any partner facilities throughout the country—will suffer the same fate. Be advised, our number one priority is public safety, and we take this responsibility very seriously."

Ashton licked his finger and turned one of the pages. He licked his finger again and adjusted his hair.

"Unfortunately, there are other matters that we must deal with simultaneously." He looked gravely into the camera. "As the public is well aware, an equal responsibility we bear at this time is the immediate apprehension of Colton Pierce. We believe he is still alive. Rest assured that we have dispatched every resource of the CTC and the local authorities in finding him. We ask you, the public, to please contact the authorities if you have any knowledge of his whereabouts. It is times like this when we must band together as citizens and fulfill our moral responsibility.

"Many people are asking difficult questions at this time. Did Colton Pierce act alone? Is there a rogue militia attempting to take people off the grid and rescue them from extractions? I can only tell you that we have our best and brightest working on these questions and rest assured, if in fact there is such an underground organization assisting in these kinds of deplorable activities, their fate will be far worse than the Aberrants who are currently in custody. We will stop at nothing until Colton Pierce is in our custody and we will stop at nothing until this underground organization—if it exists—is brought to light."

Hearing enough, Bayard picked up a remote control, clicked a button, and the screen went blank. He leaned back in a worn-out, squeaky office chair and said, "So that's what's been happening since you've been MIA. Tomorrow evening at midnight they're going to exterminate our families and our friends. And your son, Colton."

"And I'm still waiting to hear your plan," Colton said impatiently.

Bayard pointed to Aaron. "I think I'll let him explain it to you. I'm not so good at all the techno-jargon."

Colton looked to Aaron, who had remained quiet during this meeting. He hadn't done much more than listen and sip a mug of what smelled like bitter coffee.

"So you'd like to know the plan, hmm?" Aaron asked.

"Well, it would be a start," Colton said.

"I see. Hard to be thrown into so much so quickly, hmm?" Aaron took a long, loud slurp of his coffee and seemed to contemplate exactly how and where to proceed. "I am the chief technology planner for the Remnant, and we've been working on something for a long time that we'll finally be able to put to use. And you, Mr. Pierce, are going to have the opportunity to make the whole thing possible. It's a computer virus, but not just any computer virus. You might think of this as the Mother of All Computer Viruses. It's taken us years to develop it and years of waiting for an opportunity such as this to use it. It's quite simple, really. You just have to download the virus yourself, from within CTC Headquarters."

"What?" Colton nearly fell out of his chair. Now he knew these people were crazy. "You have to be kidding me! I can't just march in there!"

"Unfortunately this virus can't be implemented any other way. The firewall the CTC uses is far too strong, and even though we'd rather administer it remotely, the security they have is—"

"It's impossible!" Colton protested.

"Famous last words that always precede something great," Aaron said matter-of-factly.

Bayard jumped into the conversation. "Trust me, if there were any other way, we would love to infect the CTC's computers from the safety of our base, but we can't. Like Aaron said, the protection is just far too strong. We need someone on the inside. Someone who could access one of the servers in the lower crypts of the CTC."

Colton felt the sheer impossibility of it. To get into the CTC itself unnoticed and unmolested was one thing; to get to the servers was another thing entirely.

"You're asking the impossible," Colton said. "What does this virus do? How is it going to keep my son alive or help all of your friends?"

"That's a good question," Aaron said. "The virus has been in development for years. It has three parts, really. To begin, it will completely disable the CTC's tracking system; they will no longer be able to hunt any suspected Aberrants, but more importantly, those who are already being held captive will be immediately taken off the grid. Any accused Aberrant, such as your son, will be untraceable. Kind of like you are now."

"Then they'll all go blind for a couple days?" Colton asked.

"No," Aaron said. "Not this way. Different situation. We're not tapping directly into the NRNT chips in their skulls; we're deactivating the external trackers. The chips will be active, but the computers will have no way to track them. It'll just be scrambled signals. Understand?"

"I think so," Colton said. "But I see one big problem. If they're still behind bars, then why does it matter? It's not going to help them get out."

"Let me tell you the second component of the virus." Aaron smiled, leaned back his chair, and for a moment he sounded like a parent reminiscing over fond memories of his child. It was evident that Aaron took great pride in discussing it. "At the same time that the tracking features are disabled, the virus will instantly seize control of the CTC's security. This means all security measures will be dropped on the Island. Cells will be unlocked, communications will be shut down, and the path will be clear for escape."

Colton contemplated this. It seemed too easy. Much too clean.

"But even if all the cells on the Island are unlocked, it's not just like everyone can walk off the Island," Colton said. "You have to have something planned."

"We do," Aaron said. "And this involves the third part of the virus. The virus will allow us the ability to transmit signals through anyone's NRNT chips. *Anyone.* Until now, we've been very limited with that, and only with the NRNT chips we've scrambled. Have you ever heard of something called the Brown Note?"

"No, what is it?" Colton asked.

"It's a hypothetical infrasonic frequency that causes humans to lose control of their bodily functions due to its resonance, hence the term *Brown Note.*"

"You're gonna tap into their computers to cause people to poop their pants? That's your plan?"

"Unfortunately, no," Aaron said. "No one has ever been able to produce the Brown Note, but we've come up with something close: the Gray Note. At least, that's what we're calling it. It will cause disorientation, confusion, perhaps unconsciousness, and the virus will pinpoint every CTC worker, security, and law enforcement agent in our path. There'll be no resistance at all. We've already arranged for several of our men to prepare to head to the Island. Once security is down and every security worker and all CTC personnel on the Island are out of commission, it will simply be a matter of rounding everyone up, chartering some of the boats already on the Island, and getting out of there. But all of our plans hinge completely on the idea of you being able to get into the CTC's server room and administering the virus."

Aaron pulled a thumb drive out of his pocket and handed it to Colton. "Our hope lies in this."

Colton looked at the small device in his hand.

"But I don't know anything about computers," Colton said. "Even if I was able to access the servers, what do I do? Just stick it in one of the computers?"

"We'll be in contact with you as before. The commander will walk you through it every step of the way."

"But the whole idea is impossible," Colton protested. The idea of this virus was interesting—actually, quite amazing to Colton— but he knew the sheer impossibility of getting into headquarters. That, in Colton's mind, was where the whole idea fell apart. "It's one thing to get down to the servers with this virus, but it's another for me to actually get into the building. You guys do realize that I'm the Most Wanted Man in the United States right now, right? I can't just walk into the CTC and wander my way down to the servers and do this. I wouldn't even make it through the front door. Why not Selma? Have her do it. She can get in without tripping alarms. You should have had her do it earlier."

"Selma doesn't have the clearance that you do, Colton, and couldn't get anywhere near the servers. We think you will be able to walk through the front door just fine."

Colton looked at him, squinted, and tried to figure out if he was trying to be funny. Was this some kind of joke? What wasn't he getting at?

"He's right," Selma said. "You'll be able to get in."

"Wow." Colton shrugged. "You guys really are crazy. When did all of you start drinking the Kool-Aid? Let me know when you start passing cups of it around, okay, so I can make sure to drink something else."

Bayard rubbed his fingers along the gray stubble on his chin. "The scanners won't recognize you when you enter the building. Your NRNT chip has been reconfigured, remember? You won't register as Colton Pierce. Instead, thanks to a little reprogramming, you will appear to be Gregory Grissom, Selma's brother, who she's bringing by to see her office. The scanner will recognize you as Gregory, and this is who you will sign in as.

"As far as your appearance, a little make-up—a false set of glasses, bleaching your hair perhaps—can do wonders. One of the refugees down here used to do make-up on movie sets. He'll make sure you're not easily recognizable. And if you're still worried about going to the epicenter of where all of this began, you have to ask yourself one simple question: Do you think the CTC would expect you to come back? Of course not! It will be the last place they look."

"But...." Colton's voice trailed off. The idea had some merit, but there were so many problems, so many complications, he didn't even know where to begin.

"I know I don't have the security access that you do," Selma said, "but I can at least get us in the building. It's not uncommon to bring someone into the main offices; no one will think twice if I say I'm bringing my brother from out of town to see my office."

"But how do I get down to the servers?" Colton asked. "Any clearance I had in the building has been taken offline by now. I doubt any of my clearance codes will even work."

"Well," Bayard said, "this is where we're hoping your training as an extractor and your familiarity with the CTC will come into play. We're hoping that, once inside, you'll be able to figure out how to get down to the servers. We can get you into the building. But once there, we need you to do the heavy lifting. That's why we're sending you. We believe your long-term knowledge of the facility, the way it works, the people who work there, and all of the security procedures will prove invaluable. We need you to do this."

Colton leaned forward to make a point, but couldn't think of exactly what to say. The plan, although bordering on foolhardiness, had some merit. He had to admit to himself that if this computer virus worked, and if he could reach the servers, it was an amazing idea. It was hard to believe that the entire CTC operation could be undermined by whatever code had been written onto that tiny thumb drive, but if it could, it would give him a chance to save Marty. And he couldn't let that slip through his fingers—not when it was the *only* chance he had.

"This is a pretty crazy idea," Colton said. "A good idea, but a crazy one."

"The best of plans involve risk," Bayard said. "This one is no different."

"I'm just not convinced that I will go unnoticed. Someone could easily recognize me. The disguise would have to be very good."

"Let us worry about that." Bayard pointed out a small red button on the back of the drive. "There's something very important you should know. In the event that you are caught, and assuming you have time, press the button three times. Do it quickly. We don't want this drive and our programming to fall into the wrong hands."

It struck him as utterly ironic that such large hope could be held within so small a thing. It hardly weighed anything. "Why push the button?"

"It'll erase the drive completely. Use it only in an emergency circumstance, because we don't want the virus in the hands of the CTC. If something happens to you, we will still have the opportunity to try this again in the future. So remember, if you are caught and hope is gone, erase the thumb drive. Got it?"

"Got it," Colton said unconvincingly. "And what are you going to be doing while Selma and I put our necks on the line?"

"I'll be en route to Catalina." Bayard smiled and rubbed his hands together. "I'll be leading an evacuation team. We have several vessels and plan on confiscating several more there. I'll be leading a team of prisoners off the Island."

"To where?"

"We'll talk about that later," Bayard said. "We've also been in contact with some other cities and their Remnants."

"You mean there's more?"

"The United States is a big country, Colton. Only recently have we discovered that we're not the only underground operation. There are more. After this, we're going to unite. But right now let's just worry about what's at hand, okay? Gus will be in radio contact with you the entire time to assist you, and we have a few tools to offer you as well. But the entire Remnant here—all two hundred or so of us—will be on those boats assisting with the escape. Not a soul will remain here. There's nearly three thousand people on the Island."

"Three thousand?" Colton coughed, wiping his mouth. "That's quite an evacuation. I hope you have a lot of room on whatever ships you're taking over and whatever ships you're picking up there."

"Oh yes," Bayard said. "All of the details are worked out, and you need not concern yourself with those. Not yet. All of this is working just as we planned."

"Just as you planned? But you didn't even know I was going to be available until a few days ago. Not until I became the Most Wanted Man in America. So how could you have had this planned?"

Bayard looked at Selma, and they exchanged a brief smile. Even Aaron looked amused.

"This is something that might currently be outside your realm of knowledge and expertise," Bayard said, intertwining his fingers on the desk. "We've been waiting for you for a long time. Months. Years. Have you ever heard of prophecy, Mr. Pierce?"

"Prophecy?" Colton snickered. "I know that a group of people hiding out below ground might be a little out of touch with reality, but now you're pushing it. You're telling me that I was prophesied to help you? Your God told you this? The same one who spoke through an ass, right?"

"He can speak through other things, too," Bayard said. He laughed after exchanging a quick glance with Selma and Aaron.

"So He told you this? God?"

"Yes, and apparently He was right, wasn't He?"

"Okay," Colton said, nodding. "Okay, I'm in. I want my son back. And this is happening tomorrow?"

Bayard looked pleased. "Yes, we only have tomorrow. Tonight, you need rest."

"And where do you rest down here? You have beds?"

Bayard laughed and said, "Of course we have a place for you. We'll make sure you're comfortable."

"Good, I'm exhausted."

"Selma, why don't you show Colton where he can rest for the night?"

Colton stood, and Selma led him to the door, but Colton had one last question. He turned around before he left the room.

"What do you call this computer virus?"

Bayard appeared to like the question. He glanced at Aaron, then back to Colton.

"Exodus," Bayard said.

1.2.9

As exhausted as he was, Colton found it difficult to sleep. He had been taken down a winding cavern corridor to a small chamber with a cot. As he lay there, he could only think of Marty. What was happening to him right now? What were they doing to him? The very notion that he was going to die tomorrow evening, as the clock struck midnight, made Colton wonder if he would sleep at all. Every time he closed his eyes and started to slip away, he imagined Marty crouched in a fetal position in the corner of his cell as cyanide gas seeped in through the vents. He saw his face, heard his wailing, and tasted the tears running out of his bloodshot, terrified eyes.

Finally, accepting the fact that sleep would not come, Colton sat up in the cot and threw off the blanket. He wanted to go for a walk, though he understood little of the underground labyrinth. They had passed one place on the way to his sleeping quarters that Colton wanted to see more of; it was called the Mourning Room, and Bayard had briefly shown it to him as they passed. Now, for some reason, Colton felt drawn to it. He threw on his shoes, left the room, and walked back down the corridor. All of this, at one time, had been a sewer system, long ago abandoned and forgotten. It amazed Colton to think that the Remnant had found this place and used it as a base for their operations despite all of the CTC's efforts to extract every known Aberrant in the country.

Lights flickered along the corridor's ceiling, and water trickled down to shallow puddles at his feet. As he turned a corner, he noticed two weathered and fatigued men, both dressed in dark clothing, glance at him as he strode past. Even though they hardly acknowledged him, he knew what they were thinking; he could see it in their eyes. *This is the one we are protecting. This is the one who has been hunting us for years and now he is here, with us, hiding out. And the fact that every known authority in the country is hunting for him only makes it that much more dangerous for all of us, and everything we've worked so hard to build.*

He passed the men while looking down at his feet. He couldn't blame them for their suspicions; if he were in their shoes, he would feel the same way.

After a couple more zigzags through the abandoned sewer, he came, at last, to the Mourning Room. Giant lights hung from the ceiling, several of them dead, and a few others only offered faint flickers of momentary light, which made it feel like candles illuminated the room. The walls of the chamber were covered with pictures, many yellowed, many faded, some hardly discernible. There were hundreds if not thousands of faces here, young and old, of every ethnicity, size, and shape, which Bayard had described as friends and family of the Remnant who had been taken. Here were the sons, daughters, mothers, and fathers they could not save, who were already on the Island, who had been there for years. Even stepping into the room, Colton felt a great sadness engulf him, and he could not perceive if it was because of all of the yellowed, papered eyes glowering at him, or because he knew that his son's face might as well be added to the collage.

"He is one of them," he whispered softly as he stepped into the chamber.

A woman standing solemnly in front of the walls, looking at one of the pictures and weeping quietly, turned abruptly as Colton entered. She wiped her eyes quickly, gathered herself, and walked past him. He was sure that he saw that same look in her eyes as she passed. *You took all of these people from us. You are the reason they are on these walls, now only paper memories. Paper images. Paper souls. You took them from us.*

Colton stepped out of the way as she passed and looked down regretfully. What picture was she looking at? Was it her son? Her husband? A parent? Perhaps a dear sibling who had long ago been taken from her?

Whatever it was, this chamber seemed to have a power in

itself, and with effort, Colton walked up to one of the walls. He buried his hands in his pockets, took a deep and unsatisfying breath, and looked over the ocean of souls whose memories were entombed here.

"How many of them have I personally taken?" he whispered. There were so many: a little boy who looked Marty's age, grinning widely at a camera and straddling his BMX bike; a little girl biting into a giant cupcake; another little girl playing jump-rope; a college-age kid, standing on a podium with a cap and gown and holding up a degree; an elderly couple standing on the edge of a cruise ship, grinning ear-to-ear; a wedding photo of a pair who barely looked old enough to drive, let alone get married; an overweight mechanic, kneeling down beside the front fender of some exotic car; a well-groomed guy wearing a business suit, leaning back in an office chair with his feet kicked onto his desk.

Colton closed his eyes and rubbed his temples. *I just can't believe there's so many,* he thought. *So many faces...so many people...*

A voice startled him. "I thought I might find you in here." It was Selma.

Colton spun around. He hadn't heard her approach. "You scared me."

"Sorry, didn't mean to."

"What do you mean you thought you'd find me here? How did you know?"

"Many troubled people find themselves here," she said. "You have a lot on your plate."

"That might be a bit of an understatement."

Colton couldn't keep his eyes off the walls; everywhere he looked, the faces looked back at him.

"The faces are endless," he said. He reached out and touched one of the yellowed pictures—an elderly woman, a grandmother perhaps, holding up a pan of baked cookies and smiling proudly. Her expression seemed to say, *Yep, I just baked these cookies, and they are good. Very good!*

"Yes, endless," Selma said. "And we keep them here so they will not be forgotten. Many come here simply to remember them and to pray for their safety."

"To pray?"

"Yes, to pray. Is there something wrong with that?"

Colton found himself sneering, and Selma reacted to it. She walked closer to him and put her hand on his shoulder, and he forced himself to look away. He didn't want to be reminded of how beautiful she was, not when this whole time she had been using him to discover CTC secrets. Colton hadn't forgiven her for that and wasn't sure if he would ever be able to.

"What happened to you?" She asked in such a concerned voice that Colton looked back at her.

"What do you mean?"

"I mean, what exactly happened to you? I understand someone not believing in prayer, but I see more than disbelief on your face. You're angered by it. Something happened to you, didn't it?"

Colton sighed. *She knows my thoughts. Those gorgeous green eyes can look into me.*

"It's okay," she said, "you can tell me. I'll listen. I'll understand."

Maybe it was the way she said it with the soft voice and the mesmerizing stare. Her femininity seemed to have a power over him, and Colton found himself weakening, letting go. He looked at her—tried to look *into* her the same way she had looked *into* him—and he felt strangely safe. It may have also been all of the faces looking at him, pleading with him. Colton drew his hands out of his pockets and rubbed them together.

I guess there's no point in keep it a secret any longer, he thought. *Maybe this is the right time and place.*

"What is it?" she asked. He still wanted her and would have given himself to her if he could have. If Bayard wasn't a factor, he might have taken her at that very moment, wrapped his arms around her, and kissed her.

"I was a mess when I found out that Marty's mom was going to die," Colton said. He began to tell the story he had told nobody. The words felt strange coming out of his mouth. "We were divorced, yes. She was through with me, and when I thought of raising Marty all by myself, I panicked. I wasn't ready. I was terrified. I've never been that afraid."

"You? Afraid?"

"Deathly terrified." He tried to look her in the eyes but it was difficult. He found himself looking down at his shoes. "The last night I took Marty to see his mom at the hospital, I was overwhelmed with fear and anger. I knew she was going to die and I knew it would be soon. I watched my son sit beside his dying mom's bed and I grew angrier, more bitter, more bewildered. I didn't know what to do.

"That night, I left the house and walked for miles. At the time, I was going to find a bar, a little hole in the wall several miles down Ocean Boulevard. I think my plan was to sit there and drink myself into oblivion because, honestly, it was all I could think to do. I just wanted to be alone. I wanted to escape the world for a while. But I didn't go to the bar. When I got there, I stood outside the front door and thought about it, but I never went inside. I went somewhere else instead."

"Where?"

"To the beach. It was only a block away."

"The beach?" Selma asked. Colton could tell it wasn't what she was expecting.

"Yeah," Colton said. "I took the public access stairs down to the sand, and because it was probably nearing midnight, I was the only one out there. It was cold, and I bundled up in my jacket and walked across the sand to the water's edge, and I didn't care that my shoes were sopping wet. I didn't care about much of anything. I stood there, looking out at the oil islands, looking over at the glittering Long Beach Harbor that looked strangely like Christmas lights in the distance, and didn't want to be alive anymore. I even thought about lying down in the water and drowning myself, but it seemed too complicated, too uncomfortable. If I wanted to kill myself, I knew a gun would be a cleaner, more efficient way to go. And there was Marty. I had to take care of him."

"So you just stood there?"

Colton rubbed his right hand slowly down his face, massaging old memories. "I stood there for a long time, thinking, worrying, contemplating all of the change that was going to happen for my son. How he was going to cope. How *I* was going to cope. How we were going to cope together. And then, knowing I was alone, knowing that nobody could see me, I did it. Just that one time, only that one time."

"You did what?"

Colton looked away. He had told nobody and had hardly thought of that night until now. Returning to that place and time brought with it great pain, a cyclone of grief.

"I asked God—or whatever you call Him—to keep her alive. I got on my knees in the sand and cried out with every ounce of strength I possessed."

"You?" Selma asked, her eyes widening in disbelief. "You, Colton Pierce, prayed?"

"I did." He looked down, feeling a strange sense of shame. That night was so long ago that it often felt like a dream— something that hadn't actually *happened*. "I was at the end of my rope. Desperate people do desperate things. I only asked for two things. The first, I asked Him to save Mona's life. I didn't want my son to grow up without his mom, but I knew it was probably too late for that. So I also asked that He send someone to help me, a woman I would understand, a woman who would understand me, because I had been alone for so long, and the thought of raising Marty all by myself terrified me beyond measure."

"I'm still surprised you were scared."

"Nothing scared me more than that," Colton said matter-of-factly. "It was a different kind of scared. I wasn't ready for it."

"Wow," Selma said, clearly in disbelief. She hadn't looked away from him since he began his story. "And to think all of this happened while you were working for the CTC."

"It never happened again."

"Why never again?"

"Because I learned something else that night." Colton glanced at the endless collage of faces, and then, sighing, turned his full attention back to Selma. "I remembered that it's better to trust your own eyes and put your faith in things that you can see, that are tangible. That's what I'll put my trust in."

"I can understand that feeling," Selma said.

"Good, then maybe you should go. I feel like being alone, and I'm sure Bayard is looking for you."

"Bayard?"

"Yeah," he said. "It might not look good for us to be standing here alone, talking, especially after the pretend date the other night."

Selma crossed her arms, tilted her head, and looked at Colton in what he could only interpret as genuine confusion. He might as well have been speaking a foreign language, as he could tell she wasn't registering what he was saying. He really didn't want to have to explain this and had hoped to avoid the subject altogether, but their night out in Manhattan Beach and him being the subject of her false affection was eating away at him. It seemed silly—despite everything he was up against—but he had a difficult time letting it go.

"You think it was pretend?" she said, and Colton couldn't get a read on it. If she was denying it, did that mean she was implying that she was welcoming a relationship behind Bayard's back? Was that what she was getting at? Colton didn't even want to know and instantly regretted bringing the matter up. Besides, the more he thought about it, the guiltier he felt for even thinking of it. His son was going to die tomorrow night. How foolish and selfish to think of anything else!

"Listen, I'm really sorry I brought it up. We should go—"

"You're hurt because you think I was using you?" Selma said this almost like a statement, an *a-ha* moment.

Colton didn't say anything. With his hands back in his pockets, he looked down at his feet. It was hard to admit that he was hurt. So terribly difficult.

"Now I understand." Selma closed her eyes as she spoke, enunciating perfectly as if to be absolutely clear. She sighed, looked at Colton, leaned toward him, and kissed him delicately on the cheek.

What is this? A lover's kiss? A kiss of friendship? Colton's radar was completely broken.

Selma sighed again and began to walk away.

"I'll see you in the morning," Colton said, wondering if she would turn around to say goodbye.

She finally did when she was near the door. "Just for the record, and since you have so much faith in your own eyes and ears: I wasn't acting that night. Not at all."

Colton was nearly speechless. Frozen in place.

"But what about Bayard?" he asked, his voice echoing off the walls of the underground chamber.

A thin, crescent moon of a smile formed on Selma's lips.

"He's my brother," she said, and walked out of the chamber.

Colton was alone with a thousand faces glaring at him accusingly.

1.2.10

Colton woke up early and met Bayard and Selma in the same small command room he had come through when he first entered this underworld lair. He hadn't slept well; it was bitterly cold throughout the night, and the two blankets on his cot had done little to ward off the chill. Apart from that, his night had been filled with night terrors; twice he woke in his cot, sat up, and screamed as he imagined his son clawing futilely at the door of his prison cell.

"Why did you let them take me, Daddy?" he could hear his son say. *"Why?"*

He had given up trying to sleep around four and instead sat on his cot, bundled in his blankets, thinking of the hours his son had to live. He sat alone in the silence, listening to the sounds of trickling water coming from somewhere in this abandoned section of the underground sewer.

When he walked into the command room, he saw several men along with Bayard congregated around the holographic map. Bayard pointed at some features along the coast of Catalina, and Colton assumed he was planning exactly where to make entry on the Island and where they would be able to confiscate some of the vessels already there. Several others—three men and two women—sat at the other computers, scrolling through data. Colton felt eyes pierce him like darts when he walked into the room. Yes, he was on a mission to save these people's families, but he was still the reason they were on the Island in the first place.

He took a seat at one of the circular tables along the perimeter of the room, and Big Al placed a steaming bowl of oatmeal on the table before him. Colton couldn't eat. After one bite, he pushed the bowl away.

Selma entered the room shortly after, was also offered a bowl of oatmeal, and she took a seat beside Colton. She ate in silence while the others in the room clicked away at the computers and the group huddled around the holographic map quietly discussed their plans. Colton could hardly believe everything that had occurred in the last few days. A week ago, he was the most decorated extractor in the CTC, a stone's throw from being elected Chief Officer, and a father in contact with his son. Oh, how the tables had turned.

Bayard finally broke away from the map and walked toward the table. So did the others. When Colton looked up, there were at least ten or fifteen people standing there.

"So, how are you feeling?" Bayard asked.

He's her brother, Colton thought. *I should have seen it.* "I've been better."

"I understand. We're going to have Alex over here work on your disguise for a bit, and then you both need to get to work. Big day today."

"Yes, very big day," Colton mumbled.

"You guys need anything? Any part of the plan unclear? Anything you need clarification on? And you have the thumb drive, right?"

Colton pulled the thumb drive out of his pocket and held it up for good measure. He noticed, as he did so, that the other men and women in this cavernous room looked nearly as despondent as he felt himself; it occurred to him that many of their own sons and daughters were likely going to die this evening if the plan didn't go through. All of their hope was riding on this mission.

"I'll be in contact with you via radio," Bayard explained, rubbing his hands up and down his arms to ward off the cold.

"Okay," Colton said. "I wish I could tell you that I had some great idea up my sleeve. I'm still trying to figure out how I'm going to get down to the servers."

"You'll figure it out," Bayard assured him.

That wasn't very encouraging. Colton had enjoyed access to everywhere in the CTC, but he didn't have any means of getting down into the lower levels now. Once there, if he wasn't recognized or captured before then, he would have to be very creative about it.

"So who am I going to be?" Colton asked. "What disguise?"

"You're going to be Gregory Grissom, my brother from Portland." Selma handed Colton a thin sheet of paper. "Here's a list of some basic facts you'll want to look over on the way, just to make sure our stories are straight. Occupation. Address. Just the basics."

Colton looked over the paper. "So what is my occupation?"

"Librarian," Selma and Bayard said in unison.

"A librarian? Really? They still have those?"

"Yes, people still do read," Selma said. "You are the librarian for Centennial High School in Portland and, as such, you don't talk much. Kinda cliché, I know, but it works. So Colton, remember, Gregory is the shy and quiet type. The less you say, the better. Okay?"

"I can be the shy and humble type, no problem."

Selma and Bayard looked at him with the same frown of doubt.

"You'll wear a beard," Bayard explained, "and dark glasses and a ball cap. We can make you appear heavier with baggy clothing and such."

"That's it? Come on, I've been working at the CTC for years. I'll be recognized just by the way I walk."

"Remember, your disguise is just to get you into the building," Bayard said. "We don't want anyone monitoring the video cameras or even casual observers to suspect anything. But by no means should you approach anyone or have a discussion with anyone, unless absolutely necessary. That would surely be the end of your mission. Once you get inside Selma's office, you are free to drop the disguise or do whatever you need in order to accomplish your mission. Okay?"

Colton nodded. Bayard was right. Outside the building, Colton would only come across the rotating staff of security officers. That would be easy to get past. Once inside the building, Selma's office wasn't far from the main entrance. If he could get that far, perhaps he could figure out some means to get down to the servers—but it was going to be a challenge. The chances of someone seeing him and recognizing him felt much too high.

"There's one thing we need to do before your disguise," Bayard said.

As if this had been rehearsed, everyone in the room circled Colton and Selma. Colton's initial response was to get up and run. Why were they circling him? What did they plan to do?

Then, one by one, he felt hands on him. One hand on each shoulder, several on his back, one even on his head. He realized what was happening: prayer. Cocooned by all of the bodies, Colton looked up and watched as Bayard, his hand gripping Colton's shoulder, closed his eyes and began to pray.

Colton didn't fight it. He'd prayed only once in his life, so a second time didn't seem like it could hurt that much. He closed his eyes, lowered his head, and promised himself that he wouldn't make a habit of this. As Bayard prayed for their protection and as the others nodded and mumbled in agreement, Colton felt his mind wander.

An idea struck him. It was outlandish for sure. Colton admitted that to himself, but he thought it was a better way to get into the CTC unnoticed and undetected.

When Bayard finished his prayer, the hands fell away from Colton, and Bayard said it was time to get ready. It would take at least an hour to don the disguise.

"Bayard," Colton said, "are you open to a different idea of how to get into the CTC?"

Bayard considered this, looked at his sister, and nodded. "I'm sure we would be if a better idea presented itself."

"Good." Colton stood up. "I think I have a better idea and I'd like to try it."

"What do you plan to do?" Bayard asked.

"No disguise." Colton rubbed his hands together, ready to get this show on the road. "I'm going to the CTC as myself—Colton Pierce—and I'm going to get the job done."

Part III

1.3.1

The early morning sunlight fell like yellow rust over the rear parking lot of the CTC. Colton Pierce sat in the back seat of Selma's black Corvette and waited not-so-patiently for her to return. They had easily driven into the parking lot—a quick swipe of Selma's parking card had granted entrance. The gate opened. Selma drove her Corvette to a far corner of the parking lot and stopped beneath the cool shade of an elm tree.

Colton had told her what to do and had given her explicit instructions about what to say in case anybody asked; but chances were nobody would. The CTC had been in the midst of a fervent campaign to improve its image in the face of vocal opposition to the termination of the Aberrants. Now that it was actually going to happen, the vocal minority would most likely grow louder, and the CTC's need to remind the public of the institution's integrity and morality had never been higher.

So Colton assumed nobody would think twice when Selma, secretary to the PR Department, added a simple event to today's calendar: the filming of another public service announcement. And nobody would think twice when she noted that an outside actor would be brought onto the campus for the brief filming. It was business as usual. Selma only had to get one of the old extractor outfits—an easy prop to find amongst the recently filmed announcements—and get it back to the Corvette.

From there, Colton would make his way into the CTC with his extractor outfit on—helmet and all—and with Selma leading him through the building to his designated filming location, Colton assumed he would be about as inconspicuous as Mickey Mouse walking through a crowd at Disneyland. It was a borderline brilliant idea, and Colton prided himself on it.

Kinda funny, he thought. *I'm an extractor pretending to be an actor who is pretending to be an extractor.*

He looked at his watch: 8:17. "Sixteen hours," he whispered.

He looked across the parking lot, but there was no sign of Selma. He did see a couple other vehicles—a blue truck and a black SUV—pull into the lot. A woman climbed out of the SUV. She carried a huge assortment of red and blue balloons, so many it looked as if they might carry her away. And then it occurred to him—this wasn't going to be an ordinary day at the CTC. The Aberrants were being terminated tonight! This would be a day of celebration and merriment. This day was the result of years of political lobbying, and it would be a miracle if anyone actually got anything done today because most people, Colton assumed, would be in the mood to celebrate.

"And I would have joined them not long ago," he said.

His earpiece crackled. It was Bayard. "Are you in yet?"

"No, not yet. Waiting for Selma. But listen, where's Gus? I haven't heard from him yet."

"Don't worry, you will."

"Well, I hope so, because even if I do manage to get down to the servers, I don't have the slightest idea of what to actually do."

More static interference, but Colton thought he heard Bayard say, "Don't worry."

He was in the midst of laughing off that comment—How could he not worry?—when he noticed Selma walking hastily across the parking lot. She had a bundle slung over her back.

Colton felt his heart beating in his chest as the reality of what he was about to do hit him.

"This is the same one you used when you filmed your public service announcement," Selma said when she arrived.

Colton opened the bag and saw the extractor outfit within. He reached in and pulled out the helmet.

"You'll need this." Selma handed Colton a lanyard with an official guest pass attached to it.

Colton pulled the rest of the outfit out the bag and took a deep breath. "Let's do this," he said.

173

1.3.2

Getting into the building was even easier than Colton predicted. He made his way through security with hardly a glance. When he walked through the weapon detector and NRNT scanner, the security officer glanced lazily at the monitor, which indicated that Gregory Grissom was walking into the building, he had a clean record, and he was not armed. Apparently, that was enough. The officer did take note of the guest pass Colton wore around his neck but took such little interest in it that Colton wondered if he could have walked in without it.

Once inside, he looked over the busy lobby. Today was going to be a day of celebration. He saw three men standing by one of the coffee machines, arms folded in front of them, huge smiles on their faces, engaged in conversation. Colton had seen them before and was pretty sure he recognized them from accounting; the tall one's name was Sam, if he remembered correctly. A plump woman in high heels—Gretchen, Colton thought—strutted across the lobby with two boxes of donuts cradled in her arms. The early morning buzz of the facility was beginning; things were ramping up.

A giant banner, like a long, sadistic smile, hung from the east wall. In huge black letters: WE DID IT! CONGRATULATIONS!

Colton had hardly taken note of the banner when a man in black suspenders and a bow-tie approached them and handed Selma a small blue flyer. He looked vaguely familiar, but Colton couldn't remember what department he worked for. Was it the tech department? He had thinning hair slicked back and large, puppy eyes. Colton thought he remembered talking to him once or twice, perhaps years ago, at some department meeting. With so many people working for one organization, it was difficult to

WILLIAM MICHAEL DAVIDSON

keep everyone straight.

"Love the get up," the man said, pointing to Colton.

Colton nodded. He wanted to say "thank you" to play along, but he was paranoid that even his voice would be recognized. Why risk any more than he had to?

"The flyer is just a reminder that we'll be open all night to celebrate," the man said. "Ashton is having dinner catered, live music, drinks, the whole shebang. He's making a televised speech at midnight, and he says he has something special in store. Rumor has it there might be a fireworks show."

"Fireworks? Wow," Selma said.

"Yep. At least Ashton knows how to celebrate a good thing. It was hard enough to get Barclay to reach into the coffers to stock the restrooms with toilet paper."

"Well, thanks for the flyer," Selma said.

"Sure thing."

The man, still holding a stack of flyers, paused briefly and took note of Selma. Colton, being a man himself, recognized this expression; this was the moment when a man had a brief, casual conversation with a woman and suddenly became aware she was attractive. Date-worthy. Get-to-know-worthy. Remain-in-the-conversation-kind-of-worthy. He adjusted his bow tie and took one casual step closer to Selma.

"So," he said, "do you mind if I ask you your name? I've seen you around the building."

"You've seen me?" Selma said, evading. She looked toward her office, a clear sign that she wasn't interested in continuing the conversation, but the man didn't notice.

"Yes, and I was just wondering if—"

"Oh dear, look at the time." Selma pointed to the clock on the wall. She grabbed Colton by the arm and moved toward her office.

"Do you mind if I at least get your name?"

"So little time, so little time," Selma kept mumbling and left the man behind.

She ushered Colton into her office and closed the door behind them.

"What are you doing?" Selma asked.

Colton barely heard her. He took a seat at her computer. He threw off his helmet and began to search through the current Aberrant archives to see which Aberrants were being held in the facility, but as he expected, Selma's credentials didn't have access to their specific identities. He could try logging into the database with his own credentials, but chances were his credentials had been deactivated. If they weren't, logging into the database within the CTC probably wouldn't be a great idea. It might give away their presence.

He leaned back in Selma's squeaky chair and rubbed his hand through his sweaty hair. Colton had hoped that before he began this whole excursion into the server room, he would at least be able to validate whether or not his son was still being held at CTC Headquarters. It felt completely wrong not to know where he was. Based on typical protocol, Marty would most likely be in one of the quarantine chambers, awaiting transport to the Island. But what if Colton was wrong? What if they'd shipped him and the others off early to die on the Island with the rest of the Aberrants?

"Are you okay?" Selma asked. She sat in the guest chair on the opposite side of the desk after locking the door to her office.

"Yes, I'm fine." Colton squinted at the screen. If only he had some other means of access. If only he could check.

"Is it the servers?" Selma asked. She gripped his shoulder, and her touch felt warm—even through his extraction wardrobe. Old feelings, old thoughts returned from abandoned vaults of memory. How many nights had he sat on the edge of his bed after his wife had left him, wishing for a woman's touch? How many nights had he awoken to the sound of his son weeping in his bedroom and wanted someone—anyone—to console him?

And now, here she was.

Only he knew that even if they were able to pull this off, she would never be his. She would never choose him in that way, because as much as Colton hated to admit it to himself, he knew the truth: He was not a good man. It was the reason Mona left. It was the reason he had never had much hope of being elected Chief Officer. It was the reason he couldn't connect in any meaningful way with his son.

"I'm not a good man," he whispered.

"What? What are you talking about?"

He shook his head and snapped back to reality. "Nothing." He pointed to the computer, as if formally accusing it. "I wanted to check the database to see if Marty is being kept here, but I can't get access through your account. I just want to know that he's here."

"I thought you said he would be."

"Yes, most likely he is," Colton explained, "but with everything happening, I wanted to make sure they haven't already shipped him to the Island."

"I understand," Selma said. "Is there anything I can do? Some way I can help?"

"Not likely. I need to access the database, but right now, that's not our number one problem." He leaned far back in Selma's chair, stroked his bristly chin, and glared long and hard at the computer screen. Now that he was here, he knew he had to be laser-focused: He had to get down into the server room, and he had to get down there unnoticed. Only one question remained: How?

"Where is the server room?" Selma asked.

"Three stories below ground." Colton leaned back even further, and the chair squeaked in complaint. "I've been there, but it's been a long time. The problem is, even if my clearance wasn't removed, I'm not sure if I'd be given access to the servers. That's more for the IT people, not extractors."

Colton watched Selma. How deeply he wished he was a better man—a good man—and had stumbled across Selma in a situation that wasn't like the current one. How different his life might have been.

"Can you find someone who can access the servers?" Selma asked.

"That's what I've been thinking, but who? And what am I going to do? Walk up to that person and ask for the access code? I don't think that'll work."

Selma shifted in her seat, biting one of her fingertips. The room was quiet. Colton stared at the computer screen; Selma gazed off, child-like, into the corner of the room.

"If you can think of someone, I could call that person into my office," she said.

"Okay, but then what? What do I do?"

"I don't know. Can you steal their code if I get them in here?"

"Unlikely. Nobody's going to have their code physically on them. It'll be memorized. It's just a matter of who we call into your office."

"You must know someone here with access to the servers."

Colton thought this through, and in a sudden moment of revelation, the answer was obvious. He knew exactly who he could call into her office, and with a little more thinking and a little more planning, he knew exactly how he would extract the code from him. That was what he was after all: an extractor. Only this time he would be extracting a code from a person's mind rather than an Aberrant from the shadows of society.

He was about to tell Selma, but there was a soft knock on the door. They froze.

"Who is it?" Selma asked.

"It's Ashton."

Colton's heart nearly stopped. Without thinking, he crawled beneath Selma's desk. He had no choice, and before he had a moment to curse the situation, Selma was up from her seat, straightening her blouse, and walking toward the door.

Like it or not, they were going to have to get through this.

1.3.3

"**I** hope you don't mind me stopping by," Ashton said softly. He slipped into the guest seat on the opposite side of Selma's desk—the same one Selma had been sitting in when he first knocked on the door—and Colton could see the shiny tops of his loafers from his fetal position below the desk. Behind him, Selma slid into the squeaky chair he'd been sitting in, and he knew there was no way out.

Don't breathe, he told himself. *Don't make a sound.*

"I was just walking by and thought I'd stop to say hello," Ashton said, snake-like. Colton could hear him drum his fingers on the desk above.

"Oh, well, very nice of you to do so."

Colton was impressed with how nonchalant Selma sounded. He didn't detect the slightest tinge of trepidation in her voice.

"Are you staying for tonight's party?"

"Party?"

Colton couldn't tell if she was feigning ignorance or not.

"Don't you read the department memos?"

"Apparently not."

"We'll be open until midnight, and I'm making a speech right before we put an end to the nuisances. We'll have catering, music, even some dancing."

"Wow, you've really gone all out."

"Well, it's not every day we have special events like this." Ashton reached into his pocket, pulled out a small can of breath spray, and shot two puffs into his mouth. "And this does, of course, bring me to why I really wanted to stop by your office."

Selma cleared her throat. From below the desk, Colton saw her wipe her sweaty palms on the legs of her black pants. "And

179

why is that?" she asked.

"I know we didn't exactly hit it off when we went out," Ashton said. "Perhaps I'm not as well-versed in Shakespeare as I should be. My apologies for that. But I did think we shared a connection, perhaps just being intellectuals in a world that more and more seems to consist of non-thinkers. So I wanted to ask if you would like to sit with me at dinner tonight. I promise I won't bite. And I promise the food and champagne will be delicious."

"I…well, I …"

"I know this is awkward. When we went out before, I was just an extractor. Now I'm the Chief Officer. I know how this complicates things, and before all of the sexual harassment alarms sound, I'd like to be perfectly clear just for the record and to respect policy: I mean this in the friendliest, respectful, non-aggressive way a man could. I expect nothing in return. No quid pro quo. Just your company and a wonderful meal. What say you?"

"Uh…yes, I think so. That should be fine."

"Really?"

Colton thought Ashton sounded surprised.

"Well, that's perfectly wonderful," Ashton said. "Dinner will begin at nine. The entire lobby is being made into a dining hall."

"That sounds great."

"Good," Ashton said. "I was a little worried about asking you. Rumor gets around quickly here, and more than one person has mentioned your budding romance with Colton Pierce. In light of everything that happened, I thought you might be a little out of sorts."

"Out of sorts? But why?"

"Like I said, a budding romance struck down in its early stages can be quite displacing."

"Budding romance? We went out to dinner once. Just once. I'd hardly call that a budding romance."

"Yes, that's exactly what I told the others. There were even some here who wanted to haul you in and question you about your relationship with Colton and the remote chance that you were involved in his betrayal and disappearance. But I told them exactly what you just told me: They hardly knew each other, and Selma and Colton were not a match. Anyone could see that."

"Oh yes," she said. "To be honest, the date was borderline intolerable."

"And your impression of him?"

"A self-centered, pompous, narcissistic jerk."

Ashton laughed, and Colton was pleased that Selma seemed so at ease in the situation, despite how at ease she sounded in disparaging him. Still, it was working. Ashton was buying it.

"Very good then," Ashton said. He slapped his hands on his legs. "I'll prepare a place for you at my table tonight. That should be wonderful."

"Yes, I very much look forward to it."

"Just one question, though," Ashton said. Colton heard him lean back in his seat. "Why do you have one of the old extractor helmets here on your desk?"

The extractor helmet! Colton had taken it off when he entered the room and set it on the corner of the desk. *Idiot*, he cursed himself. *I should have snatched it off the desk when I dove down here. Fool!*

"Oh, that," Selma said, and Colton could hear the hesitation in her voice. She was fishing for an answer. Any answer that might make sense to Ashton.

"I've always been fond of the old extractor suits," Ashton said, picking up the helmet. Colton heard him turning it around in his hands. "In a way, this suit represents a simpler time for the organization. Back then, the general public genuinely appreciated the work of our agency. Now that I'm at the helm, I plan on a bright, productive future again for the CTC. I will give my soul to it."

"Well, that's a good thing. I'm sure some of the protestors are making quite a ruckus over the execution of an extractor's son."

"Ah, yes, it's made the headlines."

"I'm sure they're making a huge deal about Colton's son dying on the Island along with thousands of others."

"Yes, they are," Ashton said, "but he'll die here. He's the only one who hasn't been shipped out. With everything happening and

Colton's whereabouts unknown, we thought it best to keep him here. He'll be terminated tonight like everyone else."

"Oh, I see," Selma said, and Colton was impressed by how easily she'd gotten the information out of Ashton.

"So, as I was asking, why the old extractor outfit? A little early for Halloween, don't you think?"

Selma laughed, but Colton thought it sounded a little disingenuous. "Yes, it is much too early for Halloween. Getting ready for another public service announcement—you know, PR kinds of things. Like you said, I think the old outfits have this timeless sense to them and bring audiences back to the day when our agency was really valued and respected."

"Makes perfect sense to me." Ashton stood up. "And I suppose that's why they pay you the big bucks to figure things out."

"I guess so!" Selma said, laughing. As before, Colton thought the laugh sounded manufactured.

"Then I will see you tonight," Ashton said.

He turned and walked out of the office.

Selma locked the door behind him, and Colton crawled out from below the desk.

"That wasn't fun," he said, wiping sweat from his forehead. "Not fun at all."

1.3.4

"**I** know who you can call into your office," Colton said. "Kramer, my old assistant."

"The short guy?"

"Yeah, he's a little guy. Great at organizing other people, but looks like he can hardly dress himself in the morning. He's the person we need. He does some IT work as well. He'll have access to the server room, guaranteed. We need to get him in here, and I'll be able to get the code out of him."

"What are you going to do?"

"I don't know yet," Colton said. "But if we can get him here, I'll be able to do something. But he's the one. Trust me. He's harmless, too."

"Okay, I'll put a call into the operator and tell him he needs to report here immediately. But what reason should I give?" Selma asked.

"Don't give one. Just say it's urgent and he needs to report here immediately. He'll show. He'll probably think it has to do with one of the PR announcements that you're working on or something."

"Okay." Selma picked up her office phone, dialed the department operator, and put in the request.

Then it was just a matter of waiting. Colton paced back and forth, trying to remember exactly how to get to the server room; he so rarely went near it. But he was pretty sure he knew what to do. He would take the main elevator down to B3, walk down a long, cold corridor, and make a right. From there, the server room would be behind a glass door with a keypad next to it.

They hadn't waited long when there was a soft knock at the door. Kramer? Colton and Selma shared the same surprised expression; he'd gotten there quicker than they'd thought he would, and Colton still hadn't decided how to get the information out of him. Instead of diving under the desk, Colton stepped to the wall; Kramer would open the door, would walk right past Colton, and once he was in the room and the door was closed, Colton would figure out what to do.

"Who is it?" Selma asked in an effort to buy some time so Colton could get in position. She sounded more like a woman at home who had heard a knock at the door after getting out of the shower than a woman sitting in her office waiting for someone she'd just summoned.

"It's Kramer."

"Ah yes," Selma said, unlocking and opening the door. She glanced once at Colton as she did so to indicate the ball was completely in his court at this point. She saw Kramer outside the door, looking his usual disheveled self, a tablet clasped under his arm, and a mild sense of bewilderment about him.

"Hello, Kramer."

"Hello."

"Won't you come on in?"

"Yes, well, is there something you need?"

This wasn't going exactly as planned. With Kramer inside and the door closed, Colton would have the privacy to get the information out of him—and use whatever means were necessary to do so. But none of this was going to work with Kramer standing idly in the doorway.

"Yes," Selma said, unfolding her arms and waving her hand toward the seat opposite her desk, "but it's going to take a few minutes, so why don't you come in and sit down. I'll be brief, I promise."

Kramer waddled into the room and sat in the same guest seat that Ashton had recently warmed. Selma quickly went to her office seat, but before she got there, Colton walked up behind Kramer and tapped him gently on the shoulder. He'd already decided that there was no elegant way to do this; he would have to surprise Kramer and threaten him to get the code. There was no silver bullet in this situation.

"Colton?" Kramer said. He tried to say something else but sounded more like a dying fish. It was part gasp, part awe. His eyes were suddenly giant bug eyes.

"I need to talk to you," Colton said.

Kramer started to stand up, but Colton gently pushed him back down into the seat. It didn't take much strength.

"You need to stay here, my friend. Sorry."

"What do you…what do you…"

"I need something." Colton took the tablet out of Kramer's hand. He didn't want Kramer to hit an emergency alarm icon (if there even was one on his tablet) if he could help it. He wasn't going to take any chances. "The server room downstairs. You have a code to get into the server room, correct?"

Kramer hesitated, then nodded. "But why? Why the server room?"

"You needn't be concerned with that. I need in there, okay? I need your code."

Kramer stared at him and blinked unresponsively.

"Did you hear me, Kramer? I need your code."

"You know I can't give you my code," Kramer said. "I'm not supposed to give my code to anyone. I could lose my job."

"Lose your job?" Colton laughed. "That's really your main concern right now? I'm sure when you explain to upper management how Colton Pierce lured you into an office, threatened your life, and demanded your access code for the server room, they will be more than understanding. What else would they expect you do?"

"So you're…you're threatening my life?"

"Yes, as a matter of fact, I am." Colton reached for a pair of scissors he had seen on Selma's desk when he first walked in. "There's a number of ways we can do this. The messiest, of course, would be using this pair of scissors. Quite sharp. It would probably be much cleaner, swifter to just use my bare hands. Yes, that would probably do the job just fine."

"Okay, fine, all right," Kramer said, convulsing in his seat. "I'll give you whatever you want. Five-five-zero-eight. That's my code. Five-five-zero-eight."

Colton committed the numbers to memory. "Very nice," he said, smiling. In his heart, he'd always known Kramer was a coward. He knew it wouldn't take long to get the answer out of him.

But now a difficult question presented itself: what to do with Kramer? It would be too risky to take him with them to the server room, and now that Colton knew his access code, it would be unnecessary. It would be much better to leave Kramer behind, but how? They couldn't just ask him to wait in the office.

"I think you need to stay here," Colton told Selma.

"What? Are you sure?"

"Yes. I think you need to stay with Kramer. Make sure he doesn't leave this room. Do you have any rope, zip ties, anything?"

"Not in here," Selma said, "but I'm sure I could find some in the storage room next door. We have lots of stuff for holiday banners and things like that."

"Good, go get some, and try to be inconspicuous."

"Got it," Selma said, slipping out of the room. She made sure the door was locked behind her.

While waiting, Colton leaned back on her desk, folded his arms, and looked at Kramer. There was a long, painful silence.

"I'm really sorry it had to be like this, Kramer," Colton finally said. "I really did enjoy working with you. We had some good times."

"Why don't you just turn yourself in? You know all the resources our agency has at its disposal. You won't be able to run forever. And what are you doing in the server room? Erasing your files?"

"You don't have kids, right?"

Kramer shook his head. It was a rhetorical question, really. Colton knew Kramer had no kids, let alone a spouse.

"They say kids make you crazy, and isn't that the truth," Colton said. "At first, when you're up all night and your sleep patterns are off, you think that's what most people mean when they say kids drive you crazy. But when they get a little older, when they develop their own opinions, and when their opinions don't mesh with yours, that's when they *really* drive you crazy.

So I guess you could blame this all on fatherhood, Kramer. I'm doing this for my son."

Kramer stared at him with a puzzled expression.

There were two soft knocks on the door.

"That was quick." Colton opened it, and Selma came back into the room with two bundles of rope and a roll of duct tape. Colton was impressed. It was more than they would need to get the job done.

"It's been nice talking, Kramer," he said, uncoiling the rope. "But I'm afraid you're going to be a bit tied up for a while. Might need to cancel any appointments you have."

1.3.5

Colton pushed the DOWN button for the elevator and waited. He only passed two office workers on the way there. Dressed in the old extractor outfit, Colton garnered little attention. They most likely assumed he was just taking part in the day's festivities or, as Selma had already documented, there for another public service announcement.

It felt excruciatingly painful waiting for the elevator, and he envisioned several things going wrong. What if the elevator doors opened and it was full of people? What if one of those people, a security officer or someone of significance, asked him to take off the helmet? It was possible, wasn't it?

He took a deep breath and tried not to think about it. Selma had stayed in her office to watch over Kramer. Even though Kramer's mouth was duct-taped and he was completely bound to his chair, Colton had seen enough movies to know what happened if you left someone like that behind. The prisoner would squirm, wriggle, and break his way out of the ropes. The elevator doors hissed open, and it was empty.

He walked in, noted the camera in the corner of the elevator, and pushed B3. Would a security officer watching think it strange to see him get into an elevator in one of the old outfits? Hopefully not.

The elevator began to descend.

"Colton, are you there?"

The voice startled him. He spun around, facing the wall of the elevator.

"Colton, it's me."

Gus.

Colton swallowed the lump in his throat. He had just been

thinking about Gus, knowing that if this guy didn't make radio contact with him, Colton would have absolutely no idea what to do with the thumb drive in his pocket once he reached his destination.

"Good. It's about time. I'm on my way down right now to the server room," Colton whispered. He didn't know if the camera picked up audio but thought it unlikely. A whisper below his helmet would probably be impossible to register even if it did record audio.

"Yes, I'm tracking you."

"How are Bayard and the others?"

"They are fine. En route as we speak."

"Good."

The elevator doors opened, and Colton stepped into a long, nondescript corridor vacant of people. It was cold down here. Colton hadn't been down here in years.

"You're going to walk down the corridor and make a right at the T," Gus explained. There was mild interference, perhaps from being below ground. "Once you make a right, you want to walk all the way down that corridor, and it will be at the very end. You have means of access, I take it?"

"Yes, I just got the code."

"Good, then you're all set. I'll give you specific instructions once you're in."

"I'm glad you contacted me," Colton said. He made a right, went to the very end of the corridor, and found himself in front of a glass door with a digital keypad on the wall beside it. Within he could see the soft glow of computer lights, but the room was otherwise dark. That was good. No people.

Colton punched in the access code and heard something trigger within the door; the single red light at the top of the keypad went green. He pushed open the door and stepped inside the room. The lights flickered on. Motion detector, he assumed.

The room was smaller than he'd imagined. A large, barren table stood in the center of the room, and one wall was lined with a row of computers on a long shelf. They were all on, lights blinking, interior parts lightly humming. Frigid air poured out of the AC vent in the center of the ceiling.

Colton took off his helmet and rubbed his hands through his damp hair. Walking around in these old extractor outfits made him sweat buckets.

A thought suddenly occurred to him. How terrible would it be to have come all this way, to have endured all of this, only to find that he didn't have the thumb drive? What if it fell out of his pocket? What if he left it back in Selma's car? He reached into his pocket to assure himself that it was still in his possession. It was. But the thought of putting so much hope in something that could so easily be lost or misplaced troubled him.

"Are you in the server room?" Gus asked.

"Yeah," Colton said. "I'm here, but there are tons of computers. I have no idea what to do or which one to use the thumb drive with."

"That's why I'm here. I'll walk you through the whole thing. Just do as I say."

"Okay, fine."

"The main computer should be in the middle somewhere, kind of a workstation area. Can you find it?"

"Let me look." Colton scanned the rack of computers, and sure enough, near the center was a solitary computer—a bit separated from the rest—with a monitor and a keyboard. It certainly qualified as a workstation. No other computers appeared to be attached to monitors or keyboards. "Yeah, I think I see it."

"Okay. That's where we'll install it."

Colton took a seat at the computer, jiggled the mouse, and the screensaver—a prismatic display of lights—instantly dissolved. A green screen remained with a login request: USER ID and PASSWORD.

"Okay." Colton looked over his shoulder. Someone could walk in at any moment to find him sitting at the computer, talking to himself. "It wants a user identification and password. I should have asked Kramer. I didn't even think about this."

"That's okay. I have an identification and password that should be able to get you in. An old user account that was never deactivated that Aaron was able to hack."

Colton sat up in his seat. "What's the user name?"

"Username is Rogobot. R-O-G-O-B-O-T."

Colton typed.

"And the password is Helter414. H-E-L-T-E-R-4-1-4. You got that?"

"Yeah, I got it." Colton finished typing, hit enter, and the screen changed to a blizzard of numbers pouring down like water across the screen. It was loading something.

"It's going to take a few minutes to log you in, so you have to be patient and wait it out," Gus said.

"Okay." Colton leaned back in his seat. "A bunch of numbers are racing across the screen. It's not like I have anywhere else to go, but hopefully this won't take too long. There are not many places to hide in here."

Two or three minutes passed. The numbers kept racing across the screen, and he could hear something inside the computer churning. It was logging into something. Colton looked back at the glass door. Nobody outside. Nobody approaching.

"Are you doing all right?" Gus asked.

Colton was startled by the question. In the silence of the room, it felt as though somebody had crept up to him and spoken into his ear.

"Yeah, I'm good. I'm good."

"Okay, because you know I have your back, right? I'm monitoring the security communications at the CTC as we speak."

Not sure about that, Colton thought. *You led me astray when running down the street while blind. Remember that?* But Colton didn't say any of these things; it wasn't the time. He just wanted to get this over with.

"Yeah, yeah, I know," he said.

The numbers dissolved and now a new screen appeared. There were several icons on a blue background and lots of text below them. Colton had barely had time to start reading when he heard a terrible sound: The door to the server room swung open. Without thinking, Colton slipped out of the chair and fell onto the ground, face first. Whoever came into the room wouldn't be able to see him.

But there was more than one. Several footsteps. There was nowhere to go. He didn't even have time to roll under the table in the center of the room, and it probably wouldn't have mattered anyway—he would have been quickly discovered.

Four guards, guns drawn, walked around the side of the table and ordered him to his feet. Colton stood and put his hands up.

"Gus," he whispered.

No response.

Defeat settled over him, heavily.

Another man walked into the room, cool and confident. It was Ashton. He walked up behind the guards, picked his teeth with a toothpick, and looked at Colton like a hunter enjoying the moment of his greatest kill.

"Well, well, well," Ashton said, just before the guards ordered Colton to turn around so they could handcuff him. "Look who came by the CTC to pay us a visit."

1.3.6

"**C**an I offer you anything? A drink? A snack?" Ashton asked.

They were in Ashton's office, which used to be Brian Barclay's office, and Ashton had been unusually gracious. The officers had brought Colton directly here, had even removed the handcuffs at Ashton's request, and agreed to remain outside the office in the event they were needed. Ashton had invited Colton to sit on the couch, and Colton had the strange feeling that Ashton wanted to chat rather than see him thrown into one of the quarantine chambers. But why? There was something completely unsettling about this.

Yet his son was all Colton could think about. His failure to infect the server with the virus and his capture made one thing abundantly clear: His son was going to die in a matter of hours, and there was absolutely nothing he could do to change it. He looked at the clock on the office wall: 10:34. In a little over thirteen hours, Marty would be dead.

I hope they kill me with him, he thought. *I'd rather die with him than let him die alone.*

"I don't want anything to eat or drink," Colton said.

"Oh, come on." Ashton walked to the same refrigerator Brian Barclay had pulled a Diet Pepsi out of the last time Colton was in this office. Ashton took out a Coca-Cola and put it on the table right in front of Colton. He sat in the chair opposite the couch and folded his hands together. "Just because we're not meeting in the most ideal of circumstances doesn't mean I can't be a good host, right? Enjoy the soda. Sit back and relax."

"What do you want?"

"Nothing, really," Ashton said in a voice that sounded one octave too high. "I just wanted to talk to you. Again, I know we're not meeting under the most ideal of circumstances, but I haven't forgotten the great contributions you have made to the CTC over the years. No matter how we feel about each other and no matter what you've done, I don't think the service that you've offered to your country should be taken lightly. You deserve the same respect that I would want to be given if I were in your situation."

Colton squinted like a man who had just picked up the stench of something foul. This wasn't Ashton's normal behavior. He was fishing for something, buttering Colton up.

"What do you want, Ashton?" Colton said flatly. He didn't touch the soda. He didn't want it.

"Why do you think I want something?" Ashton asked. "Do I have to want something to sit down and have a civil conversation with you?"

"Yes, I think you do."

Ashton laughed. It was squeaky and rat-like. "No, Colton, I'm afraid you are the one who might be in need of something." He settled back in his chair in a way that conveyed he was going to tell a story. "We believe that your disappearance—that the invisibility of your NRNT chip—is the result of your joining a rogue group of insurgents that has been trying to undermine our organization for years now. We have reason to believe that this group—whoever they are—have been taking people off the grid, deactivating NRNT signals, and basically assisting the theologically ill by avoiding capture. They are a threat to our society, our public safety, and to every man, woman, and child in our country. You do realize that, don't you?"

Colton was silent, and he knew that his silence answered Ashton's question.

"Why didn't I hear about them as an extractor?" Colton asked.

"You did," Ashton said, "but I think you dismissed their ability to do any of those things because of your own confidence in yourself and this institution. Plus, it's not the job of an extractor to look into such things. The higher-ups speculate that this group has been undermining us for years. But now that you've apparently joined them, I don't need to explain that to you. And I can only assume that since you've joined them, you've become ill yourself."

"Ill?"

"Yes. As in you believe in this God delusion."

Colton started to speak but couldn't bring himself to say anything. He was instantly taken back to the beach that night so long ago, when he had cried out for some shrapnel of divinity in the universe—God, a Great Orchestrator, whatever He was called. Most likely this conversation would be over soon and Colton would be in one of the quarantine chambers. He knew it was quite possible that he would cry out for a second time—this time for his son's life—so he remained silent.

"Your lack of response answers my question," Ashton said, amused.

"So what do you want from me?"

"Like I said, I want answers." Ashton rubbed his fingers together with theatricality, like a magician about to perform a trick. "I want to know more about this group, but perhaps even more importantly, I want to make sure that you understand that they've been lying to you. They are not what they seem, Colton, and you of all people should know that. I've pegged you for many things in our time together, but gullible isn't one of them."

"What do you mean?"

"I mean exactly what I said: They're not what they seem. Let me guess—they've claimed to share in your belief in God, to be completely devoted to Him, to trust in Him, and certainly they believe He will save those who have been imprisoned."

Colton remained silent.

"They're thieves, Colton. They're conning you."

"Thieves?"

"Yes, thieves. You know, brigands, robbers, pirates? You've been completely bamboozled, my friend. I can only assume that the reason you were down in our server room is because they want you to access some kind of file so they can rob our organization of money."

"Thieves?" Colton was still stuck on that part.

"They wouldn't have told you that, of course," Ashton said. "More than likely they gave you some other explanation. I'm sure you were on some holy grail of a quest, but Colton, I can assure you that you've been completely taken in by these guys. They're thieves. They go after people targeted by our organization, take them off the grid, and send them on so-called holy quests. They're theological pirates. They take advantage of the beliefs of the theologically ill. You were a goldmine for them since you actually worked for the CTC. They sent you here to dig into the coffers."

Colton sat back in his seat and took a deep breath.

Ashton laughed and slapped his hand against the couch. "Wow, you really believed them, didn't you?"

"They're not thieves."

"What if I can prove it to you?"

"How?"

Ashton seemed to like this challenge. He clapped his hands, and the office door suddenly opened. Selma was brought into the room. Her hands cuffed behind her, and her mouth was muzzled with duct tape.

Colton almost jumped to his feet but forced himself to remain sitting.

"I take it you two have met," Ashton said, laughing at his joke. "You see, I wasn't entirely honest when I went down to Selma's office earlier today. It was a bit embarrassing, asking her to join me at dinner when I knew very well that we wouldn't have the opportunity. We've been monitoring Selma and looking through her files ever since your disappearance, and I'm afraid she's not what she seems, Colton. It's going to be difficult for you to accept this."

Selma wriggled between the arms of the two officers, and even though she tried to scream something, it was muffled by the tape.

"She and her brother have been conspiring for weeks to rob the CTC," Ashton explained. "We've gone through all of her old files and noted her searches. She's been much more concerned with digging into the company coffers than fulfilling the obligations of her PR job. It's the same reason she was so affable about joining me on a date and you shortly thereafter. She's been snooping, snooping for a while."

"You know about her brother, then?"

"Of course. They're con artists! It took some tracking, but we figured it out. Obviously, they are working for some people with technical skill who have learned how to deactivate the NRNT chips, so they're pretty good at what they do. All those myths about insurgents learning to deactivate NRNT chips certainly are true, but you already know that by now, don't you? And we don't have time for dilly-dallying, do we? Today is a big day, and time is short. We will deal with Selma, her brother, and their gang of con artists soon enough. I have one important question for you that must be answered first."

"Con artists?" Colton whispered, paralyzed with disbelief and dread. *Have I really been conned? Was this all a charade? Is there a Remnant? Or are these guys just an underground band of pirates who rolled one over on me?*

Selma was looking at him, eyes wide and terrified. But why? Colton wondered if it was because she'd been caught. Or maybe Ashton was bluffing.

"Colton, I want my question answered."

"What question?"

"I simply want to know exactly what you were doing in the server room, and I want to know where this underground operation is. You must tell me. Selma won't talk."

The thumb drive in Colton's pocket suddenly felt heavy, like a weight pushing him down in the chair. He was surprised he hadn't been frisked yet, but he would be soon, and they would certainly find it. He almost reached into his pocket to take hold of it, but he didn't. Ashton was watching his every move.

"I don't know if I believe you," Colton said flatly.

"About what?"

"About Selma and her brother being thieves. About this whole underground operation being pirates. Yes, they have broken the law, they are hiding from our surveillance, but it's not because they're thieves."

"Well, I suppose you do have the right to remain ignorant."

"So why should I tell you?" Colton asked. "What's in it for me?"

"Oh quite a bit, I'm afraid." Ashton reached into his pocket, pulled out his can of breath spray, and took two misty shots in the mouth. Then, pocketing it, he leaned forward. He clapped his hands, and the office door opened again.

Marty was brought in. Like Selma, his hands were tied, and he had obviously been crying. His eyes were bleary and bloodshot.

"Marty!" Colton gasped and without thinking, leapt across the room. The guards who brought Marty into the room backed away, and Colton scooped his son into his arms.

"Dad!" Marty cried, grabbing his father. "I'm sorry, so sorry! We were at the barbecue and Kenny's dad prayed. I did, too! We all did! For the last few weeks every time I went over to his house, I listened and—"

"It's okay, Marty. It's okay."

"I just couldn't help it, Dad. I know you wouldn't like it, and I tried to—"

"Marty, it's fine. I understand. I'm not mad at all," Colton whispered in his son's ear. Colton had never cried in front of this many people, but when he looked back at Ashton, he saw him through blurred tears. It took him several moments to gain his composure, but he refused to let go of his son.

"As I was saying," Ashton said through a pearly white, sardonic grin, "there's a lot in this for you, and it's time to start bargaining."

1.3.7

"What were you doing in the server room?" Ashton asked, a slight hint of impatience in his voice. With both of his skinny hands on his knees, he leaned forward.

"I want to know the deal first. What will happen to my son?"

"Now we're talking business." Ashton smiled. Selma, still held between two officers, continued to squirm in their grip. She screamed more into her duct tape, but remained completely incomprehensible. "I assure you that when I make a deal, I follow through with *all* of it. Every last detail. As you are probably aware, since your public and well-documented betrayal of the organization, the courts have registered you—like your son—as an Aberrant; you are to be terminated upon capture. But if you provide the information I am requesting, you and your son will live. I have been given full, legal authority in this matter. You will never be able to work for the CTC again—there's nothing I can do about that—but I can make sure that you and your son are given new identities and relocated to start your lives over. It's not a bad deal, and I would seriously consider it. You both have a lot of life ahead of you."

Colton's gaze drifted toward Selma, and Ashton took note of it.

"Do you want me to throw her into the deal as well?"

"I think you're lying about her being a thief. I think it's a story you've made up to get me to talk."

"Suit yourself." Ashton shrugged. "As I've said, you have the right to remain ignorant."

Colton paced back and forth a few steps, rubbed the palms of his hands together, and knew it was time to make a decision.

"I want her to talk," he said. "Take the duct tape off her mouth."

Ashton's eye twitched, but he otherwise remained stone-faced. "No, I'm afraid I can't do that."

"Why not?"

"Because I don't have time for these shenanigans. You have a deal to save your life, your son's, and perhaps this woman. You need to start negotiating."

"You're lying," Colton said. He felt strangely and suddenly confident. "You won't let her talk because you know that she'll explain herself, and you know it'll make sense. You're lying about her being a thief. You may have discovered that she has a brother, but they're not thieves. We're not here to steal your money, but I think you're also lying about something else."

"And what is that?" Ashton asked. His eye twitched again.

"I think you're lying that you will let me live and that you will let my son live," Colton said. "I'll give you what you want, and then you'll send us straight to the death chambers. That's what I think."

"You do?" Ashton pulled a handkerchief from his pocket, dabbed his glistening forehead with it. "Well, that's an awfully big risk to take, don't you think? Will you be able to live with yourself after turning down what very well could be the one opportunity your son has to live? I don't have any children, but that would be a difficult fact to live with…even if I only had hours to live. It would be a horrible thing to take with you to the grave."

Colton took a breath and felt his chest tighten. *So it all comes down to this,* he thought, *a game of bluffing.* One thought kept spinning through his mind: *If I tell him what I was really doing in the server room and hand over the thumb drive, they'll kill me anyway. If I remain quiet, I'll die, too. Both ways I'm dead. But if I remain silent, I save thousands of people.*

All of the faces he'd seen in the Mourning Room returned to him; he imagined them all looking at him, watching him, awaiting his decision. The whole world pressed down on him.

He looked at Marty, who was sitting on the couch, rubbing his eyes with his sleeves, fighting back tears. He looked at Selma, who was watching him. She's given up trying to say anything and succumbed to the silence of the duct tape.

Colton took the thumb drive out of his pocket. All of his fate rested in that small device, it seemed.

"I was sent here on a very specific mission," he said. "I was going to take—"

"Colton!" Gus interrupted, a small and hardly audible voice; there was a significant amount of interference. His voice sounded far, far away. "He's lying to you. Don't believe him. He'll—"

Colton ignored Gus. He ignored everything now. From this moment on, he would let his own instincts drive him.

Colton waved the thumb drive around like a weapon. "This has a virus on it. Exodus. If I had managed to install it on the server, it would have ensured that the execution didn't happen tonight."

"Really?" Ashton said, his eyes wide and luminous. "And how exactly does it work?"

"That's all I have to say. I just wish I could have seen the look on your face when you realized the execution didn't work."

"Then where is their base? We need directions."

"I'm not giving you any more information," Colton said.

"I see. You do realize, of course, that when you hand over the thumb drive, we will be able to dissect every nuance of this alleged computer virus. It'll tell us much about the rogue group you've chosen to affiliate yourself with, and it may even hold the answers as to where their base of operations is."

"I suppose. But that's something you're going to have to figure out. I'm not going to provide that information for you."

"I see." Ashton shook his head like a disappointed father. "Then you're going to hand over the thumb drive."

"Sure thing." Colton looked at his son, who had started crying again, and pressed the small button on the thumb drive three times. Knowing there was now no way back, he tossed the thumb drive to Ashton, who caught it with one hand. "But it's not going to do you any good. I just erased all of its contents. You have a blank thumb drive there in your hand, Ashton."

"What?"

"You heard me," Colton said. "There's nothing on it. You

know you weren't going to keep your end of the bargain, Ashton, and if my son's going to die, then I'm going to die with him."

1.3.8

Colton found himself alone in one of the small quarantine chambers. He had been rushed out of the room along with Selma and Marty, and although it had been a confusing blur of commotion, he was fairly confident that Selma and his son were both in their own quarantine chambers alongside him. It felt strange and surreal to be in one of the chambers in which he had locked up so many of the Aberrants. How many Aberrants had he sent to this prison? He could only imagine.

There was nothing in the room except for a small cot. He sat on the edge of it. He wondered if Ashton or anyone else were standing on the other side of the one-way mirror, watching him sit there, but Colton thought it unlikely. There was much to attend to this evening, and most likely Ashton had rushed off to deal with all of the preparations. He had made it a point to tell Colton exactly what was going to happen.

"If it is your desire to be with your son, we can provide that," Ashton had told him. "You, Marty, and Selma will die with the rest of these vermin. Enjoy your last few hours in your cell, and make all the peace you want with your imaginary deity."

With that, Ashton closed the door, and Colton heard the internal mechanisms lock.

One thing was certain: There was absolutely no way out of this cell. Colton would sit in here all day until finally, as midnight hit, the poisonous gas would seep in through the vents. After a few minutes of that, it would be over. His mind raced for remote possibilities of escape, but there were none. There were no windows. No escape hatches. No electronic keypads on the inside that he could manipulate in hopes of getting the door to unbolt.

There simply was nothing.

Maybe it doesn't matter anyway, Colton thought. *Even if I was able to escape, what could I do? I've destroyed the virus. I would have to get out of the building, and that would be highly unlikely. It's over.*

He leaned forward and sank his face into his open palms. It felt totally ironic that his life would end in the same place he had sent so many of the Aberrants, but maybe this was sweet justice; maybe this was his way of "paying back" everything he'd done over his career. He remembered that day, falling on his knees in the sand and asking for help. Maybe it was time to try again, even if he knew an answer wouldn't come.

He closed his eyes, interlaced his fingers, and took two measured breaths.

I don't really know how to do this properly, he thought. *I just have no idea.*

"I don't know if anyone's listening," he said awkwardly, as if reading from a script. He was aware of his own verbal clumsiness. "I'm in a bind here. A real bind. And so are my son and Selma. Please, please, if there's some way to—"

"Colton!"

He stopped and almost fell off the cot.

"Colton, it's me!"

It was Gus, of course.

"Gus?" Colton wasn't sure what to say. What else was there to say? No virus. No Selma. And now he was a prisoner.

"I know where you are."

"Really? Then you know how bad this is, I take it? It's over."

"Not yet."

"What do you mean *not yet?*"

"I mean it's not over. There's still a way we can do this."

"But that's impossible," Colton protested. "I don't know if you're aware, but I deleted the virus. It's completely gone. Ashton has the thumb drive, but even if I did have it, there'd be nothing on it. The whole mission is bust."

"It's not the only copy of the virus."

Colton contemplated this statement; he wasn't sure what it meant or what to do with it.

Gus elaborated: "If you can still get down to the server room, I can guide you through a way to make an outside connection and download it. It wasn't the original plan, but it'll still work. Might take a little longer, but that's okay. Tonight the CTC is hosting their big celebration party, so there won't be any visitors down there. And they think Colton Pierce is captured, right? It gives us an advantage."

"There's one problem with your plan there, Gus." Colton looked dismally at the door. "I *have* been captured. What you're saying is good and everything, but I don't have a way of getting out of here."

"I think that's about to change."

"Wha—"

Colton was startled when the door unlatched and slowly swung open. Selma poked her head inside the cell and urgently waved for him to follow.

Colton was so stunned and bewildered, he couldn't even stand. He blinked several times and wondered if he was dreaming. Or maybe some kind of hallucinogenic gas had already started seeping through the vents, and this was the beginning of the end.

"Colton, come on!" Selma said. Her voice was real. He wasn't hallucinating.

"What's going on?" he asked and stepped out onto the hall.

Marty was there, and before Colton could register what was happening, Marty grabbed hold of him. Colton scooped him into his arms. *He's getting so big,* Colton briefly thought. *I don't know how much longer I'll be able to do this.*

There was a third person: Kramer. Standing with his tablet in his hands and looking down at the screen, he looked at disheveled as ever—maybe even more so. Now Colton was really confused. He started to ask what exactly was going on, but Kramer beat him to the punch.

"Follow me," Kramer said and dashed down the hall of quarantine chambers. "There's a vacant meeting room not far from here. We can hide out there for a while to formulate our plans."

"Okay," Colton said.

He didn't understand why Kramer was helping them, but he didn't care. Even if this was a trap, he'd take his chances with this before returning back to the gas chamber.

They left the prison area. Kramer explained that he had already made sure the main guard was attending to something else. They dashed across to the other side of the building, turned into a vacant hall, made a quick right, a left, and Kramer ushered them through a door.

Kramer flicked on the lights, and Colton found himself in a small room with a meeting table and eight chairs surrounding it. The walls were white, barren, and boring, with nothing but a television screen on one wall.

Making sure they weren't followed, Kramer looked out into the hall and, satisfied, closed the door and locked it. Then, acting as if he'd just sprinted a full marathon, he collapsed into one of the reclining chairs and said, "Remind me never to do that again."

1.3.9

"You have a half-sister on the Island?" Colton asked. He was still amazed by Kramer's story.

"Yes." Kramer paced in front of the television screen. He had risked his career, his job, everything, to help them out of the cells. Colton knew that much before Kramer began to explain why. "I kept it hidden from the organization. A couple years ago it almost came to light, but I pulled a few strings to make sure that information never made it onto the desks of certain people. I thought it might jeopardize my own job and my own clearance. I was very fortunate that it remained confidential."

"Do you know her well?" Colton asked.

"Somewhat," Kramer said. "I didn't even know she was alive until I was ten years old. My mom and dad sat down and told me I had a sister. A previous relationship my dad had with a woman. Her name is Arlene. When her mom died of cancer, she lived with us. She was already in middle school and stayed with us until she graduated. We became close during that time, actually. I was an only child, always wanted a sibling, and there she was. She appeared like magic.

"So when I found out she was extracted years ago, I kept quiet. There was nothing I could do anyway, right? I guess I took some solace in the notion that on the Island she would at least live a long, healthy life, and maybe—just maybe—I would be able to see her and talk to her again. You see, my dad died several years back, and in some ways, I guess she's all I have left of him. Does that make sense?"

It was strange to see Kramer emotional. This was a side of him Colton had never witnessed.

"It makes perfect sense." Colton looked at his son. Marty sat beside Selma on one of the reclining chairs. Her arm was around him, protecting him, comforting him. "We do anything for those we love."

"I never would have gotten involved or tried to do anything to undermine the agency," Kramer explained, "but when the new legislation passed, all I could see was my sister dying. My dad dying all over again. That's all I could see, Colton. Secretly, I had always hoped the new legislation would never pass."

"Interesting," Colton said. "I always had the feeling you didn't want it to. Now it makes sense."

"After you left and I was alone with Selma, she explained why you were doing what you were doing," Kramer said. "She was caught, of course, when the guards stormed in, but in all honestly, if you had told me your plan, I would have gladly given you the access code. I would have given you anything. I don't want to see my sister die. Not tonight. If this virus can thwart the execution, I'm game."

"Wow," Colton said, amazed he was going to have a second chance at this.

"So you don't think Bayard and I are thieves, huh?" Selma asked.

"Are you kidding? I wasn't born yesterday. I knew that was nonsense. I won't put my faith in that garbage."

"Faith?" Selma said. "Interesting choice of words."

"Yeah, maybe."

"Right now I think time is of the essence," Kramer said, looking down at his tablet. For a moment, it seemed like another day at the office. Colton wearing an extraction outfit—a retro one, minus the helmet—and Kramer standing beside him and scrolling through files on his tablet. "We need to get you moving. We need to get you down to that server room. Right now, everyone is in the main foyer. There's music, dancing, lots of commotion. It's a good time to make a move. It's 8:05. Four hours until execution. Plenty of time, and it should be smooth sailing. Security will be at a minimum. They think you guys are captured."

"Okay," Colton said. A disturbing thought occurred to him. "One thing, Kramer. If this virus works, you're an employee of the CTC. The signal—the Gray Note or whatever it is called—may affect you. I'm sorry, I don't know if there's a way for me to stop it.

"Don't worry." Kramer waved off the comment. "I'll live, and it'll help my alibi. I doubt the CTC will blame me as an accomplice if I'm a victim of the same thing they are. It might be good, in the end."

Colton nodded. Kramer's bravery surprised him. "Then perhaps I should go now."

Marty, hearing this, leapt from his chair and ran to his father. Colton bent down, felt those skinny arms around him, and heard his terrified voice. "Don't leave, Dad, please don't leave, don't leave!"

"Marty," Colton said, "I'm coming back, okay? I'm coming back. But I need to go take care of this. It's the only way to save you. To save all of us."

"But I don't want you to leave," Marty pleaded. Colton looked at him and was amused; he could tell that his son was trying not to cry, was trying to be brave. Marty wiped a tear from his cheek and met his gaze. "Please stay, Dad."

"I can't, Marty."

"Can Selma stay with me?"

Selma had already gotten to her feet and stood behind Marty with her hands on his shoulders. Colton looked at her, and she nodded. *Of course*, she said without a word.

"Yes," Colton said. "I think it's best she stays, anyway. I need to do this alone. Kramer will be here, too. All three of you need to wait here. It'll be safe. Won't it, Kramer?"

"Um," Kramer said. He was looking down at his tablet. "Yes, as safe a place as any, I think. I doubt anyone is planning on having a meeting tonight. I think the dinner and celebration is preoccupying everyone. We should be safe here. But do hurry. You still have the code, right?"

"Yes."

"Good," Kramer said. "Then that's all you need."

"Okay." Colton turned his attention back to his son. "Marty, I want to tell you something. I probably should have said this a long time ago. I know I haven't given you as much attention as I should have, especially your drawing. Your art. But I do have to tell you how brave I think it is for you to do that. How incredibly strong you are."

"Brave?" Marty asked, wiping his nose. Clearly, he'd never heard bravery in this context before. Not from his dad.

"Yes," Colton said. "To create something, to pull something out of your heart, to show it to the world. That isn't easy, is it? It's like putting your heart on display for the entire world to see and judge."

Marty nodded, and Colton knew he understood. Selma wiped her cheek. What was it? A tear? An itch?

"When we get back home," Colton said, "or whatever home we make when this is all over, I'm going to take down all of those plaques in the hall. Every one of them. And I'm going to put up your work. Whichever ones you want. It'll be my new Hall of Fame, understand? That's all that will be there."

Marty nodded and said, "Are you sure you have to leave?"

"Just for a little bit. I will return. I promise."

"Okay," he said. "I will pray for you while you're gone. Dad, can I pray?"

"Of course you can, Marty. I think I'm going to need a lot of that. Maybe I always have."

Marty nodded again, maintaining his bravery.

"Okay, folks," Colton said, standing. He went to the door. "I need to leave. I'll be back shortly. Be safe."

He opened the door and stepped into the hall, but Selma slipped out behind him.

Once again, like the night she showed up at Colton's front door for their date, he lost himself in those green eyes. Two luminescent flecks of stardust, looking at him, looking *into* him. She took his hand in hers and he realized how small it was—small and delicate, like a child's.

"Are you going to be okay?" she asked.

"Yes, I think so. I'll do my best."

"I know you will. I just wanted to tell you something." She adjusted her posture, as if she were preparing to perform some kind of physical stunt. "I know I told you before that I wasn't pretending, I wasn't acting." Her fingers tightened around his. "I want to make sure that you know I really wasn't. I wasn't pretending at all, Colton. You do know that, right?"

"I know." He ran his hand over her black, silky hair and cradled her head in his hand. He felt the sudden desire to pull her toward him gently, to bend down, to kiss her, to make a promise without words that he would be with her when all of this was over. But it wasn't the right time. There would be a better time, and he decided he would wait until then.

"Are you sure you'll be okay alone?" she asked.

He leaned toward her and brushed away two strands of hair falling in front of her eyes. She looked at him expectantly and took a quick breath.

"Thank you," he said, "for everything."

"You're a good man, Colton Pierce."

He was amazed. Had she read his mind? Had she peeled back the mask to see the real doubt that lay beneath?

"Thank you," he said. "I should go." He walked down the hall. But before he turned the corner, he looked back and said, "And you don't have to worry about me being alone. If everything you and your people believe is true, I'll never be alone."

1.3.10

Colton easily made it back to the server room. When Colton stopped and listened, he could hear the sounds of bass pulsing and thumping in the walls—certainly the party in the main foyer was alive and well. No doubt current extractors, special guests, administrators, politicians, and heavy donors were seated at elegant tables and drinking champagne or spinning like drunken teacups on the dance floor. He made sure to stay far away from the epicenter of activity and avoided the extractor offices and Command Center. There were always several extractors on duty—even during a party like this—and the Command Center never slept. It made Times Square look like it had a bad case of narcolepsy.

Once again, Colton found himself standing in front of the door to the server room, looking at the keypad. Down here it really was a ghost town, and it felt like déjà vu. He couldn't believe he was going to have to break into the server room for the second time today.

"Gus, you better talk to me soon," Colton said. He knew he would need directions once he sat down at the computer. He had no idea how he was going to make an outside connection and download the virus.

Colton punched in the code. The little red light on the keypad remained red.

He tried again. He typed in the code, and the light remained red. He pulled on the door, but it was locked.

"You have to be kidding me," he said, feeling most of his strength leave him.

This was unbelievable. Here he was, ten feet from his salvation, with a single locked door between him and the computer he needed access to, and the code simply wouldn't work. Desperately hoping a third attempt wouldn't set off some kind of alarm, Colton tried one last time; the result was the same. The little light remained red and the door wouldn't open.

"Unbelievable," Colton said, and threw up his hands in defeat. He had no idea what to do.

"Colton. Are you there? It's me." It was Gus.

"Yes, I'm here."

"We've run into a little problem, huh?"

"Yes, we have." Colton wanted to strangle this guy. What a ridiculous understatement!

"They must have wiped the code after they realized you'd stolen it from Kramer."

"Yeah, I figured that out."

Colton knew Gus was right. Protocol was to wipe the code that had been used for illegal entry. Colton should have known and felt stupid for not predicting this would happen. *How did I not see this coming? How did Kramer not see this coming?*

"It's over," Colton said in defeat. He placed both hands on the door, leaned his head against it, and recognized the futility of the situation. Doubt raced through his mind. *I shouldn't have erased the thumb drive. I shouldn't have gotten caught in the first place. We should have been more careful. So much more careful.*

"Colton, what are you doing?"

"What do you mean, 'what am I doing'?"

"You can't just stand there and wallow in self-doubt. You do realize we have limited time. And it's not over yet. There's still a way."

"Oh, really." Colton backed away from the door. "I don't know what magic trick you have up your sleeve, but it better be a good one, because I don't see any possible way to get beyond this door."

"Do you trust me, Colton?"

"What?"

"You heard me. Do you trust me?"

Colton contemplated this statement. Was it a trick question? And why was he asking this? Why now?

"I need you to answer the question," Gus said, "because I have an idea, but you need to trust me. You need to trust me in a way that you have never trusted anyone before. It won't work unless you do."

"Well, let me think about this for a moment," Colton said. "You abandoned me when Ashton and his men showed up to capture me. I'm not sure you're giving me much to work with here, Gus."

"But you're here now, aren't you? You're alive. So listen, honestly, I have an idea, but you have to trust me."

"I don't know. I don't feel like—"

"Feel? What does *feeling* have to do with it?"

"What?"

"What if I told you that trust was a choice? An action. Not a feeling. What would you say?"

Colton sighed. "I would say that you better have a smoking good idea, that's what I'd say."

"You haven't considered the other code," Gus said. "The lockdown code. If the CTC was in the midst of a lockdown, all of the codes would revert to the lockdown code. Security measures. You'd be able to use the code to get in."

Colton literally felt his heart stop; it must have missed at least a couple beats, because he staggered sideways three steps and almost fell to his knees. The lockdown code? Gus was correct. Colton hadn't thought about using that, because it would mean something else entirely. An entire series of events would have to be set into motion, and it would involve risk that was borderline suicidal. The lockdown code was only used in the most severe of circumstances—if an Aberrant escaped his or her quarantine chamber—and all doors would automatically lock. The lockdown code would override all other security codes, to ensure that all present extractors could swiftly search the premises. Colton had only practiced it in training; it had never actually happened.

"You know where I'm going with this, don't you?" Gus asked.

"I think so."

"I could wire in a detailed threat that the prisoners have escaped. I could make sure that it is credible and seen instantly. The CTC would follow protocol, and when they checked on the prisoners, they would see that your cells are vacant. The agency would go into immediate lockdown."

Colton listened, knowing it was brilliant. But he also knew the risks. The horrible risks.

"The moment the agency goes into lockdown, the lockdown code would work. You could get in and still have time to create the outside connection before anyone got to you. Some of the most important people in the community are at the ball tonight, and the last thing Ashton wants is public embarrassment, so I assume it would be a quiet lockdown. They will probably sweep the entire agency quietly before dismissing everyone at the party. You'll have time to get that connection."

"But the others? They're not far from the quarantine chambers. They'll be found instantly."

Silence. Colton listened, heard intermittent static.

"Yes," Gus said. "They'll be found and taken immediately. For sure."

"But my son! I can't hand over my son!"

"This is why I asked if you trust me, Colton. You have to trust me with this one."

"But it's my son…"

"I know. I understand."

"I don't know if I can do that."

"And what other alternative is there?" Gus asked. "Stand there and mope? It's only a matter of time before they realize you've escaped and the facility really does go into lockdown. And your son's NRNT chip is still active. They'll hunt him down in seconds. This is the best chance you have. You aren't handing him away for good. Just for the moment, Colton, just for the moment. He'll be taken back to the cell, and once the virus takes effect, he'll be free. With you and Selma. You have to do this, Colton. You have no choice."

"But I don't know if I can—"

"It's an action, Colton. Not a feeling. It's never a feeling. Understand?"

"Yes." Colton's heart pounded. Sweat poured down his face. He breathed rapidly. "I just don't know how to do this. It's hard."

215

"I know it is, but I need you to be okay with it. I need you to trust me."

Colton leaned back against the wall and slid to a sitting position.

Gus is right, Colton thought. That was the hardest part to acknowledge. *Gus is right. If I don't do anything, we're sitting ducks. If I go through with this, there's a chance. A thin sliver of hope, but it's more than I have now. It's infinitely more than I have now.*

"So what do you say, Colton? What do you say?"

"Okay." Colton could barely speak. "Call it in. I'm ready."

"Okay. Let's do this."

Colton lowered his head and closed his eyes. He beat back feelings of doubt.

And for the third time in his life, he prayed.

1.3.11

It felt like an eternity passed. Colton waited in front of the door to hear that Gus had made the call, that the lockdown had taken effect, and he was clear to advance into the server room. During that time, Colton hoped he was doing the right thing. He leaned his head against the door, closed his eyes, and imagined all of the things that could go wrong. What if Kramer and Selma resisted? Could someone get hurt? Could his son get caught in the crossfire?

Colton opened his eyes and looked at the keypad. The red light flickered off momentarily and then came back.

We're in lockdown, Colton thought. *The password has reset. And Gus must be right. No alarms. They're keeping the lockdown quiet. For now.*

He knew the emergency lockdown password; he'd committed it to memory during training. Having only gone rogue a few days, he hoped they hadn't changed that password yet.

"Colton, it's me. We're in lockdown."

"I know."

He punched in the lockdown code. A moment later, he heard another clicking sound within the door, and the light went green. He pushed it open and stepped into the server room. He had a limited amount of time. Security must already be in full force, and it wouldn't take long before they realized Colton wasn't with the others. He had to move, and he had to move quickly. Time was of the essence.

He rushed over to the workstation and sat down at the same computer he had before. "I'm here."

"Okay, good. Log in. The same as last time."

"Okay." Colton typed in the login and was instantly taken to a blue screen with icons.

"Open the browser at the bottom of the screen," Gus said. "Go quickly. We don't have much time."

Colton clicked the browser icon at the bottom of the screen. "Okay, did it."

"Good. Go the following web address. You need to do it exactly, okay? You can't be off. Go to www, dot, I as in Irma, B as in Bertha, T as in Tom, B as in Bertha, I as in Irma, dot, one, three, eight, five, seven, nine, nine, eight, forward slash, T as in Tom, T as in Tom. Got that?"

Colton was still typing, trying to keep all of the letters and numbers in his head.

"Colton, you got that?"

"Yes. At least, I think so."

He hit Enter and saw a gray screen with a single icon in the center that said DOWNLOAD, RG.1, EXODUS.

"Do you see the icon to download?"

"Yes, I see it."

"Good. Click on it. At this point, it's just a matter of time."

Colton clicked the icon and saw an hourglass appear in the center of the screen. He wasn't sure if he was imagining it, but he thought he heard the computer start working harder—whatever cogs and wheels existed in the computer to download things started to lift heavier weight.

"So now what?" he asked. "What do we do?"

"We wait. That's all we can do."

"How long will it take to download?"

"Not sure. I don't know what the connection is at the CTC, but several minutes. Remember, this is Plan B. It would have been quicker to use the thumb drive."

"Okay."

Colton couldn't get the thought of his son out of his mind; by now, he assumed, Marty was most likely taken. Handcuffed. Ushered back to the same prison cell with Selma and Kramer. Only this time, Ashton wouldn't make the same mistake as before. Guards would be posted outside of their cells, just in case.

He watched the screen for what seemed like hours. The

hourglass did its thing, and the gears inside the computer churned.

"Gus, what if this doesn't work?"

Silence. Maybe Gus didn't want to answer the question.

"Gus, did you hear me? What if this doesn't work?"

"Then I suppose you will go to your death knowing you did everything you could to do the right thing. That's not a bad deal, really. Many people aren't afforded that opportunity."

Colton nodded.

The hourglass icon didn't tell him how much of the virus had downloaded. Was it fifty percent? Was it ninety percent? It was frustrating to not even know how close this was to being finished. What if the connection was too slow and the virus had barely downloaded?

The door swung open and several officers swarmed into the room with their guns drawn. Colton, startled, stood up and put his hands in the air. An entire train of people entered. Two of them, apparently computer techs, went right to the computer that Colton was on in an attempt to rescue it. They probably thought, as Ashton had suggested, that Colton was tapping into the server to steal money somehow. But a terrible thought occurred to him: *If they stop the download, then it was all in vain. No virus. No freedom.*

"Well, well, well," Ashton said, shaking his head. Two officers advanced toward Colton and handcuffed him. "This is odd. Weren't we just here?"

Colton ground his teeth but said nothing.

"I have to admit, Colton, I'm a little frustrated this time, because this is taking me away from the festivities," Ashton said. "But maybe it was good that it happened. Maybe now we'll be able to see exactly what you were trying to do. Things have a way of working out for the best, don't they? Mubarak, what was he doing?"

Mubarak was one of the two IT guys working on the computer. Colton had seen him around before. He was pretty introverted, not much for socializing, and one of the main technology workers at the CTC.

"Some kind of download," Mubarak said, clicking away at

the keys. "Probably a virus of some kind. But it shouldn't be a problem. Pretty slow connection here. Virus aborted."

"Aborted?" Ashton asked.

"Yes." Mubarak rubbed the palms of his hands together. "Just canceled it. Not sure what it was, but I can study it later. All is clear for now."

"Very nice." Ashton turned his attention back to Colton. "So it *was* a virus? Don't you know that our computers are virtually virus-proof here at the CTC? You of all people, should know that. Even if you had finished doing what you set out to do, it wouldn't have worked. You must realize that."

"Just get it over with," Colton said. "Take me to my prison so I can die in peace."

Ashton's eyes widened. He took two steps toward Colton. "I am going to take you to your prison, and you are going to die tonight, but I think I have a better plan for you first. The entire world is going to be watching tonight, and I think what the world needs right now is to see how dangerous this underground militia is and how our mission at the CTC is pure. Sometimes, Colton, people need an example. A living, breathing example. I think when the nation sees you on their televisions, their computers, their phones, and their tablets, as an extractor who was misled by a rogue band of culprits, they will be reminded of the important work we do here at the CTC."

Handcuffed or not, it took all of Colton's strength to restrain himself. He wanted to lunge toward Ashton and hurt him in some tangible way.

"Get this piece of filth out of here," Ashton said, waving to the officers. "I have a speech to make. I want the nation to see that looks can be deceiving, and we need to be vigilant because more of this scum is in our midst."

Colton was ushered out of the room.

"Gus…" Colton whispered.

No answer.

He was alone.

1.3.12

Colton was immediately taken to a different quarantine chamber. Still handcuffed, he was thrown inside and informed that they would return for him. Preparations needed to be made for Ashton's speech first. Until that time, Ashton informed him, with deliberate sarcasm, he was to make himself comfortable and enjoy the upgrade to a more spacious accommodation than his previous one.

His hands bound behind him, Colton sat on the cot and slumped his head forward. If his hands weren't bound, he might have pounded his fists against the prison door in some violent display of protest, but in his current condition, he saw no use in doing anything. He had evaded death only to be thrown back into its path.

"Gus?"

Still no answer.

But why? *Why won't he respond?* Colton wondered. *Maybe he's given up on me. He's given up hope. Just like me. And I don't blame him. Perhaps it's better to walk away and say nothing.*

A long time passed. It felt like hours. He began to wonder if Ashton had lied. Perhaps they weren't coming back to take him in front of the crowd and cameras to make an example of him; maybe that was a ruse and at any moment, the gas would seep in through the vents, and he would feel sleepy. Oh, so sleepy. He would drift into unconsciousness while his son did the same in the adjacent cell, and Selma in the cell beside that.

But eventually the door opened. Two guards stepped in and ushered him out by waving their guns. Colton didn't know what time it was, but he assumed it must have been nearing midnight. He followed the guards outside the cell, and Ashton was there waiting for him. In one hand, he held a glass of champagne.

"Sorry for the delay, my friend," Ashton said. "Much to attend to, as you know. Took a little longer than I presumed."

"Where's my son? Where's Selma?"

"Oh, I think the public has the appetite for seeing a doomed Benedict Arnold on prime time to rally their hearts to our cause, but we're not sure if they could stomach watching a woman and child. At least, that's what the PR department tells me. So while you'll be enjoying your ten seconds of fame, they'll be in their cells, awaiting their execution just like everyone else."

"And Kramer?"

"Awaiting extermination as well." He looked at his watch. "Now, if you can believe it, it's already eleven-thirty. My speech starts in a few minutes, and I'd like to be there a few minutes early."

"Please," Colton heard himself saying. "Please. Have mercy on my son. Please."

"Colton," Ashton said, sounding suddenly more serious, "do you remember how much you hated it when those you apprehended begged for mercy? You used to talk on and on about how pathetic it was. Let's not have that now, shall we?"

Colton was speechless.

"You look great," Ashton said. "And you'll do great. All you have to do is stand there and be yourself. I'll do all the talking."

Ashton nodded to the guards, and they began walking down the hall. The two officers walked behind Colton with their guns at his back.

They zigzagged through a few hallways until, at last, they came to the foyer being used for this special occasion. Before they entered the foyer, several figures stood outside the entrance, one a woman with headphones who ran up to Ashton as he approached and told him it was time for the speech; the crowd was waiting. Ashton nodded and advanced into the room with Colton and the two officers directly behind him. He walked to the stage, and Colton found himself up there as well. The lights were hot on his skin and bright in his eyes, but from this vantage point, he could look out and see the full extent of the foyer's transformation.

Circular tables draped with white linens covered every inch of the floor. CTC employees, lobbyists, politicians, and other people of importance sat around the tables. They sipped wine and champagne, chewed on bits of filet mignon, and talked over the sounds of blue jazz music that came from a small trio in the corner: a woman playing a guitar and singing, a stand-up bass player, and a drummer. Waiters and waitresses dressed in formal black and white raced like ants between the tables while balancing trays of champagne flutes, buttered bread, escargot, and frog legs. Ashton had gone all out to make this an event to remember. White and red balloons were everywhere; tied to tables, tied to chairs, tied to everything. A giant silver banner was strewn across the south wall and read: A NEW STEP FOR THE FUTURE OF CTC!

When Colton stepped onto the stage, a hush fell over the guests. The jazz musicians stopped playing, and everyone looked expectantly at Ashton as he grabbed a microphone. Most people, however, seemed more interested in Colton—the most wanted man in the country. The guests whispered over their wineglasses and exchanged shocked, bewildered expressions.

Behind the stage, a giant screen captured the image of Ashton with a microphone in his hand. It was a live broadcast, and Colton realized millions of citizens were watching in the comfort of their own homes. Below the televised image of Ashton, Colton could see the script: CHANNEL ELEVEN NEWS, SPECIAL EVENT. LIVE SPEECH FROM CTC HEADQUARTERS.

"Good evening, everyone," Ashton said into the microphone. "I apologize for arriving a bit late, but I wanted to take a moment to tell all of you how absolutely thrilled I am to have you here at what is certainly one of the most important events the CTC has catered in a long time. I also want to thank everyone watching at home for your commitment to our nation's security and safety. The CTC wouldn't be what it is without you, and I offer my sincere thanks for your continued love and support for our organization."

Ashton's introduction was met with polite applause, but most of the guests were still focused on Colton and why he had been brought onto the stage with Ashton. Colton pulled uselessly at the handcuffs that tethered his wrists behind his back.

"As all of you know," Ashton continued, "this is a landmark event for the CTC. With the extermination of the Aberrants, our agency will be more effective. No longer will taxpayer dollars be put toward feeding and housing these unscrupulous threats to our society. Instead, they can be put toward better systems of surveillance and extraction. Our agency has petitioned, fought, and lobbied a long time for this development. It is of the utmost importance to our organization that the general public not only feels safe through the CTC's operations but also knows that we are good stewards of the money we have been given to procure your safety.

"It was not long ago, before the CTC operated as it does today, when these theological threats were a great cause of alarm for society as a whole. We have strived long and hard to fight against the religious fundamentalism that has destroyed so many parts of the world as we know it, to make sure that here—in America—we do not become heirs to the same disastrous fate. We will not go back to living in caves, hurling rocks, and behaving like uncivilized barbarians. Here in America, in the Land of the Free and the Home of the Brave, we will not let those who threaten our way of life infiltrate the nooks and crannies of our society. We will smoke them out of their holes and drive them from their hideouts if it takes every last ounce of strength that we possess."

The crowd applauded, loudly this time. Colton looked at the guests, mainly overweight men clapping their puffy hands over plates of devoured food, and he wondered why he had ever believed in their so-called noble cause. These men—and some women—were gluttons, wiping the sauce from their lips with napkins as if it were blood, and grinning with crooked, fang-like teeth.

Why did I believe in this? he wondered. And he had no answer.

Ashton raised his hand to silence the guests. Obediently, they quieted.

"Sam, can you give me a little more sound in the monitors?" Ashton waved to a guy near the soundboard. The little guy, wearing oversized headphones, adjusted something and gave him the thumbs up.

"Thank you, Sam." Ashton switched hands with his microphone. "As all of you know, in about fifteen minutes, all of the Aberrants we have captured will be no more. And not only will that occur, but the possibility—however remote—of any escaping and infiltrating our society will be no more. Tomorrow will be a new day. A new day of peace. A new day of safety. A new day of public service."

The crowd applauded once again, but Colton could only think of the time.

Fifteen minutes, he thought. *Fifteen minutes and my son is dead. And Selma. And Ashton will take me back to my cell when his speech is over and I'll be killed, too. If only I could break out of these chains, reach for him, and get my hands around his throat. If only...*

"I know that with the disappearance of Colton Pierce, many speculated as to the potential of underground operations resisting our extraction capabilities," Ashton said, turning suddenly serious. He paused for dramatic effect, looking straight into the camera. "I want to make sure that every citizen of our country knows that the CTC is one hundred percent committed to removing any threats that confront our society, and if there are any groups of resistance or cells hiding in our midst, we will find them. As proof of our efficiency and commitment, and our capability to find such individuals, I want to present to you Colton Pierce—the Most Wanted Man in our country."

Colton stepped forward when an officer prodded him in the back. He imagined the millions of people watching this on their devices looking at him. The crowd at the CTC applauded, and Colton felt the irony; they weren't applauding *for* him, they were applauding because of his capture. One by one, several of the guests threw their napkins off their laps and got to their feet.

Get this over with, Colton thought. *If I'm going to die, just take me in the back and shoot me. Or put me in a cell and gas me. Whatever you're going to do, just do it.*

Ashton politely waved everyone back down, and one by one, the crowd returned to their seats.

Napkins were drawn back over laps. Flutes of champagne

refilled. Frog legs and buttered bread scooped off plates with greedy hands.

Colton looked at a large clock on the back wall: 11:47. *Thirteen minutes. Only thirteen minutes.*

"Our friend, Colton Pierce, will die shortly after the rest of the Aberrants," Ashton said, "but we wanted to make sure that the whole country was able to see that the CTC found him and brought him to proper justice. Rest assured, any Aberrants seeking to remain off the grid will suffer the same fate. Any person who attempts to—"

Suddenly, the lights in the room flickered off—all but the red stage lights. Faces, glasses of water and champagne, plates, and white linen were instantly swathed in the hue of blood.

Ashton paused. He looked in confusion at the soundboard while the sound and lighting people scrambled to solve the problem.

"Pardon me." Ashton offered a false smile. "We're having a few technical problems. Our guys will have it fixed in just a moment." He looked back to where men buzzed like worker bees around the board and controls.

"Colton," Gus said, "are you there?"

"Yes," Colton responded. Everything was still bathed in red, and Ashton shifted uncomfortably while waiting for the problem to be fixed. "You're there still?"

"Of course, I am."

"What's happening?" Colton whispered.

"It's working," Gus said. "The virus is taking effect."

1.3.13

"Sorry for that little technicality," Ashton said once the situation was fixed. The normal lights flickered back on, and the workers behind the board gave him a thumbs up. "I can assure you, that will be the end of the technical difficulties for the evening. We're not going to let a little lighting glitch ruin an otherwise superb night now, are we?"

The crowd applauded. Ashton made sure his hair was securely in place while contemplating what he was going to say next.

"Again, as I was saying, it is our utmost responsibility and goal to—"

It happened again, only this time the lights went off completely. Total darkness.

Colton couldn't believe it. Even everyone's watches and phones went dark. For a moment, he wondered if somehow all of the energy in the room had been sucked away, but that didn't make sense because there was still some electrical power. Ashton's microphone was still live, and the projector was still working, only now there was nothing to project but a strange luminescent blackness.

"Hello, hello, hello," Ashton said again, making sure the microphone still had a signal. "Can someone help with this? Maybe we have some kind of power outage, perhaps?"

"Working on it!" someone yelled by the soundboard.

Colton looked around the room, though he could see nothing. "Gus, what's happening?" he whispered.

"I already told you, the virus is taking effect. It's infiltrating the system. Give it a few more seconds." In the darkness, Gus's voice sounded louder. Clearer. Closer.

"But they said it didn't work," Colton said.

"*Who* said it didn't work?"

"The computer tech. He said the virus didn't work. He cut it off mid-download."

"And you believed him? You think they could stop it?"

"I don't...I don't know..."

"Keep watching, Colton. You haven't seen anything yet."

The guests started to grow impatient and restless in the darkness, realizing something was wrong. It was one thing for the lights to go out, but for their phones and tablets and everything else that emitted light to suddenly blacken made no sense.

Finally, as the guests' restlessness teemed, the lights flickered back on. All of the phones did as well. Happy to be in the light, most of the crowd laughed it off and chalked it up to something or other, and after some murmurs and confusion, shifted their attention back to the stage, where Ashton was waving to them and smiling. But Colton noticed him wipe the sweat off his forehead as he looked around the room apprehensively.

Maybe he knows, Colton thought. *Maybe he's figured it out. He knows the virus is in the system, and he can't stop it now.*

"Well, we definitely aren't batting a thousand tonight...not yet...but the night is young!" He raised his fist, hoping to rally everyone's attention back to him. It worked, for the most part. The darkness they had been bathed in just moments before was ancient history, and the crowd clapped their hands, whistled, and hooted and hollered until Ashton had to raise his hand again to urge silence.

"I suppose I better finish my speech quickly before the sound goes out or something else goes wrong," Ashton said. The crowd laughed, and he chuckled with them. "It's been a short time since I've—"

Again, another problem. The camera filming Ashton, which was attached to a mechanical arm, swiveled suddenly to the side, turned, and angled down toward one of the tables. Then it lowered with such sudden speed and swiftness that several people at the table gasped and fell backward out of their seats. The camera finally stopped a foot above a plate of appetizers, and the giant screen captured a montage of fried frog legs.

Ashton, in his frustration, dropped his microphone on the stage. The loud thump in the amplifiers was deafening.

Colton, although still confused, couldn't help but laugh. Millions of people across the country—across the world, for that matter—were now looking at the image of frog legs.

"It's about to take effect, Colton," Gus said.

"What is?"

"The full extent of the virus. Remember, it takes—"

Colton felt hands around his neck. It was Ashton. He leaned in close, and Colton could smell his rank breath. *No wonder he uses that breath mist all the time*, he thought. *Selma was right. He needs it.*

"What did you do?" Ashton asked, tightening his grip around Colton's throat.

Ashton gripped so tightly, Colton had to get out each word one breath—one word—at a time. "What—do—you—mean?"

"What did you do to the computer? This is something you did, isn't it? What was it?"

Ashton gripped tighter, and Colton saw the clock on the wall: *11:56*. Four minutes.

"I. Can't. Breathe."

"Tell me what you did! What did you do?"

"Can't. Breathe."

"What did you do?"

"Can't."

Colton felt lightheaded. The room started to spin. Much more of this, and he'd be unconscious.

"You know what I'm going to enjoy the most?" Ashton said, leaning toward him again. "I'm going to enjoy watching you die after your son dies. There's something unnatural about watching your son die before you, isn't there? So tragic."

"Let. Go." Little popcorn bursts of light appeared around Colton, and he felt himself slipping backward toward unconsciousness. All of the guests were on their feet now, and the camera shifted again. Zoomed in extra close. A fly, bulbous and hairy, occupied the screen. Two green, bloated eyes took up the entire wall.

"Die!" Ashton hissed, his fingers like clamps around Colton's throat.

Then the pressure released just before Colton drifted into unconsciousness.

Colton watched Ashton fall to his knees, blink in confusion, and then, spasming, collapse to the floor. He flopped around like a dying fish, and Colton realized that he wasn't alone. Every other person in the room—guests, officers, politicians, extractors—fell to the ground and, like Ashton, twitched and jittered. It was like watching an arcane and macabre religious revival, but Colton knew exactly what it meant.

He gasped for breath and tried to regain his composure, but it still felt like Ashton's fingers were around his neck. They may have made permanent impressions.

"It worked," he said.

"Yes," Gus agreed. "It worked."

With everyone in a state of semi-consciousness on the ground, Colton didn't know what to do. His hands were still bound behind him, and he had no key. No answer. He turned to the officers on the ground and wondered if he should look through their things. Perhaps he would find the key.

He didn't look long.

"Daddy!"

Colton looked up and saw Marty running toward him. Selma and Kramer were with him. His son was so excited to see him that he hardly noticed the ocean of bodies on the floor and ran toward Colton, jumped on him, and clung to him. Colton only wished he could hold him back.

"What happened to all of you?" Colton asked.

"The virus worked," Selma said, nodding at the comatose bodies everywhere. "Our cells opened instantly. The same thing is happening on the Island right now!"

Marty climbed off Colton and looked strangely at the people lying on the ground.

"But Kramer, you should be on the ground with them, shouldn't you?" Colton asked. He turned to Selma. "Why isn't the virus affecting him? Shouldn't it affect everyone working for the CTC?"

"I'm sure the Creator could make alterations to his virus as he sees fit," Selma said.

"The Creator?" Colton asked.

"Yes, who do you think designed it?"

Colton decided he would revisit that at a later time. "Can you get me out of these handcuffs, please?"

"Sure." Without being prompted, she searched the belt pouches of one of the comatose officers, pulled out a small set of keys, and unlatched the handcuffs.

Satisfied, Colton threw them to the ground and rubbed his hands up and down his throat. It felt like his esophagus was nearly flattened. "Thank you," he said.

"We need to get out of here," Kramer said. "We need to get out of here now."

"You're coming with us?" Colton asked.

"Where else can I go?"

Colton and Selma looked at each other and nodded.

"You got it," Colton said. "Let's get out of here. I'm not sure when these guys are going to wake up."

The others began to jump between the comatose people on the ground—like a game of human hopscotch—but Colton found himself drawn toward Ashton. He lay on the ground, like all of the others, and Colton bent toward him. He looked into Ashton's eyes and saw white; the very bottom of his irises drifted back and forth like two blue pendulums below his top eyelashes, trapped in a netherworld of half dream, half reality.

Colton took him by the throat, and it felt good to have his hands around the defenseless throat of the same man who could have killed him minutes ago.

Each of his fingers—as if with wills of their own—tightened around Ashton's throat.

He thought he saw some form of acknowledgement in Ashton; he twitched. Perhaps he saw Colton. Maybe he understood. He was like one of those coma patients who, after waking, remembers every word and whisper in his ear.

"I should kill you now," Colton said. His fingers tightened even more, and he heard a bubbling—a struggling—in Ashton's throat.

"Colton!" Selma called.

He looked across the room and saw Selma, Kramer, and his son waiting for him. Waving for him to hurry up.

He looked down at the face of the man he hated and forced his fingers, one by one, to release.

"What makes a man strong isn't his strength, but the ability to restrain his strength," he said, and let go completely.

Ashton twitched. One of his eyelids flickered.

Colton turned, leapt across the bodies, and found the others at the entrance.

When he reached them, he opened the front doors to the CTC and walked out into the cold night.

They were free.

1.3.14

"**A**re you sure this is where we meet them?" Colton asked.

It was nearly one o'clock in the morning and they stood on the edge of the Long Beach Pier, bundled up, waiting. Selma looked through a pair of binoculars at a constellation of yellow lights moving toward them across the water. Colton couldn't make out what they were, but he hoped they were the ships Bayard had commandeered.

"I think that's them," Selma said. "Hard to tell."

"How long does the virus last? When do the authorities wake up and start looking for us?" Colton asked.

"Not entirely sure," Selma said.

"Where do you plan to go?" Kramer asked. "Is there some kind of plan?"

"We'll deal with that once we get out of here," Selma said.

Colton looked down the pier and worried. He put his arm around his son. How tragic would it be to have come all this way only to be caught again; and if they fell into the hands of the CTC, it would be terrible. There would be no grace, no patience on the part of Ashton. They would be killed immediately.

"We're in luck, gentlemen," Selma said, after looking back through her binoculars. "They're CTC cargo ships from the Island. He's here! It worked!"

1.3.15

The sun was rising over the edge of the horizon, and Colton had been up all night. Bayard had greeted all of them with a warm, enthusiastic embrace and ushered them onto the cargo ship now carrying approximately three hundred escapees. Eight other vessels followed them, an aquatic caravan along the coast.

Colton was most surprised to see how everyone greeted him when he stepped onboard. In the matter of a couple hours, he had gone from the most hated man in the world to the most beloved. Men, women, and children hugged him, kissed him on the cheeks, and thanked him profusely for helping with the escape. At one point, several even started chanting his name, and he had to shake his head and urge them to stop. One little girl walked up to him and handed him a small flower, and Colton bent down to accept it. When he looked into her face and her brown, almond eyes, he was pretty sure he recognized her—he had seen her face in the Mourning Room. Many of these people, in fact, were probably faces that had looked at him from the shadows of that chamber.

Bayard took Kramer to have his NRNT chip deactivated; the virus had taken care of all of the Aberrants' tracking systems, but they wanted to be sure about Kramer. Colton wished him luck and told him to get used to not seeing much for a few days.

Marty, exhausted and cold, bundled up in a sleeping bag along the back deck of the vessel. Several other people were sleeping back there as well, and Colton stayed with him until he fell into a deep sleep.

He watched his son for a long time.

"I won't let you down again," he told Marty. "The old Colton Pierce isn't here anymore. I don't know what I am now, but I'm something better. And I'll give you that, Marty. I promise to give you the best of me."

Colton couldn't sleep, so he walked to the back railing and took a cup of coffee from a man who was handing them out.

"Thank you so much, Mr. Pierce," the man said after giving him a steaming, Styrofoam cup. Colton took it and realized that he recognized him: Josh Mosley, the young man he'd extracted before the madness began. The same man he'd verbally harassed while he waited to be shipped off to the Island. Colton wasn't sure what to say, but he knew he had to say something.

"I just want to tell you that I'm so sorry. I don't know how to make up for how I treated you, and I just want you to—"

"Shh," Josh said. "No more talk of the past. All has been made right, has it not?"

Colton sighed. "Yes, I suppose all has been made right."

"I knew there was a good man in there anyway," Josh said. "You just didn't know it yet."

Colton's former prisoner smiled, nodded politely, and walked away to hand out more coffees. He handed a coffee to Selma, who took it, thanked him, and walked up to Colton, who was looking out at the ocean and wondering where Bayard was taking them.

"I heard what he told you," Selma said and, like Colton, leaned against the railing and looked out at the first golden hues of sunlight rising above the horizon. "And he was right. You are a good man, Colton Pierce. I guess you were the last to know it."

He looked at her. She pulled strands of dark hair from her face with delicate fingers, and he saw those eyes, two green jewels. She was more beautiful now than she ever had been, and Colton knew it wasn't due to lack of sleep. She was truly everything he had imagined he would want in a woman. It was all right there, looking at him, within reach.

"Thank you," he said.

"You're very welcome."

"Where is Bayard taking us?"

"South for now, but there's a second part of the plan. We'll need to mobilize, of course. Once the CTC wakes up, they'll come after us, and with more of a vengeance than before. We'll need to set up a new base and a new defense, but I'll let Bayard explain all of that once we reach our destination. I think for now we just enjoy the moment, huh?"

"Yeah, maybe you're right. I guess we'll just have to trust."

"Trust?" Selma said, truly in awe. "I wasn't sure that word was in your vocabulary."

"Well, I'm learning." Colton chuckled. He sipped his coffee, and they both laughed. "I really want to meet Gus. I need to thank him. He got me out of that jam. He got all of us out of that jam. He's the real hero, you know. I more or less followed orders."

Selma grinned, but there was something to it.

Colton caught the expression, lowered his coffee, and asked her, "What's wrong? What is it? What happened?"

"I don't know if you'll believe me."

"I don't know, Selma, I think I'd believe about anything at this point."

"A long time ago, when the Remnant first formed, we were worried about being picked up by CTC surveillance," Selma explained. "So we created special words, acronyms, those kinds of things, to make sure anyone listening wouldn't pick up on what we were saying."

Colton nodded.

"And we couldn't say the word God…not in the way we were using it…so we needed another word…something kind of like it…something…"

"Gus?" Colton said.

"Yes."

"But that doesn't make sense. Why would God speak to me using my NRNT chip? What sense does that make?"

"Well, weren't you the one talking about the story of how God spoke through an ass?" Selma laughed. "So if an ass, why not an NRNT chip? That's the way He's been communicating to us most recently."

"So this whole time, it's been…"

"I guess you're the ass now."

Colton laughed, sipped his coffee, and looked up wonderingly at the stars. "Wow," he said. "It's funny, I'm surprised—I mean really, really surprised—but at the same time, it's like I knew all along. Does that make sense?"

"Yes, Colton, it does. It makes perfect sense."

He reached out and touched her cheek, and she stepped toward him. They were chest to chest, and he looked down at her. She brushed away more of her hair with her fingers and looked up at him, wanting.

"Did I not see you all along?" Colton said.

"What?"

"You're what I asked for that day on the beach. You're the answer."

He lowered his head and kissed her. Her lips were warm against his, delicious, and they held each other as the sun continued to rise. By the time they stopped and Colton released her, he wasn't sure how much time had passed. But the sun seemed higher, and the day was brighter.

"I'm glad everything ended this way," he said, looking toward the water.

Nobody was in pursuit. They had open ocean before them.

"Ended?" Selma said. "Don't forget, they won't let us run for long. This, Colton, is just the beginning."

"Yes," he said, and unable to resist her, pulled her toward him once again. "Just the beginning."

The End

.

William Michael Davidson lives in Long Beach, California, with his wife and two daughters. A believer that "good living produces good writing," Davidson writes early in the morning so he can get outside, exercise, spend time with people, and experience as much as possible. A writer of speculative fiction, he enjoys stories that deal with humanity's inherent need for redemption.